"Oh Threats of Hell
and
Hopes of Paradise"

First Edition Design Publishing

"Oh Threats of Hell and Hopes of Paradise
Copyright ©2013 John F. Gibson

ISBN 978-1506-912-72-1 PRINT
ISBN 978-1622-873-64-7 EBOOK

LCCN 2013944720

July 2013

Published and Distributed by
First Edition Design Publishing, Inc.
P.O. Box 20217, Sarasota, FL 34276-3217
www.firsteditiondesignpublishing.com

Cover Design by Deborah E Gordon

PREFACE

"The moving finger writes
and having writ moves on
and all your piety and wit
can lure it back to cancel half a line
nor, all your tears wash out a word of it"

I hope the reader enjoys the following five stories. I am vain enough to think my writings may endure as long as the above quatrain, which was written in the twelfth century A.D. by the Arabian philosopher "Omar Khayyam." However in reality, I would just like the reader to know that there are still a few "Good Ole Boys" left in the world!

Sincerely
John Gibson

Oh, threats of Hell and Hopes of Paradise!
One thing at least is certain--This Life flies;
One thing is certain and the rest is Lies;
The Flower that once has blown for ever dies.

"The old tentmaker"
Omar Khayyam circa 1120

"OH THREATS OF HELL AND HOPES OF PARADISE"

Just as soon as I discovered that dilapidated shoebox with its shocking secret, I faked nonchalance, tucked the thing under my arm and headed back up the stairs to my office. A quick glance at the contents of the box had rattled my otherwise complacent brain into overdrive. I was oblivious to the throng of folks who normally crowd the halls of the county courthouse on weekday mornings. I flung open the door to my office, then hesitated and looked about the room. I had the same uneasiness I used to get when I robbed the hen's nests so I could trade the eggs for penny candy.

Sprawling heavily into the squeaky wooden recliner, I recklessly brushed aside the half-finished report I had been working on earlier and placed the box directly in front of me on the desk. Slowly, almost surgically, I removed the dusty lid. I felt my face becoming crimson and my blood pressure rise. A great sadness gripped my very soul as I meticulously handled and scrutinized each individual item. Collectively they represented a lifetime of material gain for one simple soul, and the possibility of a one- way ticket to Hell for another. The fact of man's inhumanity to man, and the possibility of good and evil existing apart from human thought momentarily flooded my mind. The sad part, I realized, was that there was no conceivable way to rectify the situation. What was done was done and I was the only living soul this side of hell who knew the truth.

I poured myself a cup of stale coffee. It would have to do. I did not feel like making a fresh pot. I retrieved a pack of camels from the desk drawer and lit one. Yeah, I had resolved to quit yesterday but my present state of my mind would not allow me to go a minute longer without a smoke. I thought about taking the box back to where I had found it and just forgetting the whole thing but I knew I would never be at peace with myself if I did. The gravity of the situation was too great. I had to get my thoughts together- confused though they were. I was fearful that someone would burst into my office with some irrelevant problem so I eased over and locked the door. I plopped again into my chair, lit another smoke, and began to relax a bit. Slowly my memory drifted back to the events surrounding that ominous day some five years past.

It all happened on Wednesday, the fourth of September, 1942. I remember distinctly since it was my eighteenth birthday. The day began with Harley thundering into my room about 3:00 A.M. and shaking me out of a sound sleep. He had been anxious to get an early start on the day, and informed me of a million things we had to accomplish by nightfall. I tiptoed into the kitchen so as not to wake my folks and splashed a little cold water on my face. I then grabbed a couple of stale biscuits and a couple slices of bacon from the pantry and went outside where I waited for Harley near the water well. He quickly showed up carrying a pickaxe and a shovel. He handed me the shovel as he swung the pick over his shoulder and we set out down the path that led across the mountain toward Eli Hurst's farm.

There was a full moon; not a cloud in the sky. The moonlight helped tremendously and took a lot of the guesswork out of dodging the rocks and deep chug holes that littered the path. The grass on either side of the path sparkled in the moonlight from the heavy dew and I would drag my feet through the higher clumps in an attempt to remove the caked mud of the day before from my old brogan work shoes.

Harley and I had been sharecropping Eli's tobacco crop for the past couple of years. Both of us were accustomed to that type of hard work and the extra money sure came in handy, especially while I was still in school. I thanked God that we were almost finished for the year. We would have finished the week before if Harley had not accidentally killed that mule. We were on our way to bury the mule again. Yeh, this made the second time we had interred that animal. The first time, we dug the hole too close to the creek and a flash flood came and floated the corpse up out of the grave a few days later. Eli sent word by the mail carrier concerning what had happened, so we were now on our way to take care of the grizzly task. We had resolved to dig the grave on higher ground this time however!

We accomplished the two-mile trek in record time and had finished digging the five or six foot deep hole in the sandy soil before the first light of day. Things were going pretty well until we attempted to hook Eli's other mule to the rotting corpse. The mule balked and ran off. Eli finally caught him and put a set of blinders on the animals bridle. This seemed to settle the mule down a little so we hooked on, snaked the dead mule up to the hole and rolled him in without further incident. The sun was just beginning to peep over the black mountain as we flung the last shovels of dirt on the stinking carrion. I felt like I would die from thirst and we stopped at Eli's spring before setting out for home. The water was cool and sweet but the stench of the maggot-infested flesh was still in my nostrils and I had to choke the first couple of swallows down. We bid goodbye to Eli but he did not seem to be as friendly as usual.

Eli was pretty aggravated with Harley over killing his mule, and actually, I could not blame him. Harley had just let his temper get the best of him again. The incident had taken place a week ago the previous Saturday morning. We were hauling the last wagon load of tobacco from the field and had just headed down the hill toward the barn when Eli called our attention to a few of the skewered stalks on the very top of the mountain we had missed. Harley was driving the team and Eli told him we would have to turn the wagon around and go back and collect what we had missed rather than make another trip since time was money. I noticed Harley's face turning more red than it already was from the heat as he began to mumble "sweet Jesus, sweet Jesus." This had always been Harley's favorite expression when perplexed about something. He mopped the sweat from his face on the back of his hand and abruptly turned the team straight up the hill. Harley was expecting to finish before noon as he had planned a trip into town later on that day. Those mules generally worked pretty well together as a team. There was a gray mule and a black mule. They were perfectly matched in size and strength, but Harley said they had different dispositions. The gray animal would try to slack off in a hard pull leaving the black one in a terrible strain. About half way up the hill the gray began to fall behind a bit and Harley snatched up a pitchfork and began to jab the animal with it. I noticed blood spurt from the mule's hindquarters each time it was jabbed and Eli saw it too but he did not say anything to Harley. He knew Harley was already mad and did not want to make matters worse. Of course, the mule did begin to pull its share of the load and we got the tobacco in the barn without further incident. Harley and I were both surprised when we got word three or four days later that the mule had taken sick and died of the lockjaw.

The sun was fully up when we headed for home. The humidity was throttling and sweat had glued my denim shirt to my back. I trudged pantingly along behind Harley up the narrow and winding path leading to the swayback in the crest of the ridge overlooking Big Richland creek. Harley had reached the top and was leaning with his back against that gigantic white oak tree which served as the official North and East boundary marker of our farm. This was one of my favorite spots in the world; you could see for a mile in any direction. This is where I generally brought my coonhounds to turn them loose when I went coon hunting. I would sometimes spend the night there listening to the mournful sounds of those dogs on the hunt. The part of coon hunting which I did not particularly enjoy was the task of getting to the dogs after they treed. If I did not go and shake the coon out of the tree, or shoot it out for them, they would stay there and bark for a week.

I was pleased that Harley had decided to stop and rest for a while before beginning the arduous descent to the foot-log, which served as an improvised bridge across the narrow creek five or six hundred feet below. There was a fine breeze sweeping along the ridge. I turned one way and then the other allowing the wind to pass through my sweat soaked shirt as it cooled my baking body. Harley dragged a sack of "Old North State" smoking tobacco from his shirt pocket and commenced to roll a cigarette. It was blazing hot by then and I was already growing weary from the fast pace set by my big brother. "Thank yi' Jesus," Harley mumbled as he meticulously wrapped the paper around the golden flakes of tobacco. He twisted and smoothed the professional looking creation with his fingers and then put it to his mouth and licked it all along one side in order to bind the thing together. "Thank 'yi Jesus," he muttered again. He sucked hard on the fat cigarette and then slowly exhaled a long stream of gray smoke while simultaneously commenting something about the peace and serenity he felt in that spot. I muttered some halfhearted affirmative to his comment since I was too hot and thirsty to be thankful for anything at that point.

Harley was a religious man. He prayed a lot. He prayed over his food, he prayed over the crops, he prayed over the preacher, the church, and just about everything and everybody. "A man needs to walk with God," he would say. "A man needs to go a praying. A man cain't make it without God. However, if you always seek God and his will you cain't go wrong. Talk to 'im, walk with 'im, praise 'im and everything will be okay."

From this vantage point, we could see our home place about a quarter mile distant, situated in a clearing a hundred yards or so off the Knox Fork road. It was a pretty place. There was a neat six-room weather boarded house painted white and trimmed in black, and a large barn and a log corncrib nearby. Three big sycamore trees placed at just the right distance from the dwelling provided us with plenty of shade in the summer, and a tree-studded ridge to the North end of the clearing served as a shield from the coldest winds of winter. My daddy had built the house along about the time I was born. I had heard him brag many a time that he had "drove every nail and hewed every joist and rafter by hand." The family was proud of the place and we all did our best to keep it in good repair. This was home, and at this point in my life, I could not imagine living anywhere else.

Our farm of about sixty acres was located along a section of the original Wilderness Road. Daniel Boone, Dr. Thomas Walker, and subsequent early travelers to the Western United States had immortalized this road. There is a good deal of history connected with this region and I often tingled with pride when I considered the possibility that I was, more than likely, a descendent of one of those intrepid long-hunters who had journeyed over the Appalachians and on through the Cumberland Gap. These early settlers traveled along this very road in search of new hunting grounds and a way to insure their continued independence and freedom.

Appalachia is a beautiful place but at the same time, it can be an unforgiving place. It is rocky and ridged with only a few tillable acres. Most of the bottomland is perpetually flooded three or four times a year with backwater from the Cumberland River. Consequently, a good deal of the crops must be grown on small patches of flat land just slightly above the flood plain or on the lower slopes of these Western Appalachian foothills. Nevertheless, as I had often heard my daddy say, "This country is not meant to be farmed in a big way. This land was meant to bring a man peace of mind and serenity-not a pocket full of money. When a man can sleep soundly all night without being awakened by a fire engine or a police siren he is blessed! When he can walk out onto his back porch in the early morning and frighten the deer out of his backyard he again is blessed. When he can drink in his fill of unpolluted air, witness the majesty and beauty of rolling hills of lush green in summer or sparkling snow in winter, he is unspeakably blessed- whether he realizes it or not."

It was several years before I really understood what he was talking about. However, no matter how you try to justify attempting to make a living from a rocky hillside farm, you can never overemphasize the backbreaking drudgery involved. Only after I became physically strong enough to assist with some of the chores could I appreciate what Harley had done for the family since my father's accident. All I had to do in order to understand that whipped look of futility I often saw in Harleys eyes was to take hold of the handles of a hillside turning plow pulled by two obstinate mules and begin breaking the sod of a rocky, hilly, five acre new ground.

It was not easy having to slide out from between two cozy featherbeds before daybreak on a January morning and build a fire in the cook stove. You would often need to free the ice-bound dipper from the water bucket in order to get a drink of water. After you made the house nice and cozy for the rest of the family you could look forward to wading through knee- deep snow to the barn. After you fed all the animals, you would try to entice the cows to stand still with a few corn nubbins while you attempted to milk them with near frost bitten fingers. Finally, you would head back quickly towards the warm house with only a scant quart or two of milk from your two undernourished cows for your efforts. Sometimes you would cuss a little, and sometimes you would pray a little, but at least one time during that morning you would say to yourself "hell, it just ain't worth it!"

Then, there were the years you would hoe and till the crops all summer long in ninety five degree heat, and finally have to admit to yourself along about the middle of August that there had not been enough rain to produce half a sled load of corn nubbins. If you ended up with only a little corn you also ended up with only a little hay for the livestock. Our only cash crop was tobacco and if that dreaded disease called "blue mold" attacked it, there was no money with which to purchase coffee, flour and sugar. The fact is we owned this land only on a piece of paper recorded as a deed at the county seat. In reality, this land owned us; and, if we wanted to eat regularly, we had to pay conscientious attention to a grueling schedule. Cows require milking every morning and every evening; and the time for planting, tilling, harvesting, butchering and canning cannot be allowed to vary significantly. Due to that constant vigil, we were actually tied to that land. Harley and I were grown men before we had traveled more than ten miles from home.

Occasionally, and only when we were short of necessities, would we hitch the mules to the wagon and make the all-day round trip to the county seat some ten miles away. My mother had told Harley he had a registered letter waiting for him at the post office in town. Harley was nowhere to be found the day the mailman tried to deliver the letter and it was the kind that had to be signed for. I think that's why he was in such a rush that morning.

A distant roll of thunder coupled with the quarrels of a family of crows perched in a neighboring tree had brought me abruptly out of my reminiscing. Harley took one last long pull off his cigarette before tossing it onto the yellow earth and crushing it under his hob nailed shoe. The cool, therapeutic breeze had abated, and a huge black thundercloud was rolling turbidly overhead. Harley muttered something to the effect that a snake-strangling storm was imminent as he briskly began his descent towards the meandering creek below. Actually, we both knew it only appeared to be one of those light thunderstorms. I had to grin at the fact he had gotten the words "snake strangling" out without stuttering. This was the only physical defect he had as far as I knew and from what I could gather this speech impediment was the reason he had quit school in the sixth grade.

Evidently, while attempting to recite a poem in front of the class, he experienced one of his stuttering episodes and became frustrated at the teacher's prompting. He ended up breaking all the

7

windows out of the one room schoolhouse and was not allowed to return that year. He had refused to start school the following fall and eventually my folks just gave up on trying to convince him to go back. Most of the time, he only stuttered when he became overly excited or nervous about something and even though he only had a sixth grade education I knew he was smarter than me. Harley was like a daddy to me. He was the one that actually raised me. He was the one who made me do my chores, go to school, go to church and mind my manners.

Harley Vickers was a big man I thought to myself as I watched him lumbering along in front of me down that dusty path. He was six feet and three or four inches tall and weighed two hundred and twenty pounds. He was a mountain of solid muscle but his shoulders were slumped as if he had been carrying the whole world on his back. In a way he had been I guess-- his world anyway. My father had been bed-fast ever since I could remember. His back had been broken in a rock fall at the Black Diamond coal mine in Harlan County and he was paralyzed from the waist down. Consequently, too much responsibility had been placed on Harley from the time he was just a youngster and he had grown old before his time attempting to cope with all this responsibility and hard work alone.

Harley was married. He had married Evalee Jonson. Evalee was Crit Jonson's oldest daughter. The Jonson's lived back at the end of "Elam lane" about two miles from our place. Harley had always talked about how pretty she was but I didn't think she was pretty at all. Although, I guess maybe she was pretty from a physical perspective. It was just her ways that I didn't think was pretty. She was a big flirt. All through school she flirted something awful with the older boys. Of course Harley had already quit school and wasn't around to see that. But Harley was the one that got to walk Evalee home from church every Wednesday and Sunday night. She didn't flirt when Harley was around. He was not one to be fooled with, and he could whip any two his size. I'd seen him do it.

I had noticed a big change in Harley's attitude a month or so before they got married. He moped around all the time not saying anything. I figured he was just love sick but then I overheard him talking to mother. "I'm going to get married," I heard him whisper. "Well, land sake! What in the world for?" was my mother's shocked reply? "I got to mom. Evalee is going to have a baby!" Mother cried and went on something awful but finally she collected her composure and said, "Well, I reckon it's the right thing to do."

About a week after that incident, Harley and Evalee got married there at the local church and Evalee came to live with us. We all got along very well, but, after the baby came, things slowly changed. Evalee was good to my folks and me but she and Harley started to fight on a daily basis. She was constantly after Harley to supply things for her convenience that he could not afford. Finally she ran off to Detroit. All the folks said they just couldn't understand how a woman could run off and leave her husband and a six-month-old baby but to tell you the truth I was glad she left. I was sick of the fighting and the way she treated Harley. Little Molly was a year old when the incident I am relating to you occurred. Harley finally stopped moping around and things got back to normal but I know he missed his wife and he often said so. In fact, he told me more than once that he would take her back in a heartbeat if she would only come home.

We made it home before the shower came and the first thing I did was to get a clean pair of overalls from my room and a bar of homemade lye soap from the smoke house and head for the creek where I attempted to scrub that hideous stench of carrion from my body. By the time I had finished my bath and returned to the barn, Harley had the mules hooked to the wagon and was waiting for me. I bounced into the spring seat alongside Harley and with a click of his tongue the team jerked the slack out of the trace chains and we headed for town.

The first four or five miles of this journey were accomplished over a dusty dirt road full of chug-holes and washouts. Harley always drove and jealously guarded the check lines, as he was fearful the young and highly spirited team might bolt and run away from their fright of a backfiring car or truck. I generally lazed wastefully in the cargo section of the wagon on a pile of hay or just sat placidly with my legs dangling from the tailgate. Harley was acquainted with most everyone who lived along this dirt road and when we approached anyone within hollering distance he would stop and take advantage of the opportunity to exchange the local news. Usually we would find a shady spot near the person's house where we could pass the time of day over a cool drink of fresh spring water and rest the team and ourselves.

Of course, if we happened to pass along at meal time, these gracious folk would insist we join them in their humble repast and would not take no for an answer. We always accepted eagerly and graciously even if we were not at all hungry. We had been taught from an early age that it was not only bad manners, but extremely offensive, for refusing to break bread with your neighbor. Common courtesy, respect, and concern for the well being of your fellow man was just a way of life here in the "Bible Belt." I've heard the preacher comment more than once concerning the genuine hospitality of these simple people. He often called them "the salt of the earth" and although I had not always grasped the significant context of his sermons, somehow these words have stuck in my memory and I often find myself mentally applying this description to all our friends and neighbors there along the Wilderness Road. The majority of these folks are born again Christians and even those who aren't do a good job adhering to the golden rule. Even Harley, who everyone considered a miracle in this respect, had joined the church and been baptized a couple of years past.

When I questioned him about this experience he told me the Holy Spirit had put him under conviction of his sins one night during prayer meeting and that he had gone forward to the altar of God and accepted Jesus Christ as his savior. He said he needed a savior since he was afraid of going to hell when he died. He said that it was all pretty simple and that I would one day understand when the Holy Spirit began to deal with me. He said that for now all I needed to know was that all men are born sinners. That Adam and Eve disobeyed God there in the Garden of Eden simply by eating an item of fruit that God had told them not to eat. He added "you just don't disobey God and get by with it." Since the tainted blood of these first people flows in our veins, this causes all men to be sinful and unacceptable to God. He said that God is perfect and cannot tolerate, nor abide imperfection. In order for man to be forgiven, a plan had to be devised in Heaven to make naturally sinful man acceptable to God. So, God sent His own son to take upon himself the sin of the world and become the propitiation for mans sin. When a person is convicted of his sinful nature by the Holy Spirit and humbles himself and repents of his sin and confesses Jesus

Christ as his savior, God the Father only sees him through the blood of Jesus. God the father sees him as white as the driven snow and qualified to participate in the rewards and perfection of Heaven."

I remember asking him what happened if you slipped and sinned again and he said all you had to do was ask forgiveness and God was faithful and just to forgive-that once you were saved you were always saved. I remember asking Harley where God came from and how He got to be perfect, and Harley told me that was easy to figure out. "You see", he said, "God is the great "I AM." He is of Himself. He created Himself. Nothing or nobody created God. And the reason He's perfect is that while He was in the process of creating Himself, if He detected anything wrong, He would correct it immediately, so that when He was finished, everything about Him was perfect. God can't abide imperfection. That's why a sinner can never go to Heaven. Just drop a rotten apple into a bushel of perfect apples. You've no longer got a perfect bushel of apples. Also," he continued, "there can only be one God. You will understand that when you understand the concept of perfection. There is only one thing perfect and that one thing is God. Everything in existence has a flaw except the one true God."

When we merged out onto the asphalt of U.S. highway 25-E the steel banded wagon wheels rolled smoothly along and I could distinctly hear each syncopated "clip clop" of the teams shodden hooves. The clanging and banging of the loose and worn wagon, coupled with the rattling of the trace chains would diminish greatly on this smooth surface and Harley would often break into one of his favorite hymns such as "Beulah Land" or "When The Roll Is Called Up Yonder" or "The Old Rugged Cross." When Harley tried to sing I generally had to stifle a laugh since he sang off key so badly, and, if he thought no one was listening, he would stutter on some of the words. However, just the fact that he was singing made me lighten up and I would begin to try and decide what I would spend my quarter on once we got into town.

Most all the activity was centered around the courthouse in this little country town of a thousand or two, and we most generally drove around the courthouse "square" a couple of times in order to familiarize ourselves with any changes that may have occurred since our last visit. The main street circled the courthouse. On the outer periphery of the street was a wide sidewalk from which you could enter any of the numerous places of business. You could stand at any spot on this sidewalk and literally see almost every business establishment in the whole town.

A large shady lot had been set-aside at the end of one of the alleys for hitching teams and saddle horses. After securing the mules, one on either side of the wagon so they could munch on the small pile of hey we had brought along for that purpose, we would nonchalantly begin our normal window-shopping excursion. Pretty soon Harley would set about accomplishing the purchases and whatever other business we had come for and I would amble along down the sidewalk faking a disinterested attitude toward the drug store and that immaculate and delicious smelling soda fountain. You got a mountainous cone of vanilla for a nickel and it rarely endured for more than half a block from the store entrance due to the heat and my sweets starved appetite.

After this I generally just wandered around town looking in store windows and paying particular attention to any diversion that may present itself. There was most always some type of excitement going on. You may encounter a preacher standing on the courthouse steps flailing his arms and berating the evils of prostitution and alcohol, or a traveling drummer standing in the shade of his wagon awning, hawking his magical elixir. He was plaintively guaranteeing the stuff to cure every ailment from gangrene to tonsillitis. Then there was generally the scratchy voiced politician throwing off on his opponent and promising justice. Then there was always the itinerant dentist. He had his little portable office set up at a busy crosswalk. He pulled teeth at a quarter a pull. One dentist had a pet monkey. If a patient acted the least bit scared the dentist would make the monkey sit in the patients lap and make funny faces. Then the dentist would slip the set of pullers into the patient's mouth while he was preoccupied with the monkey and jerk the tooth out in a flash. The only anesthetic used was a drink of moonshine liquor if the patient was so inclined. I've seen the blood squirt for a foot or two during some of these extractions.

After a while, with all my curiosities satisfied, I would spend my last dime on a bottle of R.C. Cola and a bag of peanuts before returning to the wagon. Here, in the cool shade, while reclining in the wagon I would nurse and nibble at these delicacies, savoring every morsel as I awaited Harleys return.

It was midafternoon that day when we headed for home and near dark by the time we arrived. I noticed that Harley was unusually quiet on the way home but I figured he was just tired or something. A serious rain had threatened the entire return trip from town and just as we were un-harnessing the mules and getting them fed that "snake strangler" finally hit. Mother had just finished preparing supper when we arrived. We went into dad's room, lifted him into his wheel chair and rolled him out to his usual place at the head of the table before washing up. When we were all seated he said a blessing over the food and added a special blessing for Harley, thanking him for his hard work and dedication to the family. I had petitioned more than once on such occasions that he allow me to quit school and help Harley on a full time basis with the farming but he wouldn't hear of it. Of course this was no longer an issue. I was finished with school for life. But, as I grew older, I realized that I would not have been the quality help I had imagined since my left arm was a bit deformed. The arm had developed in size but it was a little twisted and I could not straighten it out all the way.

Mother had baked my favorite chocolate cake and my daddy had given me his pocket watch for my birthday. I was a grown man now and had graduated from Knox Central High School in June of that year. The idea of being finished with school forever was difficult for me to internalize but there was something other than just being out of school that was causing me to feel uneasy. Lately, I had noticed a great change in my mother. There seemed to be an ominous, almost foreboding look of sadness emanating from my mother's eyes. I had secretly studied her demeanor for the past few days and I got the idea she was anticipating something dreadful to happen. And then, when she turned on our old battery powered radio just before we sat down to supper I realized the object of her concern. It was the war! When the regular nightly newscast came on, she abruptly turned the volume up in an attempt to hear the familiar voice of Edward R. Murrow over the agitating static, which seemed louder than usual due to the thunderstorms. My parents never missed a newscast. Mother was "shushing" us as she slid her cane-bottomed chair a bit closer to that crackling voice. Murrow was commenting on the recent battles and casualties of the war and Hitler's apparent plans to conquer the world. Mother seemed to stiffen a bit in her chair and I noticed the water well up in her eyes as she reached out and clutched our hands. I had never paid any attention to her hands before but this time I did-they were rough and dry with large protruding veins. The years of subsistence farming had taken their toll. She looked more like she was sixty than she did her actual forty years.

I hadn't thought too much about it. That war was too far away for us to be concerned with I thought, so I had just put the whole thing out of my mind. But then, while we were still sitting there at the supper table, Harley reluctantly produced the wrinkled letter from his shirt pocket which would redefine our existence and help to hurl this God fearing family into the machinations of the proverbial world gone mad.

When the news was over he handed the letter to mother. It was obvious that this was what she had been expecting. No one but the federal government sends registered letters- especially to this family. With trembling hands and teary eyes she read it out loud to us. It was addressed to Harley and began with that ironical "greetings"-that one word message which remains emblazoned on the mind of many a mother, and its epilogue on many a distant and forsaken scab of earth in some foreign land. It went on to explain that Harley was to report for his pre-induction physical the following Monday and that if he passed the exam he would be sent directly to Fort Knox for his basic training. It went on to say that his deferment, due to Dads incapacitation, was no longer valid since I had finished school and would be capable of taking Harleys place as provider for the family. I instantly began trying to think of some way I could take Harleys place in the Army but no sooner than the thought hit my mind I realized the futility of it all. Even if I could trade places with him they wouldn't take me anyway because of my deformed arm. You can't aim a rifle with a crooked arm. Of course I knew Harley wasn't afraid of going to war. Matter of fact he had tried to join up the day after the Japanese bombed Pearl Harbor but they had turned him down because he was more or less supporting our family.

At that moment I felt a twinge of guilt. I too wanted to be a soldier and go and help win the war. I would have enlisted the very next day if I thought I would be accepted. Then, on the other hand, I just couldn't see any reason to be concerned about the war. I guess I was stuck somewhere between apathy for a conflict ten thousand miles removed from Knox county and a sense of patriotism with which we had all been indoctrinated. Who cared about Hitler and the Axis powers, and Tojo, and Mussolini? My dreams were to buy a good piece of bottomland somewhere close to home, and maybe get married and raise a family just like my daddy had done. I had never considered that too much for any man to ask. I was not interested in going away to Detroit or Cincinnati to make my fortune. I had heard too many stories about that way of life. I had never punched a time card and worked on an assembly line with a boss leaning over my shoulder watching my every move. I had heard about the tenement houses where families were packed together like sardines. I had heard about the alcoholism, dope addiction and prostitution that seemed to be by-products of the broken dreams of displaced mountain folk. My dreams were rooted in these hills where real serenity and peace of mind come from being completely independent and self-sufficient.

Yeah, that war was just too far away for us to get all excited about. But now it was different and the family was involved. Usually, when I would show a lack of concern for important situations affecting the family Harley would tell me to grow up. Well, I was growing up now, and before long I realized that often times we have little control over life's situations. I was quickly learning that we sometimes just have to give in to the insidious indoctrination of society and yield to conformity- that the tracks are laid, the wheels set in motion, and the conductor commands we climb aboard where we complacently take our assigned seats and are flung at breakneck speed to our predestined destiny.

You know, looking back on the whole situation, I can't help but believe that Harley knew if he had told the draft board about little Molly, they would not have drafted him. I guess he just wanted to get away from Knox County and the whole situation. Then again, maybe he figured if he went away, Evalee would come back to take care of the baby and by and by they would get back together. But anyway, mother hit us with another surprise after she stopped crying over the letter. She had heard gossip to the affect that Evalee had returned. Evidently, Evalee's mother had died and she had

15

come home for the funeral. I felt a bit justified in my opinion of Evalee after that news. She was evidently the bitch I had always believed her to be. If she was around, why hadn't the heartless whore been to visit her daughter? I had been taught not to judge but I had to wallow that situation around in my mind for a while. Finally I had to conclude that the woman was just pure evil and I felt justified in my belief. I believe God gives us an inherent ability to distinguish between good and evil just like he gives us the inherent ability to distinguish between ugliness and beauty.

Later that evening Harley asked me if I wanted to walk up to the Cranes Nest Baptist church with him. He explained about it being Wednesday and they would be holding prayer meeting and that it might do us both good to attend. Harley was Baptist all the way. "Once saved, always saved" was his motto. I would often try to excuse myself from these ordeals but Harley would retaliate by quoting the scripture "forsake not the assembling of yourselves together." I started to get just a little suspicious of his motives. He only had three or four days before he had to leave for the Army and I figured he would need at least that much time to get all his affairs settled around home. Of course since Evalee was back home he may have been anticipating running into her at church since that's the same church she had always attended. You could never actually tell what a man like Harley, especially with all his problems, was thinking.

It stopped raining after a couple of hours though the big black thunder clouds continued to roll overhead promising an encore of the recent deluge. As we passed the barn I ducked inside and retrieved the lantern since without it we would have been wading knee-deep mud holes most of the way home in the dark. The air was sweet and refreshing after the rain and the frogs along the creek bank had already commenced their nightly chorus. As we slogged along we seemed to be preoccupied only with dodging the numerous washouts and deep water filled wagon ruts but somewhere on the rivers of my mind bobbed an unwelcome intruder. I knew his name was "change" but I could not exactly grasp his insidious significance. I suspect Adam may have had a similar premonition upon his imminent expulsion from Eden.

It was now twilight and presently the silhouette of the church building came into view. The coal oil lamps had been lit as evident

16

from the eerie yellow light emanating from the two side windows of the building. Harley commented that in spite of the muddy conditions we had traversed the three miles with time to spare before church time. Since a convenient flat spot had not been available to erect the church building upon, the builders had positioned the front portion of the building on the berm of the road and then used huge tree trunks as props for the rear portion. This left a considerable open space beneath the building where some churchgoers would hitch their saddle horses and the younger men would congregate out of sight of the old folks in case any "cussin'" or "drinkin'" was going on. You could probably have squeezed sixty or seventy people inside the building but generally the attendance was more like twenty-five or thirty souls. The building was constructed from rough-hewn lumber with two large windows on each side and an entrance whose threshold was situated on the same level with the road. There were two rows of pews in the sanctuary with a narrow aisle between them and six pews in each row. Someone had at one time or other attempted to whitewash the walls and ceiling but most of the whitewash had flaked off long ago and the interior now had a white and brown speckled appearance. The platform on which the pulpit had been erected was considerably raised above the main floor and the huge lectern was painted solid white. A long narrow table was stationed in front of the lectern down on the sanctuary floor. Inscribed on the front of this table were the words "This Do in Remembrance of Me." It was upon this table that the bread and wine for the Eucharist was placed before being dispensed to the congregation.

Many of the older men were assembled near the entrance just standing around chewing their tobacco, whittling, and no doubt discussing the market price of their crops and cattle. Harley and I made our way around to the back of the building where several teenage boys were playing mumble peg. We sat on the ground and watched until the game was over and joined in the laughter as we watched the loser retrieve the peg out of the moldy earth with his teeth. As we were standing and dusting the seats of our britches off, old Soup Beans, whose knife the players had been using, was closing the blade and preparing to return it to his pocket. Harley asked the man if he could take a look at it his knife.Harley was opening and closing the big blade on Soup Bean's knife as we nonchalantly made our way around the building toward the front entrance. Harley pulled his own knife and handed it to Soup Beans and simultaneously asked him if he wanted to "swap" knives. Soup Beans said he didn't want to trade, but Harley was persistent and told him he would give him fifty cents to boot. Harley was honest about it. He told Soup Beans about the tip of the little blade on his own pearl handled knife being broken off but added that "it won't matter-it's still as good as new!"

Soup Beans began to scratch his head and get a little excited when he saw the shiny half dollar. Ole Soup Beans was proud of his Barlow. I feel sure the knife was his prize possession. It was a big black knife of several blades and shiny Bakelite handles. I expect he had shown it to everyone in the county. I walked on ahead of them stifling a laugh as it was easy to get tickled at the way soup beans was acting while scrutinizing the fifty cent piece.

Soup Beans was a black man about forty years old who lived alone near a place called "Cooley Gap" some four or five miles distant from the church. Cooley Gap was just a sway back in one of the higher ridges in the area. Cooley Gap was named by the Chinese who had migrated to the region some hundred years past to work for the L&N railroad. The L&N had laid a lot of track throughout the coalfields of Southeastern Kentucky and the Chinamen had hired on as tracklayers or Gandy dancers. A few black families had also settled at Cooley Gap after the civil war and I guess Soup Beans was the last survivor. He owned a shack and a little piece of bottom land where he grew a garden and hired out to the local tobacco farmers at three dollars a day. Three dollars a day was the going rate for adult farm labor at that time. I believed him to be a good moral man, and a good Christian man, since I had never heard a derogatory word concerning him. I can't remember ever attending that church without old Soup Beans being present. Someone had told me the reason they nicknamed him "soup beans" was that he lived on soup beans, collard greens, and corn bread. His real name was Lincoln Humfleet.

Pretty soon the familiar strains of the hymn "In the Sweet by And by" came wafting along on the damp air. It was near dark now and you could see the fog begin to settle in. Fanny Johnson's shrill soprano voice was raised above all the rest as usual. I had heard Harley comment that she had a set of lungs powerful enough to operate a blast furnace. Of course he had meant no disrespect. He had simply voiced his opinion during one of his more emphatic moments.

I deposited the lantern on a tree stump close to the front door and slipped inside while they were singing "When the Roll Is Called Up Yonder." The last pew near the door was empty and I sat as close to the door as I could. Pretty soon Harley appeared and in his usual nonchalant way walked on up to the front row and sat directly in front of the pulpit. The wind had kicked up some and I could feel a little breeze coming through the doorway. I had probably picked the coolest spot in the house to sit. The wicks on the coal oil lamps had been turned up as high as they would go. There were eight of the big lamps altogether, three on each wall and one on either side of the pulpit.

The light from the lamps cast flickering shadows upon the pallid faces of the men in the "amen" corner. This was the section where many of the older men sat. Most of them were regular in attendance and they usually encouraged the preacher in his message with an emphatic "amen," signifying their agreement with his description and interpretation of the scriptures. They sat as puppets staring straight ahead at the pulpit. To a man, they each wore bibbed overalls, and their faces were weather worn and wrinkled, revealing a life of hard work and responsibility. True Americans, the salt of the earth; they were stern and serious men. The dried remnants of a trickle of tobacco juice at the corners of their mouths were about all that outwardly revealed their true humanity. The women all sat in close proximity near the back of the building. They too were dressed alike. Their homemade bonnets and long gingham dresses all seemed to have been cut from the same bolt of cloth. They were all middle aged with the exception of one who appeared to be a young mother with a toddler nursing at the breast. The whole congregation appeared tired and worn out but this was the harvest season and I figured most of them had hurried in from the fields for a quick supper before making their way on to church. They were smart enough to know that not only was food for the body important but also just as important was food for the soul.

Someone suggested another hymn and while everyone was searching through the hymnal for the right page, someone reached around the door and tapped me on the shoulder. It was Evalee. She motioned for me to step outside. We stepped a few feet from the entrance and away from the faint light emitting from the door. She asked me how mad Harley was at her. I told her I hadn't noticed any difference in him. Then she asked me about her baby and told me how much she loved little Molly and how much she had missed her. She said she was sorry she had left so abruptly but that she didn't know any other way to do it. That if she had told anyone she was leaving, there would have just been a big row and that she had grown weary of all the fights and arguments.

I was starting to feel a bit sorry for her. She was acting so nervous. I told her to calm down and that everything would be all right. She told me about her mother's death and that she would be going back to Cincinnati right after the funeral. She also informed me that she was going to take little Molly with her. She said what a good man Harley was and that she felt awful about the whole affair but that she didn't love him. She said she wanted more out of life than a dirt farm in Knox County. When I informed her of Harley being drafted she started to cry. I waited until the sobbing subsided and resumed my seat inside the building. Pretty soon Evalee came in and took a seat a few rows in front of me.

When the last congregational hymn was finished, the preacher arose from the flickering shadows behind the pulpit and deliberately, gently, placed his opened bible on the wooden lectern. He looked out from between the two lamps which hung at about three or four feet from either side of his face. He was moving his head slowly right, and then left as though he were attempting to read the congregation like a book. Stillness filled the place. He retrieved a white handkerchief from his hip pocket with his right hand and wiped his brow. It was hot in there. It had to be doubly hot between those two lamps. He continued to read us awhile after the wipe.

Then, after what seemed like five minutes, he began to speak. "Judas," he mumbled. I could barely hear the word. Then in a much louder, coarse, concise tone "Judas Iscariot"- he stretched each syllable. "The disciple who betrayed Jesus our savior; the one who administered the kiss of death. The man who delivered God incarnate over to sinful man to be humiliated, beaten, and ultimately crucified on an old rugged cross. J-u-d-a-sI-s-c-a-r-i-o-t."

20

Again he stretched each syllable. "I know what you are thinking," he shouted. "What a wretch! What a traitor! What ingratitude! I could never betray one who loved me like Jesus loved Judas! I'm glad I'm not that greedy! Yeah! These are some of the thoughts running through your minds right now!" He paused and caught his breath as he read us again. "Yes, you know him, this Judas! This traitor, this man sick with the sin called greed! You know why you know him?" He paused again. "Well, do you? I'll tell you why you know him! Because he's you! And he's me! He's all of us! And that's why we can understand what he done."

"What he done was simply sin! One of the sins Judas committed was greed, and the Bible (he slammed the book hard with his right hand) tells me that greed is sin and will send you to Hell like any other unforgiving sin. God hates any sin! He hates greed as much as he hates murder!" He paused briefly after the word "murder." "Ah-ha!" he finally chuckled. "You're saying to yourself right now 'I know I've never committed murder!' Well how about adultery, or bearing false witness, or blasphemy? Let me tell you something. When you copulate with another man's wife in your mind, its adultery, just as sure as if you had committed the actual act."

It was getting mighty warm in there to me so I quietly eased out the door for a little fresh air. I wasn't that interested in religion anyway. But for some reason I was feeling guilty about something or other and I could not figure out why. A couple of my High school buddies were standing there smoking and one of them offered me a cigarette which I accepted. I have always regretted the moment. We reminisced about our High school escapades for a little while and by that time I had cooled off a bit.

I went back inside and resumed my seat but the preacher was still droning on. "We got to love one another! That was the trouble with Judas. He really didn't love Jesus. He hadn't learned how to love. Some of us have got to learn how to love. This don't always come natural. The only natural love is God's love for us and a mother's love for her child. The rest of it we have to work at. Why I can remember before I was called to preach I hated everything and everybody. But I finally saw the error of my ways and asked God to forgive me and save me and, why, today I love everybody! Yeah! If Judas had really loved Jesus he never would have betrayed Him. There wouldn't have been enough money, let alone a mere thirty pieces of silver." He began to leaf through the Bible. "For all have sinned and come short of the glory of God! Roman's 3:23! There is none righteous, no not one! Roman's 3:10! Old Judas even walked with God, talked with God, lived with God and ate with God. He was one of Gods best friends and still he sinned. So the next time you think about Judas you can put away yourself righteousness."

He motioned to the song leader to begin a congregational hymn. Then he stepped down from the platform and began to pace back and forth in front of the congregation. Finally he stopped and shouted in a strained, almost pleading voice. "I am begging you, come and give your life to Jesus." He mopped his face again. "He is the only answer! In the end He forgave Judas and He will forgive you too." He raised the bible high above his head with his right hand. "Won't you come tonight? Won't you come to Jesus tonight?" He was standing now with outstretched arms toward the congregation. He was quiet for a minute. He produced the limp handkerchief and mopped his brow again. The singers finished the hymn. The preacher began again in a low, subdued tone. "And now as we are about to be dismissed in prayer and begin to make our way to our respective places of abode, let's remember old Judas in a different light. Fear God and don't commit the unpardonable sin." He paused again and began once more to slowly look from left to right while focusing his stare on every face. "Let us go forth from this place tonight determined to follow Jesus in everything we do. Let us try not to sin, but when we do, and we will, let us try to be prompt in asking Jesus to forgive us and then determine in our hearts to never commit that sin again. Now, if you are here tonight without a savior-don't put it off. Ask Jesus to come into your heart and save you before it's eternally too late." He abruptly raised his arms motioning for us to stand and as we all stood to our feet he began the hymn "Oh Why Not Tonight." He was a pretty decent singer too, I thought to myself.

As usual, with head bowed in humility and with long slow strides, Harley made his way up to the altar to pray and two or three of the other younger men straggled along behind him. They slowly kneeled in front of the first pew with as much humility and respect as one could possibly muster. They remained there, praying, until the congregation commenced the hymn "Amazing Grace." Harley already professed salvation but he just liked to go and pray at the altar. He had related to me several times before, that getting on his knees and praying at the church altar was the place where he felt the closest to God. When they finished the last song, we were dismissed in prayer by one of the men in the "amen" corner. The preacher quickly made his way to the front door where he could shake hands with everyone as they departed and invite them back to church on Sunday.

When I stepped outside, the bright full moon seemed close enough to touch, and the cold front had pushed the humidity out of the region. Harley was standing next to the roadway talking to Evalee. I got a little nervous at the sight. I was hoping they wouldn't start a big ruckus. Evalee was talking with her hands and wiggling around like she always did. She was actually a pretty woman. She had become considerably thinner since moving away. She was wearing a thin, almost see through, blue gingham dress with a white belt girded tightly about her slim waist, and you couldn't help noticing the low cut neckline. Her full-blown head of blond hair was thick, long, and curly, and the moonlight seemed to accentuate every curve of her fully developed body. I think I may have actually had a crush on her myself at one time, but she was too old for me. As I approached them, I noticed that Harley was all smiles and did not appear agitated in the least. They seemed to be having a civil conversation. Harley told me to take the lantern and head on home alone. He said he might catch up with me later. I didn't meet up with him again that night but he was at his usual place at the breakfast table the next morning.

The last time I saw Harley he was slogging down the road toward the main highway on his way to the Army. He had to leave about daylight that Monday morning. I gave him a big hug before he left and have never forgotten that look of futility in his eyes. We didn't have anything like a suitcase so he had wrapped a few personal items in a feed sack and carried it across his shoulder on a bindle stick. He did crack a faint smile when I asked him if he had just decided to run off and be a hobo instead of going into the Army. I stood on the porch and watched him until he was around the bend in the road.

It was a sad time for us. Mother seemed to be constantly crying and my father obviously became weaker with each passing day. I didn't have time, however, to think of anything much except making sure all the crops were cultivated and taken care of. There seemed to be a thousand things that I alone was now responsible for. I did decide however to take a break and attend prayer meeting the following Wednesday night. I had noticed the Sheriffs cruiser going past our house a few times and had been wondering what had happened. News traveled slowly in that country since we had no telephone and rarely had visitors.

As usual, there were several young men congregated near the rear of the building. I missed old soup beans after I had been standing there for a while. When I inquired of his whereabouts a sudden hush came over the group. Finally, one of the boys told me that someone had lynched him. Naturally I laughed at anything so ridiculous. But then, as I assessed the demeanor of the group, I began to wonder if it could be true. Then, my friend Chuck Wagner, who I knew wouldn't joke about anything that serious, told me the whole story. Evalee had been found beaten to death over at the old Blanton barn. This was just an old abandoned barn not too far distant from the church house. She had also been raped. Her daddy and brother had found her. She had not returned home from church last Wednesday night and they had gone out looking for her. They found her about noon the following day half covered up with boards and lying face down in one of the milking stalls. She had been beaten with a two by four and then stabbed three or four times. When they rolled her over on her back they found old Soup Bean's Barlow knife underneath her. There was no mistaking Soup Bean's knife. The Barlow was as familiar to folks as Soup Beans. Then, last Sunday night the sheriff had received an anonymous call concerning some kind of mischief taking place out around Cooley Gap, and when he went to investigate, he found old Soup Beans hanging from the shade tree right in front of his shack. It seems he had been hanging there for a couple of days as the crows had already pecked both of his eyes out. The sheriff cut him down and transported him to the Jones Funeral Parlor for proper burial.

I finally got all the work done that fall but I nearly worked myself to death. I'm sure that about that time in my life was when I resolved to find a less demanding way to make a living. I was sitting on the front porch that December morning just pondering all the events that had taken place since Harley left when the black Plymouth sedan with the two soldiers pulled up in front of the house. They had come to offer their condolences and the condolences of the U.S. Army to the family. Harley had been killed in action for the battle of some island way out there in the Pacific Ocean. I don't know why, but for some reason I had been expecting that. The Army shipped his body home and gave him a military funeral with all kinds of honors.

My daddy died the day before Christmas that year and I had to enter my mother in the county home about a year later. She had all but lost her mind. Harley getting killed away off there in a foreign land was enough to drive her crazy but I'm sure the incident that pushed her over the edge was when Evalee's parents came to take little Molly.

I sold the farm, moved to town and got a job as clerk in Bill Wilson's hardware store. I liked the job pretty well and I got to meet nearly everybody that lived in the County. About two years went by when Jerry Strong, chairman of the Knox County Republican Party, asked me to run for sheriff which I did, and to my surprise was elected. I am presently in my second term of office.

The erection of a new county courthouse has been in progress now for the past year or so. My office was one of the first to be relocated to the new structure. Earlier this morning I was just browsing around the basement of the old courthouse trying to get an idea of which fixtures and furniture to move to the new location. I passed a table laden down with a curious collection of boxes, paper sacks and storage containers. All these items were marked and tagged with names, dates and other types of identification. After a minute or two I realized they were beginning the relocation of the property and evidence room to the new courthouse. I saw dates on some of these items dating back to the nineteen twenty's. As I was preparing to return up the stairs, a small box caught my eye. It was about the size of a shoebox and may actually have been a shoebox but the name scrawled on the lid was what really caused me to pause and take notice. It read "PROPERTY OF LINCOLN HUMFLEET." I thought for a minute and then remembered that this was old Soup Bean's real name. I walked over to the table, picked up the box, blew the dust off the lid and opened it. Inside I found a pair of broken eyeglasses, a red handkerchief, a gold L&N railroad watch, a billfold, which contained a faded picture of an old gray haired colored woman, a nickel and six pennies, a fifty-cent piece, and Harley's white bone handled knife with the tip of the little blade broken off.

THE END

"ONE THING AT LEAST IS CERTAIN, THIS LIFE FLIES"

The relatively flat terrain and the well-groomed fields of knee-high corn and tobacco ended abruptly as I crossed the line into Knox County. The car dropped off the smooth pavement with a thud and I was forced to throttle back to a crawl. No doubt, the early pioneers who came through the Cumberland Gap some fifty miles to the South and forged onward to this point figured they had reached the proverbial Promised Land. Laurel County stretches Northward from this county line and consists largely of rich flat farmland. I was born in Knox County and this is where the lower ridges of the Appalachian Mountains begin. I was once again on the old graveled road I had traveled so often as a growing boy. Clouds of thick yellow dust began to billow up behind my old ford and now all I could see in the rear view mirror was a thick cloud of potential mud. I did not remember the road being so full of dips and curves but then I could not remember ever having traveled this road in a car. Our family could not afford that luxury and our only mode of transportation, aside from walking, was a rickety farm wagon pulled along by a team of mules. The roadbed had been worn and scraped into the lower side of the continuous chain of ridges that form the ancient stream valley of the Knox Fork creek.

Once every two or three years the county would run a grader over the road as a part of their money strapped maintenance program. However, most of the basic engineering had been accomplished hundreds of years earlier by herds of deer, buffalo, and subsequent bands of Indians. All those intrepid beings had naturally picked the path of least resistance through these foothills of the Appalachians during their perpetual hunt for food.

This rugged stream valley had always been to me like the fabled "sleepy hollow" of Washington Irving's classic. On more than one occasion as an amorous teenager, I had volunteered to accompany one of my sweethearts home from church along this dirt road. A young man with raging hormones will go to about any length for a goodnight kiss. Nevertheless, the reward was never worth the agony of the long walk home alone, especially at night.

When darkness descends on one of these hollows here in the mountains, you can say for sure it is dark. Like Ichabod, I too would whistle a nervous tune while I feigned nonchalance and slogged along toward home. But then, when images of the headless horseman galloping out from the bushes or darting out from behind one of the big oak trees along the road became too vivid, I would run the last two or three miles with imagined steam from the horses flaring nostrils on the nape of my neck. The most beautiful sight in the world was that lamp my mother always left burning in the window when I was away at night. I would be in bed and pulling the covers up over me before our old screen door slammed behind me.

Occasionally I would come upon a ramshackle dwelling or the dilapidated remains of a rusty roofed barn or outbuilding and attempt to remember the family or the individual who had lived there when I was growing up but I could not seem to connect the place with a face. For years, I had been trying to forget Knox County and everything connected with it. Now and then I would spot a piece of antiquated farm equipment, such as a horse drawn hay rake, or mowing machine, half concealed by waist high weeds sitting abandoned alongside the road or half submerged in the shallow creek. The owner of these remnants of the past, I surmised, must have become disgusted with his lot in life and suddenly walked away from the frustrations of attempting to feed a family off the proceeds of two or three acres of bottom land. These old relics were simply castaways from a good and wholesome way of life, which was now all but forgotten.

The "New Deal" coupled with a bloody and costly world war had spawned the migration of these good-natured folk to the industrial centers of the nation like Cincinnati and Detroit. They had left the mountains in droves. They had hearkened to the sirens call and traded in their lives of freedom and tranquility for a time card, a dollar an hour, and a life of slavery to the Yankee dollar.

I was growing anxious to see the old homeplace. I figured it would look about as rundown and forsaken as everything else I had seen since I crossed the county line but I was pleasantly surprised when I discovered the property to be in relatively good repair. There was a healthy looking stand of fescue and rye grass around the little bungalow and white trellises supported the several rose bushes that dotted the yard. It appeared as though the house was sporting a new tin roof and the house, barn and tool shed had all received a fresh coat of paint. I was wondering whom mother had hired to help her with this maintenance. I jerked the shifter down into low, idled along for a minute and then stopped at the widest spot in the road facing the house. I switched the engine off and soon the awesome stillness prompted a catalogue of memories:

A winter evening playing checkers with my dad in front of the fireplace- the rattling sound of the old "Warm Morning" cook stove as my dad built the morning fire in preparation for my mother to fix breakfast-the smell of those big cat head biscuits baking and mingling with the aroma of boiling coffee. I could almost taste those delicious apple pies mother always brought out for Sunday dinner. Of course, there always seemed to be a downside, especially during winter months. Crawling out from between two cozy featherbeds during outdoor temperatures of zero was not easy. Actually, the temperature inside the house would not be much warmer during those cold mornings. I think the thing I hated worst of all was stepping out of that nice warm bed onto an ice-cold floor. I would bundle up as best I could and trudge through knee- deep snow to the barn to do my chores. I loved feeling the warmth off the body of old "jerz," our milk cow, while trying to squeeze a quart or so of milk from that pitiful undernourished animal. After a hearty breakfast of biscuits, gravy, eggs and ham, I would head out on the one- mile trek to school. If the road was not covered in a foot of snow or ankle deep mud, you could say you were blessed. I carried my lunch of breakfast leftovers in a two- pound lard bucket with holes punched in the lid for ventilation. I thought I was having a hard life at the time. Nevertheless, I would now give anything to be able to go back to what I had then mistaken for misery and start my life all over.

I could almost see my mother standing there in the yard trimming and pruning her rose bushes. She was wearing her everyday gingham dress with the hem touching the ground as usual. Her bonnet seemed a bit too large for the rest of her thin wiry frame but not quite large enough to cover the bun of iron gray hair wound up and secured neatly at the nape of her neck. She was turning now and looking in my direction. She slowly gathered the folds of the calico apron up into her tanned and sinewy hands and methodically wiped the sweat from her singularly angelic face. She looked sad. Tears began to fill my eyes and I experienced an almost uncontrollable urge to run and embrace her. I yearned to tell her how sorry I was for the heartache I had caused her. Nevertheless, it was too late now. She was dead. I read her obituary two days ago in the *Barbourville Advocate.* She reportedly had died from a cancer, but I knew her broken heart was also a factor. I had known all along that grief over what I had done would one day help to kill her, but I also realized that if I had taken any other action, matters would have only been worse. If there was a bit of solace left for me it was in knowing she had died with an unshakable faith in God. Her life of drudgery, misery, and disappointment was now over, and whatever choices I made in the future could not harm her.

There was no one stirring about the place and I seriously considered getting out of the car and looking around but I did not want to take a chance on being discovered and possibly arrested just yet. I decided to sit there in the car and enjoy that feeling of peace and serenity, which had suddenly come over me. My mind was beginning to clear, and my route of action for cleaning up my wasted life was becoming more vivid. This is all there is, I thought to myself. If a man can find a little peace of mind in this life, nothing else really matters. However, I knew that this was just one of those little snatches of contentment a man will naturally encounter now and again. My daddy had given me the prescription for peace of mind and contentment a long time ago, but I had considered his advice too simple to be truly effective. "Just do what's right," he would say. "Be satisfied with what you got and do what's right. When you got to decide what to do, just don't get angry, be good to folks and then do the next right thing."

He was a simple optimist who always viewed the proverbial glass as being half- full. He had to work hard in order to provide his family with their basic needs. He seemed to be completely satisfied with his status in life, and the idea of seeking fame and fortune had probably never occurred to him. He was born and raised in the coalfields of Harlan County and went to work in the coalmines when he was ten. By the time he was eighteen he had developed silicosis. Most people described the disease as "black lung." He started working in the logwoods after that as a teamster and finally saved enough money to make a down payment on these hundred acres of land. He married my mother in the spring of nineteen twenty-five and a week or so later, they set out for their new home here on the original Wilderness Road. The journey took them a week. It was slow going with clumsy oxen pulling the wagon. Their worldly possessions consisted of the clothes on their back, two pigs, one dozen or so chickens and a good supply of seed corn, a bushel of seed potatoes and one milk cow.

I had heard my father comment on more than one occasion that if a man had his milk and butter and a little bacon and corn bread, he could survive. I was born eight years later in September of nineteen thirty-three and by that time he had finished the new farmhouse. Mother had miss-carried twice during those years and I expect these mishaps were largely due to the backbreaking drudgery connected with subsistence farming. I was the only child and I suspect other miscarriages had occurred.

Presently I detected the sound of another vehicle coming along the road, and I glanced to make sure the driver had enough room to get around my Ford. The black Chevy sedan slowed to a crawl as it passed me. The driver stuck his head out the window and scowled at me for taking up so much of the road, and I detected a few indistinguishable cuss words as he passed, but I wasn't going to get excited and let it bother me. I sat there for a few minutes while the dust settled and then shifted into low and proceeded in the same direction as the Chevy.

The sun was high in the sky by now and it was blazing hot. The air conditioner was on the blink so I could not roll the windows up for fear of suffocating and when I rolled them down the dust from the Chevy clogged my nostrils. Within a matter of seconds, I realized I could write my name in the yellow dust, which was collecting on the dash so I dropped back down into low and proceeded on at a snail's pace.

After a mile or so of this asphyxiation, I pulled off the road in front of the "Jarvis Post Office and General Store." I sat there in the car for a minute waiting for the dust to settle. Finally, I slid cautiously out of the car and brushed the grit from my shirtsleeves

31

and the lap of my trousers. I tried to appear nonchalant and somewhat skipped up the four or five concrete steps onto the porch. Some serious remodeling had been accomplished since I last visited the place. They had originally built the store out of unfinished two by sixes and used creosote as a preservative. The exterior walls were now cobblestone, but the acrid odor of creosote was still present. A smooth concrete porch had also been added to the entire length of the building. A wrinkled and weathered octogenarian was sitting reared back in a cane-bottomed chair near the entrance. A broad brimmed, black hat partially covered his short whiskered, saddle brown face, and the bib of his otherwise blue overalls was spotted with that same brown hue. He leaned forward as he puckered his lips and expelled a long stream of tobacco juice out into the rusty dust. As I drew closer, he extended his hand and I automatically grasped it and gave it a quick shake. The hand was wrinkled, calloused, and felt like sand paper. He mumbled something about my not needing to hurry since the mail was late again. I nodded affirmatively while studying the "RC" cola and "Partridge" lard signs, which had been haphazardly affixed to a couple of the weather worn posts supporting the roof of the sagging porch.

I was surprised to see that outdated gas pump still standing majestically there at the opposite end of the building. Someone must recently have given the old pump a new coat of "fire engine red" by the way it glistened in the morning sunlight. You never had to be concerned about being cheated with this type of gas delivery system I thought. The attendant would push and pull the long pump handle back and forth in pendulum fashion as he filled the large glass bulb at the top with the exact amount of fuel being purchased. A hose was then inserted into the vehicles gas receptacle and the gas was gravity fed into the gas tank. You could tell at a glance whether or not you were receiving the correct amount.

About that time a black Chevy panel truck pulled up and a red faced, heavy breathing man of about sixty years of age retrieved a canvas bag from the cargo section which was clearly marked "U.S. Mail" and rushed pantingly into the store with it. He seemed in a terrible hurry since he was back in the truck and speeding down the road again in a matter of a few seconds. The dust from the mail truck had no sooner settled when the friendly old gentleman who had been occupying the cane-bottomed rocking chair laboriously entered the store. Pretty soon he reappeared and was nervously attempting to stuff a brown envelope into the back pocket of his overalls. He greatly resembled my grandfather who I had always held in high esteem. He hesitated for a moment at the top of the porch steps and drew in a deep breath. He was evidently dreading the walk home. As he looked about, he no doubt spied an ant or a spider crawling around in the dust and he aimed a long stream of tobacco juice at it, and then, wiping his mouth with the back of his hand he slowly descended the steps and meandered carefully along the graveled road toward home.

I approached the narrow entrance to the store and peered searchingly into the dim interior of this venerable enterprise. I immediately detected that forever familiar "tick tock" of George Jarvis's big Roman numeral clock that still hung in the same place on the back wall. For a minute, that perpetual feeling of homesickness seemed to dissipate and I felt at peace. The same big ceiling fan continued to whir over the sacks of livestock feed stacked two high in the middle of the room. I remembered that on a warm summer day you could smell the aroma of molasses and grain emanating from these burlap sacks for half a mile up the road. I caught a brief vision of myself as a lad sitting lazily on one of these sacks while nursing an ice-cold bottle of "RC" cola. I glanced again at the clock and instantly reality returned. I was wondering if that indefatigable timepiece had remained there all these years to simply click off the seconds until I returned and did something foolish enough to be arrested.

I heard someone fidgeting around behind the postmaster's cage but other than that, no one else seemed to be present. A ceiling high wooden partition had been erected to separate the U.S. post office from the rest of the establishment. I walked over and looked through the small barred window near the center of the mailroom. A thin middle-aged woman was standing there spraddle-legged with her back to me shoving envelopes into the several mailboxes along the wall in front of her. I cleared my throat and tapped lightly on the little window with a quarter. Presently the person stopped sorting the mail, came and stood across the wide counter directly in front of me. I paid her for a bottle of Royal Crown cola and she motioned for me to help myself from the soft drink cooler. When she handed me my change our eyes met and I recognized her right away.

Her name was Lucy, the youngest daughter of George Jarvis, the original proprietor of this country store and first postmaster of this little community. I was glad she did not recognize me but at the same time, I was disappointed. I had been in love with Lucy my whole life. Of course, it had been sort of a courtly love, or love from a distance, but at the least it had been a serious crush. We were the same age and had graduated at the same time; but Lucy was from a prominent family. She was not poor like me. Old George probably had more money than any man in the county. I had often thought about trying to date her, but they had sent her off to college, and I figured I would never see her again. I had never aspired to much more than just settling down there on our farm with someone like Lucy and raising a passel of kids. She was still a fine looking woman and continued to carry herself as one who demanded respect. I did not let on as if I had ever seen her before, and I felt comfortable that she had not recognized me. Then, before I turned away, I half suspected she gave me an inquisitive look.

It was nice and cool there in the store, and I thought for a minute about sitting on one of those comfortable looking sacks of feed like I used to do and rest for a while, but I had determined to be diligent and keep a low profile. I decided to go outside and find a shady place where I could relax and enjoy the cold drink. I paused briefly as I neared the exit to scrutinize a row of "Wanted" posters that were tacked to the wall near the door. I half expected to find my own image there among that row of the ten "most wanted" miscreants in the land. As I passed through the door, I glanced at George's old style calendar, which required the date to be changed every day. It read July tenth, 1992. Some coincidence, I thought. The last time I saw that calendar it read July tenth, 1972. "Twenty years of pure Hell," I mumbled to myself!

I made my way around to the side of the building and sprawled wastefully upon a lone patch of grass underneath that familiar old silver maple tree which still stood sentinel like, and impervious to time. This had been the habitual gathering place for schoolchildren on their long trek to and from the one room school building that served this community. A sleek and shiny patina on the protruding roots near the trunk of that grand old tree gave evidence of childhood memories continuing to be born here. Many a foot race had been run to this natural sanctuary from a sudden spring shower, and many a marble or mumble peg champion had won or lost his title here in the cool shade on a steamy Saturday afternoon.

The Jarvis residence was much the same as I had remembered it. This relatively large frame dwelling was situated some fifty feet to the rear and slightly to the right of the store building. It had long been the most admired home in the county. It was the first house around to get in-door plumbing. George had always maintained the little outhouse in the back however, since it was common knowledge that he felt uncomfortable relieving himself indoors. George Jarvis was one of the finest men I had ever known. He probably made a little money off the store and received a small stipend for running the Post Office but that is not how he got rich. He made his money from real estate. The Jarvise's had been among the first white settlers in the region and had accumulated large tracts of land to which George had fallen heir. Evidently, he had been smart enough to realize when the major coal seams several miles to the East were beginning to peter out. That meant, in essence, that his real estate was destitute of the black gold. George sectioned his land off into one hundred acre tracts and began to sell. My father had purchased our farm from George for twenty five hundred dollars. Eventually George sold all his inheritance but the fifteen or twenty acres on which he built this fine home and the Post Office.

He was a fair and accommodating man and well-liked by everyone. Aside from his normal dry goods business of coffee, flour, sugar and the like, he also did a good business in wholesale chickens and eggs. I had traded him many a chicken for a sack of smoking tobacco, a soft drink or a moon pie. I remembered the time I snatched up one of our old dommernecker hens and brought it to the store and traded it for a sack of "R. J. R." which was short for the "R.J. Reynolds Tobacco Company" and subsequently shortened to "Run Johnny Run" by most folks who smoked the product. George took the hen around to the side of the store and tossed it into the chicken coop. Well, the old Domernecker got loose and as I was walking home I discovered it some hundred feet or so up the road, so I just took it on home with me and brought it back again the next day and traded it for something else. I have always felt guilty about that incident and wish I could somehow make it right. I am sure I will never get that opportunity. There's no doubt the loveable old man is dead since he was at least seventy years of age the last time I saw him.

Pretty soon I noticed two men making their way down the hill from the direction of the community graveyard which was situated on a narrow plateau on the ridge adjoining the store, and at about the distance of five hundred feet to the North. As they came closer, I saw they were carrying picks and shovels. Evidently, they had been up there digging my mother's grave. She was to be buried there in the Jarvis cemetery later that afternoon. From the looks of things, they had not finished any too soon. A few dark clouds were beginning to move in promising a good soaking rain before too long. I was not sure what time the funeral had been scheduled for, but I expected it to be somewhere around one or two o'clock at the "Calihan" church some half mile or so South of my present location. It was now ten thirty, and I figured I would wait where I was. I had a good view of the road and would be able to spot the hearse as it passed.

I decided to make the best of the two or three hour wait so I folded my jacket for a pillow and reclined there on the grass hoping to catch a little nap. I was beginning to be able to relax some now that I was sure I was nearing the end of my exile. I had been alone and alienated from any meaningful contact with my fellow man for twenty years and as yet had escaped man's punishment, but not the perpetual chastisement of God. The thought of my mother having to endure the pronouncement of a death sentence upon her only son had been too great for me to bear, and if I could take comfort in anything, it was in knowing she had been gracefully and eternally spared that agony. Nevertheless, as I lay there amid those familiar surroundings I suddenly realized there would be no reprieve for me from those dreadful memories of the past until I too had in one way or another met my own demise.

I was seventeen years old when my father finally spit up what was left of his rotting lungs. It is not as if his death was unexpected. He had been sick most of his life, but he had managed to pay the farm off while at the same time supplying the family's basic needs. These were hard times for mother and me. While the loss of my dad was devastating enough, there was the extra work involved. He died in February just before it was time to start the spring plowing. Then there was school to finish. I was well enough equipped physically to handle the farming since I was a two hundred pound, all muscle lad of eighteen. Nevertheless, I did not seem to be very well equipped when it came to schoolwork. Nevertheless, I managed to graduate and at the same time accomplish all the necessary plowing and planting. Mother cried all the time, but she did manage to get the vegetable garden planted after I plowed up a little new ground near the house. She could see the garden from the kitchen window. We always had problems with groundhogs destroying our corn and beans, but since I had relocated the garden, she could now see the varmints from the kitchen window. The minute mother detected one of those critters in her garden she would simply slam the screen door on the back porch. That little trick never failed to scare the animals away.

One morning about breakfast time, I answered a knock at the front door and there stood Clyde Barnes with his bindle stick over his shoulder. He was forcing that fake smile and begging for a free meal. He was dressed in tattered army fatigues. Hobo's and tramps were a rare sight in that part of the country. I had heard stories about how plentiful they were during the great depression, but the depression was long gone, and the big war had afforded anyone who wanted it a good paying job in the killing machine departments of the big manufacturing conglomerates up North. I was not the kind of fellow to refuse a hungry man a bite to eat so I gave him a couple of biscuits and a slice of leftover ham. He shoved one of the biscuits into his mouth and the rest into his nap sack as he descended the steps and lumbered on down the road. I stood watching him until he disappeared around the curve. A strange and uneasy feeling came over me as I stood there scrutinizing that disheveled creature meandering along. He was more than just a man who had fallen on hard times I thought. His slothful gait and nasty grin instilled within me the feeling that I had just been exposed to the epitome of evil. I figured I had seen the last of him but come supper time, he was back. This time he talked to mother who gave him a few chores to accomplish in exchange for his dinner.

Clyde was a big muscular man of about forty years. He was unshaven and dirty looking. He had a wide white scar that ran diagonally up the left side of his face and disappeared under his shaggy hair. This deep scar had twisted and drawn his countenance into a perpetual smile. The color of his eyes were steely green and accentuated by dark bushy eyebrows. Those piercing eyes coupled with the fixed smile seemed to give him the ability to fathom your innermost secrets. I did not like him at all. Then, when mother agreed to his sleeping in the barn, I became that much more uneasy. He was one of those people who seemed to be everywhere at the same time. Each time I looked up, he seemed to be standing nearby with those ominous looking eyes boring a hole in me. He and mother seemed to get along fine but I figured she was just using him for his labor.

Clyde had been living in the barn for about a week when one morning I went into the kitchen as usual to build a fire in the cook stove and found him curled up sound asleep behind the stove. I did not wake him intentionally, but very soon the racket I was making in getting the fire started did. He just stretched and yawned a little and then nonchalantly ambled out the back door. When I asked mother what he was doing sleeping in the kitchen she told me he was scared to death of loud noises and thunder and lightning in particular. He told her he had been a paratrooper in world war two and had narrowly escaped death by freezing during the battle of the bulge.

Subsequently, he was taken prisoner, and during an escape attempt, the Germans had set the dogs on him. He was pretty badly disfigured all over his body. He was freed by the Russian army in 1945 and highly decorated for bravery upon his return to the States. He was still suffering from shell shock and that was the reason for his being in the house. The horrendous thunder and lightning of the previous night had driven him to seek solace and companionship among other human beings. He had intended to ask permission to come inside and wait out the storm, but his pride had prevented him from doing so. Mother had found him, cowering and terrified, underneath an old blanket on our front porch. Actually, I never bought into his yarns the way Mother did. He was just a first rate freeloader in my book.

Mother was a good-hearted woman. She was always ready to take pity on anyone with a good sob story. Nevertheless, and against all my forebodings and negativity, the inevitable romance blossomed. Within two weeks, the crops were all in excellent shape. There was not a weed in the fields. Two weeks after that, mother and Clyde were man and wife. I was convinced that this particular union between man and woman was a mistake. Funny how we all seem to harbor prejudice in one way or another but are always convinced that we are different. We believe we are fair and consistently willing to give our fellow man an even break. Nevertheless, my experiences of the past twenty years have convinced me that man in general is cast from the same mold and although we seem to be able to detect a gross prejudice in others, we never get honest enough to see this character defect in ourselves.

I must admit that I am not in a position to expect fair treatment from my fellow man since I know I do not deserve it. I realize the gravity of my sin and am ready, and I believe I have always been ready, to accept my punishment. I know I was created with a conscience and at one time considered this a cross which I had been destined to bear. Nevertheless, experience has taught me that I am one of the fortunate of Gods creations. I have learned that a man without a conscience is the ultimate loser. For that man, there is no hope. He is destined to eternal separation from God. According to the word of God, the wages of un-forgiven sin is death, and a man without a conscience is never sure if he has sinned or not. When a man with a conscience sins and knows that he has sinned, the particular act is of no consequence. In Gods eyes, sin is just sin. It is the guilt of un-confessed sin which prevents him from leading the kind of life that God intended. "A man's sins will find him out." He can continue for as long as he wants to hide and try to conceal those sins but all along, they are weighing him down to where he can find no piece or contentment. In many cases when a man dies, his folks will deliver a kind and becoming eulogy over him. Little do they realize they have buried a stranger. After carefully considering all the events of my past twenty years, I have come to the conclusion that even though I may be put to death for my sin against God and society, that when they put me in the ground, I will have confessed my sins, and they will be burying me and not someone else.

No one could ever take the place of my daddy, but old Clyde must have thought he could. He immediately began to take over as head of the family, and I was resentful of this to say the least. I had to mature for a few more years however before I realized that fact. I was jealous of the way he had so easily wormed his way into the confidence of my mother. Mother was all smiles and fluttering eyelashes from the first time she laid eyes on him. It was sickening. Within a very short time, I felt myself holding nothing but contempt for both of them. I guess Clyde could see right through me. He knew I hated him, and he made me aware he knew by piling more and more work on me. He never relinquished that hideous smile when he looked at me while barking out orders. He wanted me to break. He wanted me to leave. Then he would have my mother, the farm and everything we owned and everything my father had built.

I learned quickly to avoid Clyde when it was feasible but old Jack could not do that. Jack was my dog. I had raised him from a pup and that dog was a big part of my life. Jack would take up with anybody. The dog was continually trying to make friends with Clyde. He would walk alongside of him and try to lick his hand or run ahead and fetch Clyde a stick or run round and round Clyde in an attempt to persuade him to play, but Clyde would just cuss at him and try to kick him. If there were a rock or chunk of wood handy Clyde would pick it up and heave it at old Jack.

Jack was a smart dog and I had been training him to go to the pasture field and bring the cows to the barn for the evening milking. Without Jack, I would spend about an hour a day on this chore. The walk to the pasture field was hot and dusty and most of the time the cattle would have sought the evening shade of a briar patch or bramble thicket. I would have to chunk clods of dirt at them in order to drive them out of these dangerous thickets and if this did not work, I would have to bite the bullet and find the path of least resistance thru the briars and get closer. More than once, I had heard the rattles of a big diamond back and I had a sickening fear of those vipers. Of course, after old Jack was old enough he would go into those thickets, bring the cattle out, and put them on the path to the barn. He was becoming very proficient at his job. After a while I could walk with him to the big wooden gate at the entrance to the Pasture field, open the gate and the say "Jack, go get the cows", and old Jack would take off, and within thirty minutes you could hear the cowbell clanging around the side of the hill. Jack would be herding the cows along in single file toward the barn.

Of course, Jack was still a pup and occasionally a rabbit or a skunk caught his attention and Jack would become sidetracked. At those times, I would have to go to the pasture and find him and the cattle, but he was getting more and more dependable as he got older. It took me about six months to teach him how to lift the big leather ring up over the pole and open the gate but he finally got the hang of it. Most of the time after that all I had to do about sundown was just say to him "Jack, go get the cows" and Jack would make a beeline to the pasture and before long you could hear the tinkle of the cow bell as old "Jerz" and the other four cows trotted down to the gate.

Then old Jack un-latched the gate and marched them right on to the barn. Occasionally, old "Jerz," that was the lead cow, would balk, and for no good reason refuse to walk on through the gate. Of course, when I was there this was no problem. I could just holler, wave my arms, and she would lead the herd right on through the gate. But old Jack could not do that. He barked and nipped at her hooves but the cow usually turned and run in the wrong direction. When Jack ran and nipped at her heels the cow just naturally lowered her head in defense. If I were present when this happened, I just calmly walked up to the cow, grabbed her by the ear, and lead her through the gate. After Jack saw me do this several times, much to my surprise and delight, he began doing the same thing. If Jerz hesitated, Jack would run up in front of her and wait. Then when she lowered her head as if to butt him, Jack went into action. He grabbed her by the ear with his teeth and led her right on through the gate. Actually, old Jack got so good at his job that all I had to do was rattle the milk buckets along about milking time and Jack would go into action.

Clyde hated us for that. He was jealous beyond description. However, I could tell; he mainly hated me - I was in his way. Little did he know or suspect the feeling was mutual, and I was intensely bothered by that feeling. I had never known the real meaning of hate. A loving mother had taught me better. The golden rule of "do unto others" and "love thy neighbor as thyself" had been instilled within me. But again, there was something else about that man. In the final analysis, I actually believe genuine, bona fide, hate and jealously to be the motives for what eventually happened. I can remember having wrestled with my deeper feelings for several weeks prior to the incident. I often cursed, and whispered my hate for him. Then I always felt guilty and began trying to analyze that uncomfortable feeling within. On more than one occasion, I concluded that Clyde was just plain evil. I believed him to be evil incarnate. After all, I had not really committed any outward act to make him hate me, or for that matter to cause him to dislike me. For this reason, I began to ponder the real root of his problem. I then concluded that Clyde was the devil himself. The evidence of this was not in his spontaneous tantrums and fits of temper, or his cursing and ravings. The evidence was in that hideous perpetual smirk on his face and the penetrating gleam in his steely green eyes that always told you he could see right into your very soul.

Clyde continued to be the perfect gentleman around my mother and I was careful not to cause her any alarm concerning my attitude toward him. Saying anything to her in that regard would only serve to make matters worse. But, when he killed my dog, that primordial evil nature which I was able to so articulately conceal gripped my very essence and the primitive man within me, which socialization will never completely obliterate, sprung newborn from those dormant genes and temporarily turned me into the very beast that I had so readily detected in him.

It was not a spur of the moment thing. It did not happen in a fit of rage. It was deliberate and preconceived. I considered trying to make it look like an accident, but that would not do. He might not see it coming, and I wanted to see that ugly smile turn into a look of terror. I wanted him to see me and to realize, if only for an instant, that I was about to kill him and to realize that he was about to die.

As I look back on my life, it is hard for me to understand just how my thinking could have taken such a detour. I had been raised a Christian and basically brought up as a church going believer, and it had never occurred to me that a spirit of evil had suddenly clutched my heart and mind concerning this one individual.

While on my way to the barn to take care of the milking about daybreak one Sunday morning, I suddenly realized that old Jack had not been there to greet me when I stepped out the kitchen door. I just figured he was off chasing an early rising rabbit somewhere, but all my surmising about him faded when I reached the woodpile. Jack was lying there with half of his head missing. There was a big stick of blood stained stove wood lying next to him. I knew Clyde had killed him, but grieved as I was, I did not let on. I just carried the blood soaked carcass to the feedlot and buried it in the relatively soft earth just beyond the fence. This did not take but a few minutes, and then I went on into the barn. I noticed the fresh wound on old jerz's ear. The wound was not too bad and would heal just fine in a few days according to my calculations. It certainly was not serious enough to justify the murder of my dog. Nervous and grief stricken, I proceeded with the milking but was so distracted I barely was able to retrieve more than a quart each in the two buckets I had brought with me. As I plodded along toward the house, I noticed Clyde standing by the woodpile. When he turned to face me that hateful countenance produced within me an indescribable rage. I automatically reached the milk buckets toward him, and he instinctively grasped one bucket in each hand. In an instant, I picked up a stick of the freshly split and jagged edged stove wood and struck him square in the face with all my power. He fell headlong onto the pile of wood. A sheet of blood ran down his forehead and began to puddle up in his eye sockets.

Thoughts of the penitentiary, the electric chair and a brokenhearted mother began to bombard my mind. I stood motionless for several minutes then turned and looked toward the house. There was no one in sight. I glanced at Clyde. The smile was gone. A distinct taste of copper filled my mouth and a tingling numbness immobilized me. Presently a faint but audible voice advised me to run to mother and confess the deed, while another prompted me to flee-that he had deserved what he got, and that if I stayed around my life was over. I wanted to cry, but I did not have the time. I started walking, slowly at first, but then as the instinct of self-survival took over I lit out as fast as I could across the fields in the general direction of the state highway some four miles away.

By the time I reached US 25 East, I was out of breath and drenched in sweat. My jeans were soaked to the waist from the dew I had collected as I ran through hay fields and weed thickets. I had tentatively been planning to hitch a ride north but as I began to think more clearly, I realized someone was sure to turn me in before the day was over. I then decided to try boarding one of the North bound freights out of Baily's Switch. There was a coal tipple near that little community and freights were being loaded and un-loaded there all through the day and night. The L&N Railroad ran parallel to the highway for a couple of miles in that vicinity. I waited until there was not a car in sight before darting across the four-lane highway and down the graveled escarpment towards the tracks, which were some two hundred yards distant. I paused near the bottom of this incline and tried to get my bearings. There was a small stream on the other side of the tracks. The cool water proved to be a lifesaver as I was by now dying of thirst. The sun was now at about forty-five degrees in the East and most of the fog had dissipated. Five hundred yards or so up the track was a water tower, and I decided to find a place near that solitary structure to hide. I tried to conceal myself by bending forward and cautiously waded upstream in the knee-deep water. I had just enough sense left to remember I wanted to go north. I don't really know why I wanted to go North, but I suppose I felt I could lose myself in one of the big cities I'd heard about like Cincinnati or Detroit.

I finally made it to a concrete culvert near the water tower and slid myself inside. I was scared to death. I did not pay much attention to the mud or having to sit in a couple inches of water all day. I just wanted to be out of anyone's sight. I prayed for nightfall so I could crawl out of that concrete sepulcher. I prayed to die, for God to simply let me die, but nothing relieved my misery. Sometime along in the afternoon reality hit me. I was going to have to make it on my own. That was the first time I had ever actually been in real trouble. Things were up to me now and no one else. Do it or die. Get away and make a new life for myself or go to the Sheriff and turn myself in. It was my day of decision, and I'll never forget the loneliness and heartbreak I felt there in that hole in the ground. I was the paragon of misery. I was woe incarnate. Finally, darkness fell over that little prison and with every joint in my body aching, I somehow managed to slither forth into the night.

I still had enough of my wits left to know North from South, and the locomotive on the first set of tracks I came to just happened to be headed in the right direction for me. At first sight, I thought the locomotive was attached only to coal gondolas but a hundred or so yards away I could see the beginning of several boxcars. I remained concealed within the stubbly trees and bushes along the tracks as I approached the boxcars. I quickly hoisted myself inside the first one I came to with an open door and stealthily made my way to the end of the putrid smelling carrier. I found a corner and slid slowly down on my haunches as I waited for my eyes to become more acclimated to the near pitch-blackness. I tried not to move or breath but I had no control over my heart, which was pounding with the rapidity and sound of the proverbial jackhammer. I sat there in that exact position and condition for at least an hour. I heard nothing and saw nothing. Then suddenly, with the shrill grating sound of tons of metal rubbing against tons of metal, my escape vehicle was jerked into motion. I did feel a bit of relief as the time between clicks of the wheels became shorter and shorter, but I could not stop the tears from streaming down my face. Pretty soon we were rattling along at what I estimated to be twenty-five or thirty miles an hour.

It was a warm humid evening, but the air was beginning to circulate a bit through the open doors and slatted walls of the boxcar. I had sat on my haunches for so long that my legs were going to sleep so I finally stretched out and leaned back up against the wall. I was rigid as if rigor mortis was already setting in. I just wanted to melt, to fade away and disappear off the face of the earth, but I knew my demise would not be that easy, and I knew I did not have the guts to expedite the situation. A bright full moon came from behind a cloud and I welcomed the myriad shafts of light that came streaming through the boxcar. I assumed from the smell and the hay-strewn floor of this ominous vehicle that it was a cattle car. Many a beast had been delivered up to the executioner by way of this pungent crate, and I couldn't help but wonder if they would be able to add me to the tally in the final analysis.

Pretty soon I thought I detected a movement from a pile of hay situated in a corner of the boxcar at the opposite end, but after a couple of minutes I assumed it to be only the wind. But then it began to move again. Could it be a snake, or a polecat? I started scooting toward the door, and it too slithered in that direction. My heart was totally unprepared. It crawled closer. Most of the hay had fallen off the figure by now, and I could see that it was human. Finally, I got the courage to move closer, and as I approached it I detected heavy, raspy breathing. Pretty soon it was in full view. I

45

watched undetected as a young man about my own age tried to brush the straw and dust away from his face and gulp in as best he could mouthfuls of fresh air. He was finding extreme difficulty in breathing, but finally the gasping and gurgling began to subside, and he started to get his breath with a little more ease. He had some difficulty gathering himself up into a sitting position but finally made it and leaned wastefully back against the wall of the swaying boxcar just inside the door. It was only then I spoke to him, and no doubt he was as startled as I had been, but evidently he didn't have the strength to show it. I told him I had just boarded the freight and this was the first I had noticed him. It was then he laboriously began to tell me his story.

He lived in Cincinnati and was on his way home. His mother was critical and near death at the University of Cincinnati hospital. His uncle was a coal operator and part owner of a small mine somewhere around Hazard, KY. The uncle had hired Charley, which was his name, Charley Manus, some three years ago. He said he had been aware from his first day of work in that coal mine that if he stayed there long, breathing in that nitrous smoke and dust, that he would die since he had chronic lung problems from birth. He had started throwing up blood some six months ago, but he couldn't bring himself to quit since he was still broke. He had been sending most of his money home on a regular basis and had been hoping to get a few dollars in his pocket before leaving, but when the news reached him that his mother was dying he hopped the first freight North.

Charley was an old hand at hopping freights. He had used this mode of travel between Cincinnati and Hazard many times and was very grateful for the accommodations of the L& N railroad. He had a denim knapsack strapped about his shoulders and began to gather it up into his lap while at the same time wiping the dust and straws from it. Presently he removed a couple of tins of potted ham and a few packs of saltine crackers from the traveling kit. He then uncapped a large canteen from the other shoulder. He passed a container of the canned meat to me along with a packet of the crackers. I was beginning to realize just how hungry I was. Charley fished an old Barlow knife from the pocket of his overalls, opened it, and handed it to me handle first. I was never to forget that act of kindness. That scene became emblazoned upon my memory for some unknown reason. From that time forward, every time someone was kind to me, that moment flashed across my mind. I guess it was because I had realized that some people were just naturally kind and thoughtful and some were just naturally unkind and cruel, and the question "why" often flitted around the outskirts of my mind. I sawed the top out of the can of meat and handed the knife back to Charley. That little meal of potted meat and crackers wasn't much but it sufficed to fill the "holler" spot in my belly as my daddy used to say. After a long drink of water from charley's canteen I began to relax a bit and was anticipating his question of why I was hitching a ride. I simply told him I was having problems with the folks at home and he accepted that explanation and never questioned me further.

We had been clipping along at about the same speed for a few hours. Now and then we would slow down a bit and you could tell we were near some small town by the several lights scattered here and there. At these times a world of shadows seemed to flit in and out, and around the wide door of the boxcar. Charley continued to breathe raspingly amid sporadic coughing spells. I had just begun to doze off when he suddenly startled me by asking if I saw it? I told him I had not seen anything, and then he told me he had seen the hand. He told me it was the hand of God, and he thought he had been seeing it a lot lately. I became uneasy and felt like he might be going out of his head, and I didn't know what I would do if he did. But then he explained that his mother had told him about the un-seen hand of God a lot of times. He said the hand of God was always around, and the hand of God was always leading us, and directing us, if we were attempting to do the right thing. It was a good omen, he said, and he seemed to relax and be pleased. We rattled on through the night, and I think I dozed off for a time.

When I awakened you could see just a tinge of blue on the horizon. Charley woke at about the same time, and after he looked around and got his bearings, he told me we would be crossing the Ohio River soon. We were going up an incline and it seemed that we instantly ran out of ground. We were on the top deck of a tressel, and the side rails of this bridge only extended up as far as the level of the floor of the boxcar. We had a perfect view of the river. It was beautiful. I told Charley it was the biggest creek I had ever seen. He became strangled a bit while attempting to choke back a laugh. Little did he know I wasn't joking? But the most amazing and beautiful sight of all was the great myriad of lights that seemed to cover the city of Cincinnati. It was a scene that I would never forget.

The sun was just coming up. I realized briefly, that if I were home I would likely be heading for the barn to do the milking and the rest of the morning chores with old jack at my heels. Pretty soon we seemed to make a sweeping arc back into a Southerly direction and then straightened out and traveled parallel with the river about fifty feet from the shore. Charley was now sitting in the door of the boxcar with his feet dangling. He said we were nearing the stockyard and would have to jump out as soon as the train stopped if not before. He said if the railroad dicks caught us they would send us to jail after they beat the shit out of us. Pretty soon we began to slow down, and Charley told me to get ready, and jump when he did. When he gave the signal, I jumped and landed on my feet, but Charlie's legs gave way, and he fell forward with a thud right on his stomach.

The fall had knocked the wind out of him, and he just lay there as still as a dead man. By the time I got to him the caboose was just passing us. I hoisted him to his feet, and he swung an arm around my neck. He was almost limp, and I too was weak from the long ride with only a can of potted ham and a few crackers to eat since the previous morning. When I looked over my shoulder, I saw a big burly, ugly looking man with what appeared to be a baseball bat in his hand crossing the tracks toward us. He waved the bat in the air and hollered that it was the end of the line. Charley mumbled something like "ah shit," as the ugly man approached us. I believe he must have seen our weakened condition since he stopped fifty or so feet short of us. After hurling a few more cuss words at us, he told us that if he ever saw us in that switchyard again he would take us to jail. We thanked him and achingly made our way to the opposite side of the tracks.

We passed along the edge of a holding pen for what seemed to be a thousand cattle. These potential steaks and briskets all seemed to be bellowing at the same time. Within a few days they would be forced to run single file through a narrow chute where a man would hit them in the head with a sledge hammer, after which, another man would slit their throats and then hoist them up by their hind legs so their blood would flow freely out of their bodies. Yeah, the ugly man with the club was right; it was the end of the line all right.

We cripplingly made our way through a lot of back streets and alleys and ended up at his mother's basement apartment. By the time we reached the place, Charley was bleeding from his nose and mouth. He went immediately to the bedroom and collapsed on a bed. I went back to wondering what I should do while giving the place the once-over. The apartment looked a lot better inside than I had expected. There was a kitchen, living room, a bedroom and a small bathroom with a shower. The place was well secluded from the street and prying eyes. I began to ponder my next route of action. My only alternative was to hit the road again. I figured I would rest for a while first, so I found a comfortable chair in the living room and sat dozing as I waited for Charley to wake up.

He had a long sleep and did not awake until around 10 P.M. He sent me down to the corner delicatessen for some bread, lunchmeat and Coca-Cola. When we finished eating, Charley said he wanted to go to the hospital to see his mother. He seemed so weak and frail. I thought to myself that he was the one who needed to be in the hospital. His cough was becoming more frequent and strained. It was more like episodes of retching rather than normal coughing. It was eleven O'clock when we set out for the hospital. We had to walk since there were no busses at that time of night, and it seemed every step was uphill. It was hot, and there were piles of garbage and debris collected all around the storm drains at every corner signifying a recent summer deluge. There were still a few stragglers on the streets, and many of them appeared to just be wandering aimlessly over the dirty sidewalks. These were mostly the homeless, as I would learn later. They were pitiful in a way, but at that time I considered them to be just dirty people on a dirty sidewalk in a dirty town. Snotty nosed kids eight and ten years old rummaging through garbage cans, and passed out winos asleep in every doorway. This was a section of the city where streets were lined on both sides with multi story brick buildings jammed together. Each building had a stoop of concrete steps six or eight high with an iron railing on each side. Now and then the buildings were separated by a narrow slit just wide enough for a man to walk through. There was always a cool draft coming from these walkways. The breeze was cool but it carried a stench with it that I had never experienced anywhere. It smelled moldy and rotten like curdled milk, or a baby that needs a bath.

Charley was very weak. We would stop and sit on the curb or lean up against a building every hundred feet or so. The hospital, a big monstrous limestone building, had floodlights all around it. People were lounging all along the front of the building especially where the lights were brightest. Charley said they were mostly whores and pimps. In fact, before Charley passed, he had pretty well clued me in on how to identify each member of a particular lifestyle in that skid row section of the Queen City. Whores, pimps, gays, lesbians, cross dressers and armed robbers. These lifestyles, as I would later learn, were accepted ways of life to many city dwellers. All these people had one thing in common- they slept all day and started coming out of their holes and dens about dusk.

I waited inside by the elevator while Charley went up to visit his mother. A few minutes later he returned. She was dead. She had died that very night. Charley was muttering something to the effect that he was sure he had seen the unseen hand of God at about the same time of her death. He was mostly blubbering and incoherent. Her remains were at a local funeral parlor where she had prearranged all the necessities for her cremation. A week or so later an urn containing her ashes was delivered to Charley. He never spoke of her again.

Charlie's lung condition got worse by the day. He struggled for every breath, and finally he just quit trying. I had looked after him night and day and did all I could to make him comfortable, but he had been in constant agony the last week. I was saddened beyond description since he was the only friend I had. Charley returned my kindness by giving to me the only thing he had left in the world-his identity. He gave me his social security card, his driver's license, and the name and address of the corporation his mother had rented the apartment from. He informed me I could live there as long as I wanted just so I sent the landlord sixty dollars every month.

Once again I was alone. I had been flung instantly into another world consisting of what at first seemed like hordes of frantic people rushing wildly to and fro over sheets of concrete and asphalt. I sat for what seemed days in that little apartment just reminiscing about home and the peace I had once known. I had always believed in God, and my conscience was eating me up. I frequently thought of the unseen hand of God that Charley had mentioned and hoped that God would give me a sign of some kind--a sign that I wasn't lost and eternally separated from Him. I had committed an abominable sin, and there was no feasible way to make amends. The constant threat of impending disaster was overwhelming. My transgressions permeated every waking moment. Like my long removed brother, Cain, the spirit of god had found me guilty, and I had been banished from Eden. I found myself doubting the reality of God one minute and then praying to him the next. The thought of suicide came to my mind with great frequency. I figured if I was right, and God did not exist, I would be better off to jump in front of one of those speeding trucks, or climb to the top of one of those skyscrapers and take the plunge, but I knew that deep down I was only kidding myself. More than anything, I still wanted to live, and I didn't know why.

How could a person in my situation want to live when he could end all that misery in a couple of seconds? The answer I got from that question removed any doubt from my mind concerning the existence of God. God has instilled within all men the overpowering desire to survive. It was as simple as that. I also believe Charley had sensed something of my plight even though I had never let on to him anything about what I had done. He had mentioned the unseen hand of God intervening in the lives of men several times, and once or twice I got a notion he had mentioned this just for my benefit. During one of my more depressing times after Charlie's death, I remembered the rest of the story concerning Cain. He was to be a vagabond, and no matter what he did, the earth would not yield up its full strength to him, but he also would have a mark set upon him, which would protect him from harm.

Once I got up enough nerve to venture out of the apartment, things began to sort of fall into place. I found a job washing dishes at a small diner in the neighborhood. I had to work a split shift, but I didn't mind since it sort of broke the monotony of having to remain in the apartment too long at a time. I finally came to terms with my situation and accepted things the way they were. Nevertheless, all my prayers seemed to ring hollow, and I wrestled with the thought of being lost and perpetually separated from God.

I read the Bible and prayed on a regular basis. In short, I lived a monk's life, avoiding any semblance of sin. I avoided lengthy familiarity with people, but from the askance glances I received from those who I had a need to encounter in my daily life, I realized what an ignorant country bumpkin I must have been. I finally made the decision to correct that image.

The local library was only a couple blocks from the apartment, and I became a voracious reader of history and philosophy and pretty much remained abreast of current events. I aspired to no higher calling than dishwasher, short order cook, bicycle messenger or janitor. Any higher position than that would, to me, have been all vanity.

I saw the decadence of society and wanted no active part in it. Sure, I was on the lam, a term I had become familiar with since lighting in this metropolis, but I soon realized that everyone was on the lam from something or someone. Genuine honesty and morality seemed to be nonexistent. To be sure, folks tried to project the similitude of honesty and morality. They were in large part cordial with one another; they attended church on Sunday, but if you were truly objective and witnessed their dealings with one another you had to conclude that Charley had been right. Deep down inside, and this side would show up only if you pushed them into a corner, they were whores and pimps in large part, attempting to act like legitimate, god-fearing people. All I ever wanted to do was go back home - back to where I was born and raised. I wanted to be able to wake once again to the smell of new mown hay and fresh turned new ground. I longed to be away from the shrillness of emergency sirens and bumper-to-bumper traffic and the anticipated knock on the door in the middle of the night that would signal the end of my freedom.

After a few years I subscribed, by mail, to my hometown newspaper in hopes of learning something of my mothers' circumstances or just some news from home. Well, my mother's circumstances are no longer a mystery. She had gone home to meet her maker three days ago.

The sky was turning darker as those big black clouds rolled in front of the sun and the wind was picking up and making little whirly gig tornadoes in the dusty parking space in front of the Jarvis store. I decided to take refuge from the oncoming deluge on the porch of the post office. I just made it up the steps as a torrent of rain came sideways at my meager shelter. I pushed the rocking chair the old gentleman was occupying when I first arrived there as far back as I could out of the weather and sat there staring out over the surrounding bottoms of corn and hay blowing in the wind.

Pretty soon Lucy came and stood for a minute in the doorway and then stepped out onto the concrete landing. A gust of wind suddenly welded her long skirt against her tall sinewy and voluptuous body. Old memories of the crush I had on her as a teenager came flooding back. She had always been a handsome lady and now this unexpected revelation of what a beautiful object of eroticism she was, stirred within me my long suppressed feelings of a natural desire for a woman's companionship. It had become second nature for me to suppress those urges, but this time I couldn't. My longing to live a normal life and to give vent to my natural drives as a man was about to get the best of me, but just in time the storm was over. The rain had stopped as suddenly as it had started, and after staring intently at me for a moment, Lucy turned and disappeared back inside the store.

A few minutes later the hearse came by and my thoughts returned to the business at hand. I longed to see my mother, and she had just passed by in front of me. The downpour had thoroughly washed my old ford appropriately enough for a funeral, and I took my time driving the mile and a half on down to the church. I noticed right away that about ten feet had been added on to the length of the church building. I just assumed they had added a baptistery. I remember how the congregation used to meet on the creek bank a few hundred yards to the East of the church for the baptizing of new converts, and how we would sing "Shall we gather at the river" while the preacher waded out into the middle of the creek and led in single file those to be immersed. After all the handshaking and singing of hymns, we would gather back at the church for an "all day meeting and dinner on the ground", or a sort of a picnic as a way to celebrate the new additions to our "flock." I thought of how times had changed. The preachers and the converts are too uppity or too lazy nowadays to walk to the creek and be baptized according to nature, and now the parking lot was blacktopped and there was no grassy spot to have a picnic or "dinner on the ground".

Across the boxed wire fence and a couple of hundred yards to the North stood the one room school I attended through the seventh grade. Someone had remodeled the cobblestone building and turned it into a family dwelling as evidenced by the black chevy coupe in the driveway and the two bicycles leaning against the fence. The county had long since lost the need for a local school, and all students were now bussed the ten miles to the centralized schools. I had always thought of the one room school as a very efficient way of teaching. Students in the upper grades would assist those in the lower grades, which, in my estimation, reinforced retention of subjects. Of course there was no indoor plumbing and that lack of luxury was probably the cause of most of the daily distraction from the curriculum. When a student needed to go to the out-house, he or she would prop a book against the doorpost, and this would alert anyone of the same inclination that the outside facility was occupied. Many an opportunity was taken advantage of due to that situation. It was not uncommon for one of the older students to slip outside and commence throwing rocks at the wooden outhouse while another student was inside making an honest attempt to do his business. And on more than one occasion the little building had been overturned by one of the more radical students while it was being occupied.

The mourners were beginning to gather now. They would seem to stop briefly at the entrance and turn to shake hands with those behind them before entering the building. Many of them looked familiar to me but I could not seem to put a name to the face. They were, no doubt, related to folks I had once known. Pretty soon it began to sprinkle rain again, and I figured I had better get on inside if I didn't want to get soaked. As I was walking to the entrance of the church a Sheriff's cruiser pulled in to the parking lot and my heart skipped. I slowed down and waited. I had no trouble recognizing the occupant. It was Sheriff Jones. Arthur Jones had been a longtime friend of my family. He was getting pretty old, but as he made his way up the driveway he seemed to be in good health. I waited for him to get inside before I entered and took a seat near the entrance. I was amazed at how small the sanctuary seemed. I had often heard how small a place becomes when you haven't seen it for a while, but nevertheless I was still stunned. This had at one time been the biggest building in the world. The interior seemed to be about the same except for the big potbellied stove that used to occupy the very center of the sanctuary. The stove was missing. Of course they had probably graduated to propane or natural gas. The casket had been placed in the customary place directly in front of the pulpit. I suppressed the urge to walk on up and view my mother's remains but thought it best not to draw any unnecessary attention to myself just yet. I had waited twenty years to see her and I could wait a few minutes longer.

The song leader came to the microphone, and the choir joined him in the opening verse of "Amazing Grace." Just then, to my surprise, Lucy Jarvis squeezed in and sat beside me. She looked directly into my eyes and told me how sorry she was for my loss and called me by name. That taste of copper came back in my mouth, and my heart nearly stopped, but I just kept on trying to sing and remember the words to the song. After that they sang "Beulah Land" and "When the Roll is called Up Yonder." There was a short pause, and then an older baldheaded fellow with a rich baritone voice came to the podium and sang the hymn "When We All Get To Heaven."

Then the preacher slowly came forward and opened his bible. I had known this man all my life. He was a local farmer with a large family of a dozen or so kids. I remembered being classmates with some of his children. He was a good man whom I had always held in high esteem. After a few conciliatory platitudes about my mother and what a pillar of the community she had been, he said something to this affect.

"The remarks I'm about to utter are not for the benefit of the dead. The dead have already gone to their just reward. Their soul is either in Heaven with the Lord or lost somewhere in eternity and separated from God. There are some who believe in a place called purgatory. I too believe in purgatory. But purgatory, in my humble estimation, is a state of mind. A state of mind where the prideful, arrogant, selfish and sinful folks of this world have to go before they die. I said b-e-f-o-r-e they die. It is a place where they go to remember. It is a place of solitude where they are forced to contemplate their transgressions against God. A place where there is wailing, and gnashing of teeth, and bewilderment. They have always been too proud to admit that there just might be a God. These are ungodly people and not hard to detect. The people they have known all their lives have shunned them and rejected them oftentimes for one or more of the foregoing reasons. They just wither away and die alone since they have been too proud to call on God. They go to their graves alone, unwept, un-honored, and unsung. I know! I have witnessed such heartbreaking sadness. Yes, there are those who think they are too smart and too educated to believe in an almighty creator, that is to say, God! And again I say these fools will be eternally separated from paradise."

"Now I've known this fine lady who is laid out before us here all my life, and I can attest to the fact that she is now in Heaven. I am the man who had the pleasure of leading this fine lady to the Lord several years ago. This book," and he held the bible high above his head, "this book tells me that to be absent from the body is to be present with God! That is to say, if you're saved by the blood!" He paused for a minute "That is, if you're saved by the blood of Jesus Christ!" He paused again while he retrieved a handkerchief from his shirt pocket and wiped his mouth. "God, in His infinite wisdom, gave to mankind free will! The ability to make choices! Without an inherent ability to choose, man would be pre-programmed like a mule. A mule just automatically, by instinct, seeks out its basic needs and has no use for free will. But because man is God's most wonderful creation, and He loves us, and doesn't want us to be puppets like a mule, or a cow or a goat, He gives us the ability to make our own choices. And God in His infinite omniscience also knows that due to this gift of free will, man is sometimes going to make some bad choices. And God also knows, and every man knows, if he will just stop and think about it a minute, that man cannot be good enough to work his way into heaven. God is perfect and cannot abide imperfection. If God could associate himself with imperfection he would not be God. You all know what happens when you've got one rotten apple in a barrel. God has to be perfect in order to be God. God is the author and creator of all things including Himself. For He describes Himself in this book as "I am that I am." If, like some of the heathen say, "I too have a god." How can that be? Only God, the one God, is perfect. And we must be perfect in order to abide with God in Heaven. No, you will never be perfect in the physical, but you can be perfect in the spiritual. You can be perfect of soul. He has made a way for you to achieve that perfection. He sent his son to earth in the form of a man, and his name is Jesus Christ. He was sacrificed there at Mount Calvary so that you and I could have eternal life. And now, when Jehovah God, looks down at us from Heaven, He looks through that blood of the supreme sacrifice, the blood of his son Jesus Christ, and if we have been covered by that blood, and have accepted Jesus Christ as our savior, and have contritely asked forgiveness for our sins, He will see you through that blood as if you are as clean as the driven snow. And, He will take you on to Heaven when you die. Now, if you plan to wait until you are in one of these boxes to come to Jesus," he pointed at the casket, "we all know it's going to be too late. Today is the day of salvation, sayeth the Lord. I suggest that as we carry this dear saint to the graveyard you seriously consider my words, as a word to the wise is sufficient."

As the preacher closed his bible and stepped back from the pulpit the choir began the hymn "Oh Come Angel Band", and since I was seated in the back row, we were first to be instructed to proceed forward in single file for the viewing. I passed slowly in front of the casket. I choked back the tears as long as I could. I couldn't resist leaning forward and placing a kiss on that beloved forehead. A thousand thoughts of days gone by raced through my mind. And then with head bowed, I retrieved my handkerchief and wiped my eyes as I slowly made my exit and across the parking lot to my car.

It was hot. I rolled down the window and sat waiting for the church to clear out while the preacher's words rang in my ears. I was under a more heavy conviction than ever. My debt to society had to be paid. I was becoming more apprehensive and nervous as I sat there. Lucy had remembered me, and I didn't know if there were others or not. The idea that the Sheriff might have remembered me was my greatest concern. If he had, he may come out and arrest me on the spot, so I decided to drive on up to the cemetery and wait there for them to bring my mother along. I remembered there was a dirt road leading up the hill to the graveyard, but that it was so steep that at least on one occasion, the casket had to be snaked up the hill on a horse drawn sled. I found the turnoff leading to the graveyard but realized right away the road was too steep and slippery for my car so I turned around and parked by the side of the Post Office. Pretty soon the hearse arrived and took the same course I had taken. The driver evidently realized right away that the road was impassable so he backed up and parked near me.

I had made up my mind. As soon as my mother was in the ground I would turn myself in to Sheriff Jones. I sat there wondering just how bad prison life would be and concluded it could be no worse than the life I had been living. At the very least it would be an open confession to man and would be in compliance of the biblical edict "render unto Caesar that which is Caesars."

It looked to me like the rain had ended as the sun was trying to peep out over the trees on the ridge behind the graveyard. Someone was driving a team of mules pulling a sled up to the hearse. In a couple of minutes the pallbearers had mothers coffin loaded onto the sled, and a handful of the faithful mourners fell in behind as the team began the slippery trip up the steep and winding roadway. It was just a small country cemetery of about fifty feet wide by a hundred feet long. It was bordered on the north and west sides by some pretty tall pines. There was a four-strand barbed wire fence around the entire perimeter. The place had been cleaned free of weeds and brush, and flowers were in bloom all around the fence line. I was thankful for the strong fence, as the local farmers had always been pretty lax about letting their livestock roam too freely. There was a doublewide gate at the entrance, and I waited there while they carried the casket up to the gravesite. A person couldn't ask for a more beautiful place in which to abide thru eternity.

Finally, I walked up and joined the little group standing around the coffin. I only recognized three of them and these were Sheriff Jones, Lucy Jarvis and the preacher. The undertaker slowly and reverently opened the coffin as we stood tearfully viewing my mother. Finally, as I had anticipated, Sheriff Jones walked over to me and put his hand on my shoulder. My mother was lying there dead but the copper taste came to my mouth again with a vengeance. "Why, you're Bertha's son Robert, ain't you?" he said. I was too choked up to make an audible reply so I just nodded my head in the affirmative. "Well it's good to see you son. Glad you could be here. Your mother was a fine lady!" After the preacher said a few more words the little group joined him in the Lord's prayer, and he informed us that the ceremony was concluded. Sheriff Jones was now talking to another fellow several feet from me. I turned to walk in his direction when a shaft of sunlight filtered through the tall trees and seemed to illuminate a brass plaque affixed to a tombstone directly in my path. I had to read the inscription a couple of times through my tear dimmed eyes, but then the implications of that simple message suddenly exploded in my brain. This was the grave of a man who had received the Congressional Medal of Honor. He had been awarded the medal for heroism "above and beyond the call of duty" at Normandy France, nineteen hundred and forty four. On the granite stone was inscribed:

BARNES, CLYDE

BORN APRIL 5, 1925
DIED AUGUST 8, 1991

THE END

"ONE THING IS CERTAIN AND THE REST IS LIES"

I see that you too my friend may be seeking a diversion from this layover in space and time that we have collectively labeled "life." Well then, let us savor the moment and agree to agree on at least this one definition of existence. For after all, what is time without life and what is life without time? Let us just call "life" a quandary and be done with it! This may well be the only concept upon which we will ever be able to completely agree. There are many who seem convinced of the infallibility of the principle of cause and effect. Their philosophy is that history will perpetually repeat itself lest we learn from our mistakes. If you consider this philosophy correct then count yourself among the fortunate. You have evidently been successfully indoctrinated by society. Therefore, unlike me, you will probably escape the hangman's noose.

On the other hand, we only become indoctrinated "dumb driven cattle" if we choose to be. You know, self- will and all that crap! There still exists a few, such as myself, who are compelled by a gene driven propensity to think outside the proverbial box. Folks with this malady attempt to escape the shackles of conventionalism. We unwittingly descend into that maelstrom which engulfs the nonconformist in our effort to escape the slavery of peer pressure and custom. Our roles could easily be switched here you know. You could be doing the writing and I the reading. You could be pacing the confines of this jail cell awaiting the hangman's noose save for that cruel trick God has played on a few of us humans. Some of us did not get the right combination of amino acids during the creation and lack the ability to suppress our dark side as well as others.

While the vast populous of the world has been busy slaving and trying to keep body and soul together, there have always been a few, who by some stroke of luck were able to acquire an excess of money and power. These rich and famous have insidiously indoctrinated the less fortunate into thinking and behaving in ways that allow the wealthy to hang on to their excessive fortunes. You must admit however, the rich and powerful are smart; they allow the underdog just enough of the world's amenities to keep them from revolting.

I do not know why I am going off on this tangent! In a few days, it will not matter to me; I will be gone. My lawyer is preparing my last appeal but that is his idea and his alone. Personally, I welcome the end of my sojourn here between the eternities. The hangman will appear, slip the black hood over my face, fix the rope around my neck and drop me through the trap door. I've had plenty of time to think about death- and I'm ready for it. My only regret is, I do not believe anyone has understood me during this ordeal; not even my lawyer. Of course, he is also rich. You will meet him in a little bit and you can judge him for yourself. On the other hand, maybe you will be able to understand me--I hope so. All I really want is to be understood.

When you have finished your perusal of this, my last written communication, you will indubitably ask yourself "what in Gods name would motivate a man to commit such a deed and then be stupid enough to set it down in writing! Doesn't he know this is tantamount to an irrefutable confession?" I am aware of your concern. Nevertheless, you see, I have already confessed. It is my lawyer who wants to appeal-not me! I am free! I have nothing left to lose, and want no more of this life! It is my lawyer! He continues to seek fame and fortune by representing infamous miscreants such as myself! You will ultimately ask yourself "does this person have no shame, no remorse of having committed such a diabolical deed?" I would emphatically answer yes! Of course, I have a twinge of guilt! However, my embarrassment is not in my having done the deed. It is in my inherent inability to conceal my dark side. Yes, my propensity to do evil is great but so is yours! You have this penchant for evil but you are very skillful in keeping it suppressed. I know there have been times in your life when you have disliked someone very much and said to yourself "Id kill that son of a bitch if I knew I could get away with it!" However, you see, you perish the thought right away. That does not make you any less guilty than I am! Even the Good Book tells us that if we look upon a woman with lust in our heart it is as sinful as actually committing the lustful deed. Of course, the sin of lust was never a part of my makeup, as you will later see.

All the philosophers from Plato to Sartre, folks of deep discernment, have delved headlong into the meaning of "meaning;" especially the meaning of life, and have come up empty; or at their best "inconclusive." The smart ones will go right to the bottom line, throw their hands up and announce that life is but a "quandary." However, occasionally we must admit to the efficacy of the ramblings of those old philosophers. They have the ability to pluck the sensitive strings of our soul, and then motivate us to plunge even further into that black abyss of "meaning." After long years of assimilating and internalizing this nonsense, if we are lucky, we will take a time out (just as you are doing at this moment my friend) and find a quiet place where a more profound reflection concerning "life" is possible. After such a time out, we are then forced to ask ourselves, "What new thing have I learned about life?" The honest answer can only be "nothing new." I have only learned to quote or paraphrase that which another has thought or stated many years before. However, we do learn one thing for sure; we have lost many years and most of our freedom, since the more we know, the less freedom we have. With great knowledge comes great pride and when you have finished reading this you can be the judge as to whether my real sin is pride, murder, vanity, or whether I was simply predestined to commit the act.

Excuse me for a moment please but I think I heard my lawyer's voice. Yes, there he is down at the other end of the cellblock. This paragon of a sophistry spouter intends to plead me temporarily insane. Well let him plead, as he will! The deed goes unaltered as the rolling of the ages and I will stand sane, insane, good or evil in the mind of a jury of my so-called peers who will ultimately hold my fate in their hands. Yes, let him make his argument. I am looking forward to the trial. I enjoy watching a gifted theoretician pull out his bag of rhetoric and ply his trade. I like to listen as they wring and render obscure symbols from everyday language while a simple straightforward statement eludes their tongue. No wonder the ancient Greek deplored, yet, somehow adored the sophist- that learned master of manipulation whose silver tongue could create or annihilate a standard. Moreover, for a fee, they will change a lie into the truth.

I met the woeful barrister only on one other occasion and that was on the morning they clapped me into this eight by eleven dungeon. I am still a little foggy about the meeting and the man. I distinctly remember that he had only one ear. I get nauseous at the thought. I do remember his telling me that he was once a soldier and that while in Korea he had stepped on a land mine and part of his face had been blown away. The surgeons had successfully reconstructed his face but they could not find what was left of his ear while it was still viable. A hole in the side of his head, which he intermittently dabbed at with a handkerchief, was the only sign he had ever had an ear in that spot. Actually, what I am saying may all be fantasy since I was either in or near a state of delirium tremens when they incarcerated me. I may have still been on "the other side" as I call it when I talked to this man. Of course, you would not know what I mean by "the other side" unless you had been there on at least one occasion yourself. I am sorry. You may not want to hear about such tripe. I know you will never be able to commiserate with a man who would willingly subject his body to such torture for no good reason. However, you see, I must tell my story to someone. Whether it is to you or some other fellow creature-I will be heard! But hush. I must hurry along.

I will tell you straight up! I did it! Let me get through this as expeditiously as I can-as thoroughly as I can and then you become the judge.

I was born in the ridge country of Southeastern Kentucky on a rocky hillside farm. Wait! Don't lose interest yet! Poor farm boys also have a story! Remember Lincoln? Well, let us get on with it then. I attended one of those often- reminisced about but seldom applauded "one room schools." A single teacher taught from tried and tested lesson plans and covered materials which satisfactorily educated children from the "primer" to the eighth grade. The students were kept busy, busy, busy all day long every day. Whether you know it or not this is the greatest method of teaching man has ever conceived. It is true there was only one teacher but if that teacher had fifteen students she also had fifteen assistants who tutored one another and reinforced the learning every day. If a student did not show proficiency and perform at the eighth grade level by the time he moved on to the ninth grade, it was simply because he was mentally deficient, the curriculum was insufficient, or the teacher needed to be replaced. You know, you can molly coddle a child too much!

I am mentally gifted, and under this one room system, I was able to complete the primer through the eighth grade that first year. I know you will probably be disgusted with what I am going to say, but you see I was a genius; I could do algebra and quote the Constitution and the Gettysburg Address as well as other long documents during my first year of school. Of course, it did not matter much to anyone. My parents had only completed the ninth grade. I had a brilliant teacher when it came to book learning. However, she did not know a whole lot about how to handle a gifted student. She somehow instilled within me a profound sense of inferiority. Thinking back on it, I could fluently read and understand the most esoteric of literature and philosophy, and solve all the math problems I encountered by Christmas time of my first year of school. It seems that about then was when my teacher began to ignore me. She would not talk to me, look at me, or call on me to respond. She simply ignored me as if I were not alive. I never really paid much attention to her attitude toward me at the time. After all, what does a first grader know about the diabolical intricacies of the human mind? I thought perhaps I had been offensive in some mysterious way or that she just did not like me.

Consequently, I worked hard at keeping a low profile and making sure I did not let on as if I knew all the answers. Since I did not have to exert myself in the least to learn, the hours I spent in school were consumed largely in daydreaming and meditation. I became a voracious reader and by the time I had finished with that one room schoolhouse I was deep into metaphysics and the philosophy of man. For the next four years, we were bussed to the joint High School in town where I continued to keep my philosophical meditations to myself.

I graduated High School with the one distinction of being a straight "A" student. Up to that point, I felt as if I had just been floating through life. I had no real initiative or ambition; life just happened to me. It was about this point in time when I understood what Ahab, that intrepid captain of the *Pequod* meant when he asserted, "the path to my fixed purpose is laid with iron rails whereon my soul is grooved to run." I knew I did not mount this fixed track on my own accord and by some ominous intuition, knew that try as I may, I could not dismount. I was like Jonah who was regurgitated from the belly of the whale onto dry land. However, unlike Jonah, I had no Nineveh to save.

The cool outward demeanor that I perpetually maintained belied the internal churning and vexation of my soul. I saw the incompleteness in creation, and constantly sought the missing pieces. It must have been about this time that the germ of futility was born in me. I secretly felt that I had discovered completeness in a very simple construction, the circle. I first became infatuated with the circle upon reading Dr. Jung's article on the "Mandela" and his theory on the "Collective Unconscious" in the mind of man. The circle having apparently been used all down through recorded history as the symbol of perfection and completeness and the implication that knowledge and experience could be genetically propagated, consumed a great deal of my meditations. Then, when I discovered through mathematical exploration that a perfect circle could only exist in essence, that is, only in my mind, I became quite despondent and even more withdrawn. I did not know there was nothing perfect in creation.

I also worried Plato's doctrine of reminiscence around in my mind for long periods. Plato believed that learning and remembering are basically the same when it comes to a-priori, or original questions. This led me to the conclusion that man has so confused true knowledge by expanding and obfuscating the substance of original questions that the bare- naked question no longer exists, and cannot be verbalized in its a-priori context. Perhaps original man inherently knew the answers to all the so-called metaphysical questions we ask today on truth, knowledge, good, evil, reality, beauty and God. Perhaps man, due to the innumerable opinions, elaborations, revisions and fallibility of language and variability of expression is regressing, rather than progressing toward the understanding of nature and creation.

Could it be that there is no knowledge ever forgotten or lost to the human race? Oh, I know we keep records, but these records are not always true or correct, and many a man goes to the grave with at least one well- kept secret or idea. Do we, through our collective ancestors know all the past? Could that ninety percent of our brain, which is supposed to be dormant, contain that knowledge to which our ancestors had attained? As far as we know, the healthy individual never really forgets. This is evident when we start the process of re-learning something we thought we had forgotten. Are we unknowingly making an attempt at education in this way? That is, remembering. If we could ask the a-priori, valid question, how could we ask such a question without knowing the answer? According to Plato, Socrates proved to his young student that he already knew and understood the Pythagorean theorem on the solution of right triangles. Socrates simply asked the young man the right questions proving his student already understood the theory. If we did not know the a-priori answers, we would not be able to think of the a-priori questions. Perhaps the only things complicated were not so until "thinking" made them so.

I asked you to be the judge in this matter earlier on and I expect you are beginning to lean toward the conclusion that I really am insane. Of course, it is common knowledge that genius is akin to madness. However, I beg you- hear me out! Prejudging a person to be insane is a serious business. We need to consider exactly what sanity and insanity is before we pass judgment. So, let us digress a bit and reason together.

Everything must be simplified and reduced to its lowest terms in order to be perfectly understood. Would you not agree? It follows then if we choose to speak of sanity/insanity or any other generally tenuous concept with authority; we must first establish a concrete definition of the concept in question. A very simple example of insanity would be when a person continues to commit the exact same detrimental act repeatedly, while each time expecting a different result, is, by definition insanity. However, this definition will not hold water: the individual in question may be a sadist and enjoy inflicting pain upon himself or others. Of course this is only one of many examples. And then, there are those who contend that an "operational definition" will suffice. However, this can only hold true for the empiricist or the pragmatist. In order to truly understand anything by definition, we must somehow arrive at a universal definition, that is, perfect objectivity, which, at this point in time is non-existent. On the other hand, total subjectivity is one hundred percent, since subjectivity involves only one mind. (I have never heard of anything so preposterous as the contention of this school of "analysts" of recent times who have somehow mustered the audacity to infer their ability to "analyze" the exact substance of what an individual "means" when he makes a statement.)

The real significance here is that we are becoming hard pressed for "theories." Do not get me wrong; philosophical speculation is not always futile. Let us briefly consider two of the more plausible philosophical concepts. First, let us look at John Locke's theory of the "Tabula Rossa" or the idea that man is born with a "blank tablet" for a mind. In other words, when a person pops out of the womb his mind is completely blank, and that he immediately begins to acquire "knowledge" by way of sensory experience. For example, the child quickly learns that sucking on his mothers' breast can satiate his hunger. This fact and all other experience is then recorded on this original blank slate and we act, react, and make inferences by way of memory and imagination while individual bodily actions are initiated or suppressed according to the pleasure or pain these actions entail. Add to this Humes theory of "cause and effect;" that in essence the new born would not be surprised if when his parent released a ball that the ball fell "up" instead of "down," did not move at all or remained suspended in mid-air can only lead to one conclusion- the a-priori catalyst to all physical action is simply faith; faith that all our actions, whatever they may be, will produce pleasurable results- will be beneficial in some way, thereby producing pleasure and avoiding pain or unpleasantness.

Now if we will just stop and think, both Locke and Hume are touching only on the material side of life, only the mechanical; they are totally leaving out the spiritual side of man. From out the depths of this spiritual side, this gray side, or this dark side flows the real man- his essence. If man were only viewed from the significance of the cause and effect, memory/imagination analysis, and then photographed in slow motion, he would be mistaken for a mime. His movements would be viewed as a series of jerks-thought interspersing each jerk. Not understanding the spirit/soul aspect of man is where all our alleged difficulties lie. Nevertheless, you see, we cause these difficulties. All we have to do in order to free ourselves from this dilemma is to rid ourselves of pride and all the other deadly sins- get outside of ourselves and include God in the cause/effect explanation. No matter how you analyze, no matter how often your analysis may diverge, get sidetracked or run up those blind alleys, the only alternative is to realize we are on this inevitable track; that railroad of the great circle, which, no matter how many detours you may take, will always end up at the first cause, which is God. He is the beginning and the end of that eternal train ride and we are on that train whether we want to be or not. The only variable we have the power to change is how we behave on the trip.

Please allow me to apologize again for this digression. I know you are becoming impatient and anxious for me to get on with my story so you can judge me but I feel compelled to give you a perfect explanation, which you must have if justice is to be served. I am not pleading my case here. I am just giving you the facts so you can judge. Nor am I looking for sympathy. I have the sense to understand the need for unbiased law and convention. I am guilty, and I emphatically believe in the axiom of "an eye for an eye" and that this law should never be compromised. I suppose it is my eternal soul with which I am concerned. Perhaps my crime could very well have been condoned or even praised under different circumstances. After all, I once heard of a pacific island society that held a prolific thief in high esteem. The more an individual in this society could successfully purloin, the higher his status in that society! If you will then, indulge me this one last diversion and I promise to hurry along to the end.

Let us briefly consider a hypothetical-- that a – prior concept-ualization of the two opposites "malevolence" and "benevolence," or "good" and "evil" if you will. Visualize "Moe" who lived on the banks of the Euphrates River some eons past and his cousin "Joe" who lived on the banks of the Tigris. These men, each unaware of the others existence began to consider the Sun; that big ball of fire which somehow was mysteriously suspended overhead and appeared with amazing regularity at the same time and place every day, and then moved stealthfully, deliberately and ominously down to the horizon where it slowly dropped out of sight. It does not take a modern imagination to realize that this thing; the sun that is, produced a lot of heat. Now both "Moe" and "Joe" had, by that time in their lives, experienced the effects of fire on the human body. "Moe" and "Joe" undoubtedly lived in constant anticipation of this huge ball of fire descending to the ground and consuming them.

Then one day when the Sun was directly over Moe's head a nearby volcano erupted. The ensuing red- hot lava was immediately attributed to the presence of the red- hot Sun. Fire and brimstone rained down on Moe and he never trusted that big ball of fire in the sky again. Thus was born the concept of malevolence, or evil, or something hurtful. Of course, this is only one of ten thousand analogies. Now there were no volcanoes in the immediate proximity of Joe's abode, and after a few years, Joe began to attribute many beneficent amenities to the Sun's appearing and disappearing. As this big red circle became warmer, the leaves on the trees became bigger and the edible plants ripened. Thus, the concept of benevolence or "goodness" was born.

Now just consider the facts in this case; malevolence and benevolence were both attributed to the existence of the same physical object. However, if you will just stop and think, benevolence could not exist without malevolence and visa versa--these opposites define one another. No one of these conditions can exist apart from the other. Therefore, there is evidently some gravity in the Bards statement that "nothing is good or evil but thinking makes it so." "Good" cannot exist without "evil" and "obedience" cannot exist without "disobedience" and so on! Perhaps the original sin, which lost for us Heaven on this earth, has been misinterpreted. Give a kid an ice cream cone on a hot sunny day and tell him not to eat it.

But enough of this dead philosophy! Enough of these dead words from a dead man!

My father, an illiterate sharecropper, could not succeed the rigors of city life. He had been ousted from his dirt farm and thrust upon the big city. In spite of his ignorance, he was a presentable man, and well-liked by everyone. Nevertheless, for some reason he did not fit in. He just could not compete. He could not hold a job, and when I was twelve years of age, he left us. He just packed his things and disappeared. We were the proverbial sharecropper family, minus a father and husband, attempting to survive in the big city of Baltimore. My sister became a drug addict and a prostitute, and my brother was shot right between the eyes by an irate merchant during an attempted holdup the very day he turned sixteen. This left only my mother and me to cope the best way we could. The loss of a husband, son, and daughter in quick succession had a devastating effect on mother. However, she was no stranger to adversity. She had labored her entire life under a severe handicap. She had only one eye. Her left eye had been sealed at birth. Apart from this, she was a beautiful woman with flawless skin, jet- black hair, full lips, and a perfect Roman nose. She was a tailor of high renown and managed to acquire enough work to support the both of us.

I received an academic scholarship to a local university there in Baltimore and majored in architecture. I graduated first in my class. Upon graduation, I secured a position with the most prestigious architectural firm in the Mid-West, and mother and I began to realize the meaning of the American dream. I was driven by beauty and perfection. I lived to design and create magnificent structures and felt in my heart that this muse had touched me. I had great reverence for anything beautiful, especially beautiful women. However, I found early on in my life that I could only deal with women on a superficial basis. I could not bring myself to become intimate with them. There were only two kinds of women to me- beautiful, and ugly. The ugly I detested and the beautiful I worshipped. However, I could only worship them from a distance, since I knew I would never willingly be able to defile, ravage, or desecrate this beauty in any way. Although I must admit, there were occasions when the natural drive to procreate would consume me and I would carry on a brief affair with the least appealing female I encountered. These affairs were always short lived and by the time I was twenty five I had totally resigned myself to bachelorhood and celibacy. I had successfully freed myself from amorous lust and could now devote all my time and energy to my work and to seeing that all my mother's needs were met.

My reputation as a designer and builder of grand structures snowballed, and my architectural services were in great demand. My name was on the cornerstone of many a wonder, and synonymous with "majestic." Then upon the completion of this, my most beautiful and elaborate design, I was asked to participate in the grand opening and dedication ceremonies of that counterpart of the Taj Ma Hal. Under this one glorious roof were housed department stores, museums, exquisite eatery's, fine frescoes and fountains-- all the essence of perfection incarnate. When the ceremonies ended and the main doors were flung open to droves of humanity, a sinking feeling of impending disaster gripped my soul with a furor that caused my body to literally quake. A concept of death and the finite overwhelmed me. I could not seem to free myself from this gloom as I meandered throughout the building witnessing the desecration of this beautiful work of art by multitudes of ungrateful bodies pushing, shoving, spitting, and scraping along the immaculate halls. Something seemed to be flowing out of me little by little- like the way it must be when the body is only a few minutes from death and the soul slowly departs. I instantly lost my desire to create, and the futility of life consumed my thought. My head buzzing with that incoherent sound of the multitudes of humanity, I sought the nearest exit and wandered through the backstreets of the city trying to make some sense out of my despondency.

By and by, I passed the door of a dimly lit tavern. I heard for the first time in my life the upbeat sound of titillating music and excited voices intermingled with the smell of stale beer and cigarrette smoke. A cool but mysteriously inviting draft of this acrid air pressed upon me as I passed the shady entrance. I retraced my steps several times in front of this tavern each time squinting to try catching a glimpse of the apparent merriment inside. Finally, I mustered the courage to enter that den of iniquity. It was dark and cool and smelled like a public toilet, but somehow I was drawn to a stool at the far end of a long shiny bar. Once established on the stool my eyes began to become acclimated to the darkness and I saw several men and women seated at the bar and tables. They paid no attention to me and were either engrossed in low toned conversation or just sitting there relaxed either holding or sipping their drinks. I felt as if I were in another world. I had no idea what kind of refreshment to order.

When the bartender asked me what refreshment I would have, I hesitated. The nearest person to me was a disheveled man sitting about three stools to my left. I told the bartender to bring me the same thing as this man was drinking. I ended up with a glass of beer and a glass of whiskey. I imitated my neighbor, tossed the whiskey down my throat, and followed it with a long drink of beer. Within a few minutes, a warm glow enveloped me and my cares seemed to disappear. I had no problems, no inhibitions, and no fear. Time stood still. I no longer had to be anywhere in particular, do anything in particular or say anything in particular. I had discovered what man cherishes above all privileges-- freedom from care. Moreover, for the first time in my life I was free. I bought the disheveled man a drink and for a little while, we became the best of friends.

The leveling effect of alcohol never ceases to amaze me. I never saw the man again that I know of, but somehow, I felt that our inner lives, our very souls, had intertwined. I felt better about life. This experience was short lived however. Within an hour, the alcohol had rendered me near helpless but my newfound friend called for a cab and sent me safely home.

The next day at my office, I tried not to think about my diversion of the night before but could not stop my brain from projecting me back into that dingy barroom. The attraction I felt for the place was ironical and totally against the standards I had always lived by. Little did I realize it but I had become like the Apostle Peter. I had taken my eyes off my goal, and even then had begun to sink. That same evening I found myself in a different bar, but mostly, it was the counterpart of the other. As a matter of fact, as the months rolled on, I found all these havens of rest for the wicked to be about the same.

Nevertheless, I was drawn to this atmosphere like Lazarus to paradise. Certainly, it was not those unscrupulous and nasty people who frequented the places that drew me there. Who wants to associate with drunks, whores, pimps, rapists and murderers? Of course all of those I encountered in these obsolete opium dens did not fall into these specific categories but common sense will tell you that all who enter there are only one step away from perdition. I am convinced that it was the freedom from the shackles of any and all responsibility I felt. At some time during my formative years, I had been indoctrinated into the mindset that I could make a difference. Someone had instilled within me the notion that I could find success and contribute my part to the human race. Like most who have been struck by one creative muse or another to contribute or create, I had hearkened, much like Isaiah to the voice in the wind which asked "Whom shall I send?" I had subconsciously answered, "Send me-I can make a difference. I can help to bring gladness and lightness of heart through my creations of beauty and perfection." Then with the desecration of my masterpiece and my first drink, I had apparently repented of this philosophy and determined along with the sages of old that "all is vanity" and man, along with all his creations, must eventually succumb to a dusty death.

It was not long before I stopped going to work. As I was chief executive officer and majority stockholder of my firm, I simply delegated all my responsibilities to others and began to consume great quantities of alcohol.

Consequently, after about a year I was forced to desist from the bar routine. I began to encounter too many unpleasant episodes. The police officers and municipal judges were beginning to call me by my first name. I was arrested several times each for drunk driving, public intoxication and vagrancy. I very soon became apprehensive of setting foot outside my own door. Occasionally, during some of my more lucid moments, a glimmer of my past dedication to life and a belief in my own resiliency would cross my mind, but such thoughts were fleeting and soon futility would once again flood my very essence. Then I would inevitably clutch the wretched bottle and guzzle myself into oblivion. There were times while in a state of semi-delirium that I would once again search through the writings of ancient philosophers. I was always hoping to find an answer to the age- old questions of man's purpose concerning his earthly existence, and the possibility of his eternal soul gaining an eternal paradise; but all these queries were inconclusive since they required dying for the answer.

I do not know what I would have done without mother. She continued to stick by me and to see that my basic needs were taken care of. Nevertheless, and by and by, it all became too much for her. Her once compassionate smile turned into a perpetual scowl accentuated by that ghastly slit she had for an eye. She hired a huge, buxom, and masculine looking nurse to take care of me, and thereafter mother seemed to avoid me like the proverbial plague.

It was about this time that I too came to realize that it was hopeless. Alcohol had such a grip on me that there was no escape. I had dropped off the normal side of the world onto the side of hopelessness and futility. For some time I lived to drink, but eventually I discovered I had to drink to live. Finally, I decided to just go ahead and drink myself to death and the sooner the better. Anything was better than a perpetual hangover. I would order a case of whiskey and a case of strawberry brandy for my chasers. Using beer for a chaser had become intolerable, as I would regurgitate as soon as the cold beer hit my raw stomach; whereas, the brandy used as a chaser seemed to be more compatible with my en-fevered physical condition and the alcohol would remain on my stomach until absorbed by my system.

Before my first morning drink, my hands would tremble to the extent that I could not hold a glass to my lips and I would often have to pour the whiskey into a saucer, and then get down and lap the poison up like a dog. When my system would no longer tolerate the alcohol and I continued to force it into my stomach I would heave until I could feel my insides becoming detached from their moorings. I would not have been astonished at seeing what was left of my liver gushing out into that putrid pail all in a piece. Finally, all spent and out of breath from this retching, I would fall back near lifeless onto the sweat soaked mattress and pray to die.

Eventually, I would just have to begin to suffer it out. I was experiencing a living hell that cannot be explained. After about three days and nights of lying near motionless in this disgusting state, I would force myself to crawl to the kitchen and attempt to ingest a morsel or two of nourishment. After about a week I would be able to manage something like a fried egg, a slice of toast and a half glass of milk. After about two to three weeks, I could keep a normal meal on my stomach. I hated alcohol during these times. I would earnestly swear off the stuff and vow with all the sincerity I could muster that I would never take another drink, but eventually I would. Soon, the pain of the last drunk would fade and during one of my weaker moments, I would again yield to the demon. At some point in time, I began to consider alcohol as having a life. I imagined this stuff to be lying in wait for me. On more than one occasion, I have sat at a bar, sipped a soft drink, stared at the bottles of liquor on display and imagined these distilled spirits beckoning to me. "I'll get you yet!" they would whisper, and a cold sweat of droplets the size of thumbnails would form upon my brow. I would often sit and nurse the soft drink for hours but old John Barleycorn would ultimately win out and before long the bartender would be standing there pouring him into my glass.

Eventually I detected a conspiracy between my buxom nurse and mother to wean me off the dreadful stuff. Instead of the unlimited amount I had been accustomed to, they began to ration my liquor. I was appropriated just enough to sufficiently keep the demons and ghastly apparitions which accompany delirium tremens at bay. My nurse brought a bottle of liquor early each morning along with the admonition to see that it lasted until the following morning since I would get no more until that time.

The great majority of my time was now spent lounging in my overstuffed chair in front of the fireplace. Occasionally I would read bits and pieces of the old philosophers and then spend hours or days turning these transcendental postulations over in my enfeverished brain until I rendered them of all their phantasmagoric implications- until the futilities of life would once again engulf my being. The fire in the grate seemed to be the only thing that afforded me the least semblance of serenity. I would gaze for hours into the flickering flames and embers while I pondered many a curious question.

Early one morning I awakened with unbelievable alarm from my normal state of inebriation. My body quaked as one with the epileptic seizure. I was unbelievably cold. The embers on the grate had died to a dim glow. I reached for the poker in order to stoke and invigorate the fire but to no avail as the dull embers turned to ashes. I called out to mother for assistance. I reached for my bottle of whiskey but found it empty. A feeling of inescapable dread overwhelmed me. Once again, I clutched the poker but it suddenly turned into a three-foot long diamond back rattlesnake. Screaming, I flung it into the fireplace. Mother came quickly and rekindled the fire and in a few minutes, it was glowing red-hot.

The poker was once again a poker. I picked it up and once again began to stir the coals. Mother added more fuel and soon I began to feel warm and comfortable. I begged her to bring my daily ration of liquor. As I lifted the bottle to my parched lips mother turned and glared at me. Her face was only inches from mine. Her expression of disgust overwhelmed me. I hit her straight on in the back of the head with the near full bottle. She fell heavily at my feet. I gazed down into her imperfect face. The poker was standing in the red-hot coals. My hands no longer trembled. With great agility and grace, I withdrew the poker from the flame and buried its red-hot tip as deeply as my strength would allow into my mother's good eye. She never wiggled. A puff of smoke and the stench of burning flesh wafted up to my nostrils and I sank back, spent and satisfied, into my comfortable overstuffed chair. I had finally mustered the courage to remove her only flaw. Her features were now congruent. Both sides of her face were symmetrical. She was perfect.

Well, here is my lawyer! He once again assumes that pleasant unhurried demeanor as he is admitted into my cell. He sits on my bunk, opens his briefcase and withdraws a manila folder containing my pedigree. He begins to apprise me of certain defense tactics he proposes to utilize at my trial. I'm impressed! I like this person. He seems sincere. He even has himself convinced of his usefulness and importance. As I pace back and forth the length of this confine, attempting to assimilate and grasp the gravity and significance of what he has to say, I spy, clipped to one of the compartments of his briefcase a silver letter opener. There is no immediate significance to this. But, as he drones on and I begin to consider the vanity of his synthetic eloquence, once again that forlorn impulse to set things right, to bring about congruence, that yearning for symmetry and completeness grips my spirit and my inner depths. Futility explodes in my brain as my hand instantly clutches that shimmering blade, thrusts forward and severs that ghastly ear. The unearthly howl from his pallid lips has brought a host of guards and I'm standing limp, and spent, as they systematically enshroud me in this straight jacket. The lawyers' bloody ear stares up at me from the floor. I turn and look him straight in the face. His countenance is pallid but symmetrical. I have once again accomplished my little bit toward creating conformity to the universe-------------.

But please, my new found friend, perhaps you will allow me this one last digression as I feel my purpose for bearing my soul to you will remain obscure and futile lest I allude, at last, to another of Baltimore's heroes who, in spite of his propensity to do battle with the demon rum and opium, was imbued with an unsurpassed ability to create wonderful tales, and poesy, only to eventually fall victim to his own *"Imp Of The Perverse."*

The End

"THE FLOWER THAT ONCE HAS BLOWN FOREVER DIES"

When I was a little boy, my grandfather told me if I had the faith of a mustard seed, I could move a mountain. Of course, he told me a lot of things; like if I played with frogs I'd get warts, or if I wandered out of view of the house I'd be eaten up by a mad dog. But despite all those admonitions I would forget and play with frogs every chance I got and now and then I would slip off and go a mile down the road to the store for a sack of smoking tobacco or a sack of penny candy. Well, I never got warts and I never saw a mad dog. However, I have to admit; I wrestled with that mustard seed idea for quite a long time. I never was able to make any sense out of it and eventually stored the idea in the back of my memory along with a lot of my granddaddy's other famous sayings. It was not until several years later when I was near morally and spiritually destitute, and my best friend had lost all hope, that the concept of faith became a prominent theme in my life.

Ty Hardy was my friend. We had always been good friends. We had known one another all our lives and in fact born only a few days apart. I am not very sure, but I think I am just a day or two his senior. The Hardy place was the second farm south of ours. My great aunt, my granddad's sister and her husband Rousseau, or Rusaw, as we called him, owned the farm in between. Therefore, there was about a half-mile distance from my house to Ty's. We were born during the "great depression." We were not only born in hard times, we were born in a hard country. What folks called farms there in those Appalachian foothills was more like five acres of tillable bottomland and a hundred acres of rocks and hillsides too steep on which to plant a hill of corn.

An example of that I believe was the proverbial straw that broke the camel's back and caused my daddy to give up on farming. He had spent the better half of a fall and winter clearing one of those hillsides in hopes of growing a decent crop of corn the following year. He fell all the big trees, chopped them up into stove wood, dynamited the stumps out of the ground and burned them. I remember the stumps burning all winter long. Then in the spring, he turned the ground with a hillside plow, disked and dragged until that hillside was as smooth as a pancake. Then along about the last week in May he plowed nice straight rows, then dropped and covered the seed corn. About a day or two later there came a rain like Noah's flood. Then, two or three weeks later when the corn came up, it appeared the seed had been broadcast and scattered more like grass seed. The rain had washed the seed out of the furrows and the corn was un-tillable as there were not two rows left that you could get a cultivator between. That is when my daddy decided to quit the farm and move on up to Cincinnati.

Rumors of war were rumbling over the world in those days and one dollar an hour wages in the defense plants up North was far more enticing than the three dollars total for daylight to dark backbreaking farm labor. My folks, along with hordes of other dirt farmers heard the sirens call. My parents and my older sister moved to Cincinnati, where factory jobs were plentiful. They left my older brother Dale and myself on the farm to assist my grandparents. There was little or no money available but my brother and I did not know the difference. You just do not miss something you never had or do not know much about to begin with. The only cash crop we had was four acres of tobacco, the proceeds from which provided us with coffee, sugar, clothes, and a few minor necessities. The remainder of our essentials we grew or produced ourselves. Our farm equipment consisted of a pair of mules, a farm wagon, a hay-rake, a bottom plow, a hillside plow, a bull tongue and a double shovel plow, hoes, pitchforks, shovels and miscellaneous items. We worked from daybreak to nightfall during the spring, summer, and fall. We always had some chore to perform. It was do or die! Work or starve! Nevertheless, looking back on those times I realize they were the happiest times of my life.

Ty and I were near inseparable during those early years. Of course there were things that had to be attended to on our own farms, but when we got caught up a little we would often trade a day or two of labor. If my brother Dale and I were any ways near ahead with our work, we would pitch in and help Ty and his folks; and when we got behind, the Hardy family would reciprocate. Therefore, between work and school, Ty and I were together most of the time about like brothers.

The highlight of my early days on the farm was that special time in the evenings after I had finished with all my chores. I would feel like I was finally free. That is, after I had finished with the milking, chopping stove wood, kindling, and feeding the livestock. There was a long driveway from the house down to the main road and with nowhere to go and not much to do to occupy my time, I would generally amble down to the end of that driveway until I was out of sight of the house and crank myself up a cigarette. My folks did not allow me to smoke. Of course, they knew I did, but I could not stand my grandmothers look of disappointment when I smoked in front of her. They were always afraid if I got too persistent with the habit that I would become careless and set the barn ablaze and that would have bankrupted us.

By and by, I would here that familiar whistling. That would be Ty. He liked to whistle. Fact is, he whistled about all the time he was not talking. Sometimes he would whistle, "Yankee doodle, or "Buffalo gals" but mainly he liked to whistle hymns, like "When the roll is called up yonder" or "Shall we gather at the river" or "When we all get to heaven." TY and I attended church together about every Wednesday and Sunday night. I think he knew every word of every hymn in the book. Sometimes Dale, and Ty's older brother Jack, would gather there with us at the end of the driveway and we would get up a game of mumble peg; although most of the time we would just sit around and tell jokes, smoke cigarettes and throw rocks at the bats. The bats always came out just before dark. They were hard to identify from ordinary sparrows or barn swallows. However, when you threw a rock in their direction several bats would dive after the rock. We must have thrown a million rocks at those bats but were never able to connect with a single one of them.

Occasionally Ty would ride his little mare when he came to visit. He had named his mare "Fanny." She was sort of a peculiar looking animal. Frank, that was Ty's father, had taken old Fanny in on some kind of trade. He was always swapping animals. I saw Fanny the day Frank brought her home. She looked to be undernourished and most of the hair looked like it had been scraped off her sides and belly. Ty said they had worked her in the coalmines. She was small and docile enough for the job I figured. Ty said she would be a right pretty mare when he was finished with her. He doctored her bare spots with a mixture of linseed oil and some other chemicals he found around the barn and believed that concoction to be a cure-all for any sore or laceration an animal might incur. I always made him hitch her downwind of us as that "dukes" mixture of medicine he had applied to the mare smelled awfully like rotten eggs. Ty said as soon as she was healed he was going to train her to be a five-gaited saddle mare. I choked back a laugh when he told me that. Later on, when I told Dale about Ty's intentions for old Fanny, we laughed so hard we actually got down and rolled on the ground. After about a month, the mare did start to perk up some. Ty was feeding her that high protein horse feed and the linseed oil poultices were working. She was beginning to look like a different animal.

One evening Ty rode up on old Fanny at a full gallop. He was wearing a shiny new pair of cowboy boots and a set of leather chaps. I noticed a new lariat attached to the saddle and a little bell dangling from the saddle horn. Old Fanny was sporting a new set of shoes along with shiny shellacked hooves. Dale and I cast a sidewise glance at one another and rolled our eyes a little bit but we didn't say anything. Then Dale asked if "Tex" and I wanted to play a game of mumble peg. When the game was coming to a close and Ty had set the knife in the ground getting ready to "spank the baby" I mentioned something to the effect that I thought Roy Rogers had a Palomino. I had not meant to, but I knew right away that I had hurt Ty's feelings. The game was not over but he stood up and put the knife in his pocket. He puffed up like a blowing viper and slowly walked over and got on his mare. He rode slowly up the hill, and Dale and I thought he was just going up that way to pout. Soon he was out of sight, but a minute or two later we heard this loud "ya-hoooo" and here he came down that hill as fast as the mare could run. Sometime in the past, my granddad had planned to install a gate at the mouth of the driveway but had only set one post. Anyway, Ty had his lasso out twirling it over his head like a professional. Dale and I watched wide-eyed as they passed us at full speed. Ty lassoed the post but had forgotten to loosen the rope from the saddle horn. When the rope ran out old Fanny and Ty hit the ground simultaneously. We didn't laugh at him that time. Fanny had landed on Ty's leg and broken it in three places.

I rode the mare up to Dr. Crit Jone's place, which was about three miles North on the Knox Fork road. He was the closest thing we had to a doctor in that area. He had been a medic in the military and was generally the first person we called on in an emergency. He did his best to set the leg but something was not right. Ty walked with a serious limp for the rest of his life.

Our lives seemed to take on a different course after that incident. Ty was laid up in bed for several weeks. He couldn't go to school so he failed the tenth grade. After four months on crutches he graduated to just a cane. I stopped by now and then to check on him and during these brief visits detected a radical change in Ty's personality. There was little for him to do while giving the leg time to heal except sit by the fire and read, and there was very little reading material available there in the mountains except a Sears & Roebuck catalogue and the bible. More than once during these visits I noticed that big family bible lying beside his rocking chair. I also became aware during those days that he had stopped cussing. He had always been bad to cuss. About every word in fact had been "sum-bitch or mu-fuka." He also had stopped smoking. In fact, I even offered him a store bought "Camel" a couple of times and he turned them down. I knew right away that something was wrong. Then, when the weather warmed up, Ty once again resumed his evening visits. That old familiar whistling would once again brighten my otherwise solitary existence. He walked a little slower and with a quite noticeable limp but, by and large, he was the same old Ty from a physical standpoint.

I'm glad he sprang the news on me when no one else was around. It happened on a Wednesday night as we were walking home from prayer meeting. It had been one of those halleluiah breakdown meetings. A lot of the old folks, women especially, were in the spirit and dancing and shouting and speaking in tongues. Ty was right in among them. He was baptized in the spirit, danced, and shouted all over the place. I had never seen him act that way. Of course, shouting and going on was normal for the old folks. When he told me that the Lord had called him to preach I was shocked. Actually, I was at a loss for words. He said that one day, and he told me to mark his words, that he was going to be the pastor right

83

there at the New Bethel Baptist church. Of course, we were alone and had been talking in such serious and personal tones that I could not just bust out and laugh. In fact, I just said "yeah," and began trying to imagine Ty standing behind the pulpit there at New Bethel preaching. I thought it was one of his many fantasies and that he would forget about it over night. However, the next evening when he rounded the bend there at the little hill below the barn, I noticed right away he was not whistling. He walked a bit slower than usual and was motioning with his hands as if he were trying to explain something to someone. As he came closer, it became clear that he was talking to himself; he was practicing his preaching technique.

There was a great change in Ty during those times. He was not the person with which I had grown up. For those few minutes while he expounded on Jesus, God and the Bible, he would go through a total metamorphosis- from a timid and scared farm boy to a highly intelligent and skillful orator. He used many words I had heard before but their meaning had never been clear. Afterwards, I often found myself looking up the definitions in our old dictionary just because he had used them, and I did not want the reputation of being more ignorant than Ty. Once he started preaching I could not stop listening. I was terribly interested as well as amazed at his apparent intellectualism. When I asked him where he learned all those big words, he said he did not know- that God had called him to preach and given him the necessary words. He said that the words had to be just right so that anyone who listened could understand the good news of redemption, salvation, and forgiveness of sin.

Of course the atmosphere, scenery and setting, for those orations was optimum to say the least. Our tobacco barn was a perfect backdrop for a speech. Ty's words seemed to echo throughout that dry rotted old structure and reverberate from every timber. These mock sermons generally took place at about the time the sun became a huge orange semi-circle against the tree-lined ridges to the West. As the sun sank lower, the barns shadow crept steadily in my direction. More than once Ty's description of Hell as a place where the fire is never quenched and the worm never dies was enough to produce a strangely ominous feeling in my very soul. Many times the shadow of the barn had already overtaken me by the time he had finished his sermon.

I had long since stopped doubting Ty's ability to preach. Dale and I had cracked many jokes between ourselves at Ty's expense but we finally stopped with the derision. He had convinced both of us concerning his ability, and we accepted the idea that he would one day be a successful "man of the cloth." I had finally conceded that one day he would likely become the pastor of "New Bethel;" the church where all my family, and Ty's family, and, in fact, all the believers for miles around had been baptized.

Things began to move fast the following spring. My grandfather's kidneys began to fail, so my uncle, who was a police officer in Covington Ky., Entered him in a hospital there where he died a month later. Dale enlisted in the Army and the week after I graduated from school my grandmother sold what livestock we had, closed up the old house, and before I knew it we were on a Greyhound bus to Cincinnati. I was a big strong kid and had no problem getting a good paying job as hod carrier on a construction gang, and my mother and father had both found factory jobs and could now afford to care for my grandmother.

I moved into a small-furnished apartment and was doing very well until the first snow fell and there was a lay off. I loafed around for a week or two and then got my first of many jobs as a bartender. During the following ten years, I worked in about every skid row joint in the city. This was an exciting job for a green country bumpkin- for a while at least. I grew street smart and made many fair-weather friends. I learned fast how to hustle drunks and pimp out a few whores. However, there was always a twinge of remorse in the way I lived. Of course, everyone was doing it. Everyone was tapping someone. It was fast becoming a way of life for me as well. There was no loyalty; it was dog eat dog; it was all smoke and mirrors. Actually, I knew I had been raised better, and resolved more than once to straighten up and make something of myself. I even enrolled at the University on a part time basis and completed a few courses but eventually that "who gives a damn" attitude would take over. Then after two failed marriages and the handwriting on the wall every morning warning me of impending alcoholism, I figured I had better start to make some changes. I started to miss the simple life. I yearned for just a little contentment and peace of mind. I longed for the life I had known back there in the mountains.

It was during one of these homesick moments that I visited my grandmother. She was by that time in a nursing home. I rather poured my heart out to her. She said nothing would please her more than to know I was living at the old homeplace. She told me if I would promise to go home, she would give me a clear deed to the farm.

My last divorce had been final for over a year. Since all the trouble between my wife and I had been largely my fault, I had made several attempts at reconciliation but to no avail. Maggie was a very independent Woman and she was an honest woman. I tried to talk her into moving back to the hills with me but she was not ready to give up her job. She did agree to try to sell my house in which I had considerable equity. I somehow got the feeling she was softening a bit and that there was a possibility of our getting back together if this new venture of mine became viable.

I knew that at best, I would only be able to eke out enough money to keep body and soul together, but fame and fortune was something I had never considered attaining. Some would call that philosophy a lack of ambition but I was more concerned with lying down at night with a clear conscience. The few times I had broken the law or become involved in some type of shady deal had made a believer out of me. During those times, I became so paranoid I decided to be content with what I had and could acquire with my own sweat. I learned quickly that a fast buck and easy money always entailed the possibility of losing one's freedom, and freedom meant more to me than anything. Besides that, it had always been hard for me to lie or to be unfair. I'm sure if I had been born and raised in the city I would not have been aware of the fake smiles, the insincere handshakes, the prejudice, and the looking down ones nose at those less fortunate. My moral heritage was old fashioned, and quickly becoming outdated but it was my greatest strength and possession. That's why I was dissatisfied with my life; that's why I longed to get back to my roots; a place where I wouldn't have to be trying to second guess every person I encountered and analyze their motives.

Within a week after visiting my grandmother, I had the deed in my pocket and had paid what bills I could remember. On a bright and sunny morning in Cincinnati, I loaded what clothes I had into my old pickup and headed back to the place where I was born.

I arrived at the old homeplace about five in the afternoon on that early spring day. I tried to drive up close to the house but was stopped about halfway up the driveway by overgrown elder bushes and briar thickets. Only the upper half of the house with its rusting tin roof was visible. The total scene put me in mind of a newly discovered Inca temple and the surrounding area, which I had recently come across on the cover of "National Geographic." I got out of the car and eased my way through the brambles to the side porch. From what I could see, at least on that side of the house, the windows were still intact. Honeysuckle vines seemed to be slowly encapsulating the old structure and a few of these dauntless creepers had made it to the roof. I knew from experience that a thick growth of honeysuckle was a copperhead's utopia so I kept a stealthy eye out for one of those poisonous vipers. I tried the door and much to my surprise, it was still locked. I forgot for a minute that I had left that horde of unscrupulous thieves some two hundred miles behind me. Folks here in these Appalachian foothills were largely honest but it was still hard to believe that the old house had been sitting locked up and unmolested for ten years. I found the skeleton key I had placed in a cranny above the door when I left and let myself in. I could not believe it. There was dust, cobwebs and spider webs and rat droppings galore but everything else was exactly as we had left it right down to the dishes in the kitchen cupboard and the quilts on the beds. I thought about opening all the doors and windows to let the place air out good but then on second thought, I figured I best get that jungle of bushes around the house cut down first. I slept in my truck that night; in fact for the next several nights and spent my days attempting to restore the house to what I would consider my personal minimum living standards.

During those first few days as I looked around and considered the monumental task before me, I must admit that I felt like giving up. For years, no real physical exertion had been required of me. My body had become flabby and every cell of my being was thoroughly saturated with alcohol. It was the first week in April and still very much on the cool side but after ten minutes of physical exertion, I was near out of breath and sweating profusely.

However, after about a week of that hard labor I began to feel like a new man. The excruciating soreness in my joints and muscles began to dissipate and I was starting to breath like a normal human being. I washed down the ceilings, walls and floors of every room in the house. On my first trip into town, I rented a sump pump. I pumped the well dry, treated the cavity and steel casing with the necessary ant-bacterial chemicals, then waited twenty-four hours and repeated the process. After pumping the well dry and applying the purifier three different times, I felt the water was safe enough to drink. That well had been hand dug by my grandfather and had always produced a continuous supply of clear, near ice cold, sweet water. The stovepipe for the old warm morning kitchen stove had completely rusted out and I was surprised to find that the new postmaster had remodeled and expanded the post office to include a line of general merchandise. This would save me a ten-mile trip into town every time I needed something. Within about three days, I had the inside of the house in good enough shape to live in.

Now came the hard part. When I began the task of clearing the jungle of weeds, vines and saplings from around the place I was soon overwhelmed. I mentioned this problem to the clerk at the general store and he referred me to a fellow who was an out of work strip miner. I was vaguely aware of the economic problems within the coal industry over the past few years. Coal prices had sharply increased and coal operators were no longer going underground for the black gold; they were simply scraping the tops off mountains in order to get at the mineral. I had noticed many bald mountain peaks during the trip back but it held no real significance for me at the time. When coal prices drastically dropped, many operators went bankrupt and holding a lot of heavy equipment they could not give away. I found a guy who lived a couple miles North of me who owned a medium sized bulldozer that had been sitting idle for two or three years. That man was happy to get the work and within a days' time he had the whole area around the house and the barn looking like a new ground. I seeded the whole area with a good grade of fescue. Actually, I was beginning to become very pleased with the way the old place was shaping up. However, there was still the rat infestation with which to contend. The place was crawling with the critters. The first night I slept in the house, I woke up abruptly when one of those big rascals ran right across my face. One of those big rascals ran right across my face. The next day I rigged a five-gallon lard can around each leg of the bed, set traps, and sprinkled rat poison in every room.

All the old horse drawn farm equipment was still there in the barn right where we had left it. Of course, everything was pretty well rusted but I figured it was still in working order and with a little grease and oil would hold up long enough to cultivate at least one crop of tobacco. Of course, all the wooden parts like the wagon tongue and the plow handles were dry rotted and would have to be replaced. I just was not sure I could accomplish all the necessary repairs in time to get a four-acre tobacco crop in the ground by the first day of June. It was now the first of May and time was against me. However, I was feeling more alive and getting stronger by the day. The best part of all was, I was sober, and that in itself was a miracle.

Things were fine during the daylight hours. I had plenty to keep me busy and the manual labor and profuse perspiration was like a tonic. However, when the Sun went down I often felt like I was the only person alive. When darkness falls there in the mountains, it is the epitome of darkness- especially on a cloudy night. My nearest neighbors lived a mile away. My great aunt and uncle who had lived a quarter mile down the road during my teenage years were now dead. Of course, Rusaw had been invalid all the time I was growing up and that had left my aunt Vinney to accomplish all the necessary chores around the farm. She had always seemed so frail. Many times in the past, I had been near their home and witnessed aunt vinney, long dress and bonnet, wending her way through the pasture. She was heading out to do the milking. She would be carrying a three-gallon bucket in each hand. I figured that chore alone which had to be accomplished morning and evening in all kinds of inclement weather, would have been enough to kill the poor woman and I often wondered if she hadn't just fallen dead from sheer exhaustion during one of those long treks. Nevertheless, they were hearty people of good mountain stock. They were way up near eighty years old when they died.

Evenings would find me there at my favorite spot on the driveway below the house where Ty and I used to meet. Nothing substantial had really changed during the ten years I had been away. Once all the sapplings and underbrush had been bulldozed, things virtually looked the same as the day I had left. The old barn seemed to be a bit more weather worn as a few of the sheating planks had come loose and were leaning sideways a bit but all in all, things hadn't changed much. The bats were still coming back in droves just after sunset and the familiar "hoot" of an occasional owl could still be heard from the woods on the other side of the creek. The only thing missing was Ty's visits. When I had inquired of his whereabouts shortly after my return home, his daddy informed me he was up in Harlan County pastoring a church at one of the coal camps near Benham or Lynch. I planned to go and visit him as soon as I got my tobacco crop planted.

I had a coal oil lamp in each room of the house but only used one of them at a time. I had not quite decimated the rat population and was afraid if I left a lamp burning un-guarded, that one of those big vermin might knock it over and consequently set the house ablaze. Therefore, if I had to move from room to room, I would just carry a lamp with me. Obviously, the poison I had spread around the premises when I first arrived was having some effect on the demise of the rodent population but I could still hear them squeaking all through the house at night. I had a nice little twenty two-caliber rifle and was a dead shot with it at close range. I would spend hours sitting in the lamplight shooting those bastards. Their eyes shine purple in the dark, which made them perfect targets. The lamplight was sufficient for me to get a bead on them. I must have killed two or three dozen with that twenty-two. I continued to spread poison and set traps but finally realized the traps I had been using were too small. I was dealing with big cliff rats- some of them as large as a half grown cat. I found the steel traps Dale and I had used years ago to trap rabbit. I oiled them up and started setting them around the periphery of the house. About every morning, there would be three or four cliff rats dead in the traps.

Then one morning I discovered a rattlesnake caught in one of the traps I had set near the kitchen door. The thing had coiled around and around the trap almost concealing it. However, the snake was still alive as I could hear the rattles as I approached. I backed up a few steps and the rattling stopped but as I walked again towards the thing the rattles began to sing. The rattles were sticking straight up in plain sight and I counted ten of them. There was a five-foot circle of freshly disturbed dirt around the scene and it looked as if the snake had been pulling the trap around over the ground. I had anchored the trap to about a five-foot length of chain. On closer examination, I saw that the jaws of the trap had closed on a portion of the snakes head as well as about a two-inch portion of the body behind the head. I was well aware of the strength of one of those traps in good working order. Upon closing, the trap should have crushed the snake's head but evidently, because of its rusty condition, the trap had lost some of its tenacity and had not completely closed. Still, the old rattler had been secured fast enough to prevent his escape. I decided to leave the thing where it was since I could not discern how much injury the snake had sustained, and anyway, I had always heard that a snake would not die until the Sun goes down. However, I was not about to try and open the trap. I went on about my business for the rest of the day and it was already dark before I thought about the incident again, so I decided just to wait until the next morning before removing the dead snake and resetting the trap.

But the next morning as I approached what I thought would be a dead rattlesnake I heard the rattles begin to hum again. Several things went through my mind; like how long would the thing live? How could I release the trap without taking a chance on being bitten? I could not even see the latch that would allow the trap to be opened. The body of that big snake had it concealed. I finally decided to put snake, trap and all, into some kind of a box or something. I found a couple of wire meshed rabbit traps that Dale and I had made years ago. The openings between the wires were too big so I added a layer of screen wire from a role I had been saving for repair of the screen doors. I then scraped the snake, trap and all, into the cage with a hoe and wired it shut. I waited for a couple of days and when I went to check, the snake was still alive so I stuck a poker through the cage and pried the trap open enough for the snake to wriggle free.

I always thought the thing about the snake to be preposterous. I hated snakes. So I thought about taking the thing back into the woods and turning it loose. On the other hand, I guess I was just curious. How long would it live? How badly had it been injured by the trap? How much and what did it eat? I guess I was just naturally curious about such things and decided to keep it around for a while. It was not long before I would catch myself saying, "Well, better go see about on old rattler." My granddaddy had taught me a song once about a blind dog. The song went something like this: "Once I had an old houn'dog as blind as he could be, but every night about supper time I think that dog could see. Well here rattler here, here, here rattler here, call old rattler from the barn - here rattler here." Therefore, I decided to call the snake "ole rattler" and I had a good laugh after having thought up such an appropriate name.

I had heard that a snake's diet is generally birds and mice, so I caught a mouse in one of the small traps one morning and threw it in with the snake. I waited a couple of days and the mouse was still there. I got to thinking that maybe a snake would not eat carrion so I caught a live mouse and managed to get it inside the cage. Old rattler didn't do anything but the mouse was going berserk. I watched for a few minutes and had to leave to attend to something else but that evening the mouse was gone. I noticed a good-sized bulge about half way down the length of old rattler.

Feeding Ole Rattler proved to be quite a chore. It was not easy trying to stick a wriggling live mouse into the small door of a cage with one hand while trying to close the door with the other before the mouse could escape. One morning I got careless and shoved the mouse in too far and ole rattler nailed me on the hand right around the fleshy part of the thumb. He got me good. There was a splotch of blood around the entry point of each of the fangs. I was alone and ten miles from a doctor, so I just poured rubbing alcohol over the wound and headed for town. The doctor, luckily, was in his office. He gave me a shot and a liquid antidote to drink and sent a blood sample to be analyzed. I kept expecting my hand to start swelling. I sat there in the doctor's office for hours waiting on the results of the blood test and expecting to become deathly sick at any minute but nothing happened. My hand did not swell, and I felt completely normal. The doctor finally informed me that there was no sign of venom toxicity in my blood and that the snake was evidently sterile. I was naturally thankful and told God so. Nevertheless, something else crept into my mind. Was I just lucky or was it a sign-a sign that I was doing the right thing by moving back to these hills? I was secretly hoping that was the case because common sense kept telling me how stupid I was to keep working from sun-up to sundown on a venture that probably would not keep me in smoking tobacco. However, in spite of all that negativity, I was determined to persevere.

Everything seemed to be coming together. My farm equipment seemed adequate and the necessary repairs on the old house were coming along as planned. Unfortunately, there was a key ingredient to this enterprise that I had been putting off, and finally, I was determined to put it off no longer. I was in dire need of a team of mules and I had been delaying that purchase because I knew how easily a novice in dealing with horseflesh could be duped. I knew ty's dad Frank, was an expert when it came to mules and horses so I persuaded him to accompany me to the weekly stock sale in London, Kentucky. I was well pleased with Frank's selection of a pair of iron gray mules of about sixteen hands and four years of age. These mules had been broken to the harness and that was a plus.

There came one of those proverbial cloudbursts the day the stockyard promised delivery of the mules. Knox County is famous for their devastating flash floods and the truck hauling the mules had become stuck somewhere around the Frank Hardy place. Ty just happened to be there and had accepted delivery of the mules, and kept them in his barn for a couple of days while waiting for the water to recede. Two days after it stopped raining, I became anxious to get on with the many tasks at hand. I went down to the barn and began whittling on one of the unfinished plow handles. I dragged a dilapidated cane bottomed chair out onto the easement between the barn and the road. As I sat there, I began to drink in the peacefulness and serenity surrounding me. At times like these, my thinking would often drift back to city life but I always tried to put those things out of my mind. I would automatically direct my eyes toward the heavens and thank God for inspiring me to return here to the mountains where there was no smell of exhaust fumes-no bumper to bumper traffic-no throng of people all trying to talk at the same time- no scream of a police sirene or a fire engine. There was no one around here to give you that crooked and deceitful smile-no limp handshakes while starring at your naval area, afraid to look you in the eye-no flashing of those pearly whites and trying to take your mind off the fact that they had their hand in your pocket. Such memories only served to reinforce my commitment to this new way of life.

I had about finished whittling and fashioning the hickory handle to the rusty plow when I heard a faint singing sound coming from around the bend in the road there at the little hill. Pretty soon Ty rounded the bend singing at the top of his lungs. He was riding one of my mules and leading the other one. Both mules seemed to be fully harnessed, and soon the little band was close enough for me to hear the tinckle of the trace chains. Ty had a red and white bandana tied about his head and a long turkey feather protruding, Indian style, from one side of the headdress. He was singing "Goodbye Old Paint" in a very drawn out and slurred resonance. He was sounding as if he was drunk, and I prayed I was wrong. He rode up near the hay rake and attempted to slide off the mule but got his right shoe tangled in the harness and fell to the ground. I ran over and helped him to his feet. He reeked of moonshine whiskey and he was still attempting to sing. He wobbled over to the chair and sprawled out in a spraddle legged fashion. There was a white coagulation of saliva in the corners of his mouth and a dribble of the same running off his chin. "Well, heres your mules" he said. "Nice team-niiice team". He put a long drawn out emphasis on the second "nice." His face was red and little beads of sweat had collected on his forehead and underneath his eyes.

"Whew! It's hotter'n hell," he rasped. He attempted to wipe the sweat from his forehead with his left hand while producing a pint of whiskey from underneath his shirt with his right. "Wanna drink," he said as he thrust the bottle toward me. "No, I quit" I replied. "Quit! Hell, you cain't quit! Who am I gonna drink with around here if you quit? Ain't anything but bible thumpin hypocrites around here!" He hic-upped a couple of times and I thought for a minute he was going to throw up. He took a couple of deep breaths and began again. "All I hear around here is "thank yi' Jesus, halleluiah and praise the lord." I was dismayed to say the least. I thought for a second I was going to be the one to throw up. I could not believe it. This guy had always's sort of been my idol when it came to morals and ethics and here he was acting like one of the skid row drunks I abhorred. I walked around my mules, scrutinizing them intently and making sure all the harness was there and intact. Evidently, Ty had brought them through some pretty high water as there was a muddy ring around them near the tops of their flanks and the leather breeching of the harness was soaked. Ty just sat eyeballing me as he waited for me to speak. "Hey, man" I said in a questioning tone, "I thought you were a preacher. I've never known a preacher who got drunk!" "Whatcha' mean?" was his quick retort. "I ain't drunk! Jus' take a lil' nip now an' then for this pain in my leg. Hell, I ain't drunk. You know, little wine for the stomach's sake as the good book says--that's all." I couldn't help but chuckle at that familiar comeback.

I led the mules into the barn and removed the harness. I had expected them to be a little skittish and nervous due to these unfamiliar surroundings but for the most part, they were docile and well behaved. I had previously repaired and prepared individual stalls for them. I added new slats to each stall and the hay manger, which separated the stalls. The slats, or dividers, of the manger were stationed vertically on about a thirty-degree angle with enough space between the two by fours for the mules to get at the hay. The top of the manger opened into the loft. This was a fast and efficient way to feed the animals. There was no carrying or lugging hay around. All I had to do was slide the hay into the manger from the hayloft above. The solid wood corn and oat troughs my granddaddy had fashioned and whittled out when he built the barn were still usable and I had nailed them back into their original places. Sometime along in the nineteen twenties, representatives of the major oil companies had come into Appalachia buying up the mineral rights to the farms, and one of these companies had drilled a four hundred foot deep oil well near the back of the barn but all they hit was water. As far as I know, oil has never been found in that area. Anyway, my granddad fastened a hand pump to the well and it had always produced sufficient water for the livestock.

After I finished getting the mules situated, I found Ty sound asleep in the chair where I had left him. He was still sprawled there with saliva oozing out from the corners of his mouth. He looked and smelled as though he had not shaved or bathed for a week. It had been ten years since I last laid eyes on him and apparently, those years had not been good to him. He was flabby, and his wrinkled face was aged far beyond that of most thirty year olds. I just stood there staring at him-trying to make some sense of what I saw. I think I was hurt more than disappointed. He was my friend and always would be. We had endured and survived the poverty of our childhood together and in this at least, we had a common bond. I could forgive him for anything but I could just not understand how any man could be a "God called preacher" and end up in the shape he was in. Nevertheless, called by God to preach or not, I thought-- he's still just a man.

The air was heavy with throttling humidity as it always was after a series of those prolonged thunderstorms. The setting sun produced that familiar orange glow in the West and served as a perfect backdrop for the silhouette of tree lined mountain ridges. Pockets of smoky mist was gathering and floating about the treetops and the hooting of a barn owl, and the lowing of cattle in some distant pasture signaled that night was falling. While gazing about me at that beautiful sunset, an indescribable feeling of being at peace with, and being a part of, the puzzle of creation, humbled me to the point of tears. The total silence of the approaching night and the majesty of the aged mountains seemed to whisper that they had been there forever-that they would be there forever and were pleased with my brief intrusion and my sincere adulation. I felt as though I could survive forever with nothing more for sustenance than the beauty and wonder of Gods magnificent creation. It was times like this, which had made me very much aware of my many indiscretions against God and all my futile attempts to achieve righteousness. As I stood looking down at Ty in his fallen condition and being very aware of his sincerity concerning things spiritual, I wondered how my own vain attempts to realize spiritual sanctification could ever come to pass. I felt sure the diversion Ty was experiencing was only temporary-that all men at times are destined to succumb to various and sundry temptations and indiscretions. The abrupt interjection of something human, Ty's snoring jarred me out of my reverie.

I began to contemplate how I could get him home when the intermittent half howl, half barking of a dog pierced what remained of the solitude. Pretty soon a little black and tan beagle whizzed past me and jumped squarely onto Ty's lap and began furiously licking the man's face. Ty blubbered a few times and began flailing his arms in astonishment. When he realized what was happening he let out a squall and jumped to his feet. "Get off me you sum-bitch" he bellered. "What the hell you doin' sparky? You tryin' to eat me up? You scared the hell out a' me." The little dog fell with a thump to the ground. When Ty had collected his composure, he reached down, picked up a clod of dirt, and heaved it at the dog. The clod hit the ground within inches of the beagle. "Git, git home! Git on down the road you crazy sumbitch. I thought somethin' was about to eat me up." Ty shook himself violently like a dog just out of the creek. The little beagle tucked its tail between its legs, but instead of running away, crouched, and slowly crawled over to Ty and began to lick his boot. Ty abruptly lifted his foot and sent the dog end over end into a clump of weeds where it lay yipping and whimpering, afraid to show itself. "That's a worthless sum-bitch" Ty said. "Won't run a rabbit! Last time I took him huntin' he embarrassed the hell out of me. I had told my daddy what a great huntin' dog I had. Told him I had the best rabbit dog in the county. The other morning we got our shotguns and headed out through the pasture with the beagle there. Daddy and I were just walkin' along talkin'. We unlatched the gate and walked through. We just assumed the dog had plenty openings in the fence to be able to follow us, but when we looked back that damn dog was standing there at the gate crying. I finally had to go back and help the dog through the fence. Talk about being embarrassed! I came in a pee-diddle shooting the lil'" sum-bitch then and there but daddy talked me out of it." I finally went over, picked the beagle up, and sat down in the chair with him in my lap. He quit shivering after I had stroked his head and back a few times. Ty was beginning to sober up a bit by this time and his empty bottle was lying there by the chair where he had dropped it. I realized his decision to bring the mule's home through high water to be the spontaneous decision of a drunk. I suggested he just stay all night with me since he was evidently in no shape to wade through the high water after dark. I made a pallet for him on the kitchen floor and ten minutes later, he was snoring like a hibernating bear.

I was awake and had a fire going in the cook stove before daybreak. I set a pot of coffee to boiling first and then squeezed out a pan of sourdough biscuits and put them in the oven. I must have awakened Ty while scooting my big cast iron skillet across the iron stove. By the time I had boiled the grits and fried a half dozen eggs he was standing there at the washbasin washing and rubbing the sleep out of his eyes. He sat down at the table and produced a can of Prince Albert from his shirt pocket. I watched him out of the corner of my eyes. His hand was shaking pretty badly as he tried to roll a cigarette. The kitchen windows were wide open and a nice breeze was circulating through the house but little beads of yellow sweat was collecting on his face that for some reason reminded me of a freshly baked chiffon pie. I slid a couple of fried eggs out of the skillet onto his plate and followed that with a heaping scoop of grits. Ty coughed a couple times and backed up from the table. "Oh God man," he mumbled. "I can't eat anything right now. He sucked in a deep breath and added "Maybe later." I poured the coffee, sat down, and started to eat. Ty was still fumbling around trying to roll a cigarette. I pulled a pack of camels out of my pocket and tossed him one. "Thanks man, I gott'a get a little fresh air." He cleared his throat loudly and walked toward the door. I had about finished eating when he returned and resumed his place at the table. I was well aware of his physical condition. He was suffering from a severe hangover. Those rotten hangovers were a major catalyst in my desire to stop drinking. A good case of dry heaves and uncontrollable shakes from the withdrawal of alcohol is the epitome of physical misery.

I knew he needed a drink but there was no alcohol available. I left the food on the table and began to clean up the mess, which I had created in preparing the meal. I was hoping he would eventually choke down a few bites and drink the coffee. After a little while, he took a long last drag off his cigarette and flicked the butt out the nearby window. I waited patiently while he forced down half the food on his plate and drained a second cup of coffee. I was proud of him. I could not have gagged down a bite of food in his condition.

I was running out of time. I had a million things to accomplish if I was going to get my tobacco in the ground on time. But, I thought, first things first. I had just bought a fine pair of mules and I had to feed them. I met one of my high school classmates at the County seat while I was recording my deed not long after I arrived back in Knox County. He himself was a retread, or to put it another way, he too had moved north and tried big city living but had also found that he was not cut out for that way of life. His name was Steve House. From my memory of our school days, Steve would fit into the category of the "gentle giant." He was quiet, polite, and always kind and considerate of others. I had not been surprised to learn that immediately upon graduation he had enrolled at a bible seminary and moved to Baltimore. I just happened to run in to him there at the County clerks' office.

We had a little time to kill and reminisced at length over a cup of coffee. He told me his folks had died and that he had decided to return and take over the family farm. He had inherited a good-sized farm "up there in the head of huntin' shirt" as he described it. I was familiar with the name "huntin shirt" as my grandmother had referred to that place very often when I was growing up. Steve had returned to the old homeplace about five years before our meeting and had in his words "the old homeplace in pretty good shape." He told me he had plenty of corn, hay, pigs and cattle for sale and that if I ever needed any of those items to look him up. To be honest about it, I was getting pretty hard up for money. I was in need of at least fifty bales of hay, twenty bushel of corn on the cob, a good milk-cow with calf, and a couple of pigs. I was hoping I could purchase these items from Steve with half down and payment in full when I sold my tobacco around Christmas time. However, even if I were to be lucky enough to acquire these necessities I was still only one man and I was in dire need of physical help. Getting back to my roots and delving my hands into the soil once again had seemed quite romantic, but reality was now setting in.

After I cleared the dishes, I poured another cup of coffee and sat back down at the table. I lit a cigarrete and started considering what to do next. I suppose the deafening silence was telling. "Hey man, whats your problem?" Ty blurted. "I guess I'm going to be heading up huntin' shirt directly," I responded. "Gotta go up there and see if I can buy some corn and hay off 'a Steve House. I must get some feed in here for my mules. Thinkin' about getting a milk cow and a coupla' pigs too." "Looks like you are serious about this farming business." Ty said. "You actually think you can get a crop of tobacco in the ground in time for it to do any good?" "I don't know, but I'm sure as hell gonna try" I responded. "Well, gimme another one of them tailor mades" he said. I tossed him another camel. He lit up and blew a few smoke rings while staring intently at some imaginary spot on the ceiling. I could almost see the cogs turning in his head. He had always been so predictable. He was getting ready to come up with a solution to the problem he had just proposed. "Tell you what!" He commenced, after a long silence. "Make you a deal! I am planning to stay around here for a while. I could stay with my folks, but if you agree, I'll stay here and help you with the farm this summer. Fact is, I'll even stay and help you get your tobacco to market up in Richmond when the time comes. I'll do it for room and board and maybe a small percentage, whatever you say, of the profit." I studied about his proposal for a minute. "O.k, sounds like an offer I can't refuse. You're a true friend Ty and I won't forget this." "Ok, he said. Let's shake on it." We both stood up and shook hands like we were two important businessmen.

We had the mules fed, watered and harnessed before the sun was fully above the horizon. We pulled the wagon inside one of the shed additions to the barn where the hay frame for the wagon had been leaning there against the wall for ten or more years. It had been out of the weather and seemed to be relatively in good repair. Ty found a hammer and reseated a few nails that appeared to have loosened their hold over time and then we lifted the frame onto the wagon and strapped it down. With this frame extending over each side and the rear end of the wagon by about three feet all the way around, the hauling capacity was actually doubled. Before we headed out I went back to the house and retrieved my twelve gauge pump and secured it under the spring seat on the wagon. You never knew what type of critter you might incur back in those hollows.

I was more curious about whether or not the mules would work as a team than anything else at the moment. I found out immediately that they were well trained in recognizing the standard commands of "get-up," "whoa," "gee and haw." Whether or not they would pull in concert under a heavy load was yet to be seen.

Ty and I didn't talk much for a while. We were paying more attention to the road condition, the attitude of the team, and whether or not the wagon would hold together. Water was still axle deep at the dip in the road near the bridge but we had no trouble fording. Water did cover the wheel hubs and I was a little concerned since I had not regreased the wheel bearings. About a half-mile below the bridge we made a hard left and headed up Huntin' shirt hollow.

Since the time I was a little ragamuffin running the hills and hollows here in these Appalachian foothills I had developed sort of a fascination for the name and the place folks referred to as "huntin' shirt." When I first heard the name of the place pronounced, that person, and I believe that person to be my grandmother, pronounced it as being one word like "huntinshirt," and I had not considered it to be actually two words until I was much older. I remember pondering long and hard on the idea of why anyone would attach such an odd identity to a wagon road.

When I was probably ten years old I slipped off one day and was gone until late in the afternoon trying to explore and discover more about what I considered must be a fascinating place- this place called "huntinshirt." I had made it back home just before dark and when I told my grandmother I had been up on "huntinshirt" I thought sure she was going to wear me out with a switch. She told me it was a wonder I wasn't dead and I was lucky to say the least that I had not been eaten up by a mad-dog or worse. I was near ready to graduate from high school before I realized that the threat of being bitten by a mad-dog was just a scare tactic used by the old folks in that part of the country to keep kids close to home. They told us that if we were ever bitten by a mad dog that we would start foaming at the mouth and then go mad or crazy and have to be tied to a tree and left there to die. No one would be able to get close enough to us to feed us as we would be out of our heads and try to bite them, and, if we did bite someone, they too would go mad and so on. I can tell you it worked. I was more afraid of a mad-dog than anything I could think of and after all those admonitions about wandering far from home; I was seldom out of sight of the house.

Hunting shirt had not changed much from the way I remembered. It was still just a sled road; originally an animal trace tromped out during eons past by herds of buffalo and deer. Stunted willow bushes largely concealed the choked up stream that paralleled the road. The flat expanse of wasteland which made up the original stream valley was four or five hundred feet wide but useless to any type of agriculture. Yearly flash floods maintain these bottoms as perpetual swamp. This area is still only sparsely settled and today's man can understand why. You might wonder why anyone at all would want to settle here and I suppose the answer lies in the way you define the word "settle." Sometimes you just "settle" for the way things are- for the hand God deals you. If a man had been among those first pioneers who came through the

Cumberland Gap from Virginia or South Carolina he probably would have been sick of the hardships of travel by the time he advanced this thirty-five or forty miles into Kentucky. I suppose that if he could find a spot where there was plenty of water and a flat spot large enough to grow a crop of corn, he would just "settle" for that. He would be able to raise his family unimpeded by anyone telling him what to do and how to live. These rough hills and roads are a testament to the stoic and tenacious disposition of those first settlers. They were survivors in the largest sense of the word. These mountain people and their ancestors are genuine bonafide people. They can withstand any ordeal which man or nature can throw at them.

Actually, many of these people are descendants of Desoto's Conquistador's. According to history, Desoto and his band of intrepid adventurers, largely of Persian and Turkish descent, landed somewhere on the West coast of Florida during the early fifteen hundreds and made their way inland. They discovered the Mississippi River and made it on as far as Nashville Tennessee. During the return trip, Desoto died of a fever, leaving these soldiers of fortune leaderless. It is said there were about five hundred of them who scattered out and intermarried with the Indian tribes of the area. The half-breed descendants of these folks are called Melungeons; the dark skin, green-eyed people who can readily be identified today by those very obvious features. Matter of fact, I am a descendant of one of those half-breeds. The dark skin and green eyes are prevalent among of my uncles and several cousins. Melungeons are very private, solitary people who just want to be left alone. They are self-sufficient and experts at improvising. They have always been able to take care of their families even though they were only a steel plow away from twelfth century Europe.

Then there are the Scots-Irish, those who migrated to America due to the devastating Irish potato famine. Many of these folks pushed westward from South Carolina and Virginia through the Cumberland Gap. These families began to settle along every tributary and stream that feeds the Cumberland River. Anywhere there was a sufficient water supply they would build their cabin. All they owned was the clothes on their backs, a wagon, a pair of mules, and if they were real lucky, a pig or two and a milk cow. Their self-reliance and desire to be left alone is a testimony to an inherent disposition among them which put simply is "mind your own business and let other folks mind theirs." These mountains that taught them all they wanted and needed to know about life, is a heritage we can only hope will prevail as the ages roll. These folks have adhered to a philosophy best summed up by John Keats: "Beauty is truth, truth beauty. This is all ye know on earth and all ye need to know."

There have been several attempts by the Northern "do-gooders" during the twentieth century to call attention to the so-called "poverty" of these mountain people. They came here to Appalachia taking pictures and filming documentaries in hopes of getting the government to take steps in lifting these people out of their perceived poverty. There's always a group of bleeding hearts around hoping to make a name for themselves, or acquire a degree of righteousness in the eyes of God by "helping the poor." Actually, it's laughable. These people are not poor. They have everything they want. Sure, if the so-called philanthropist or the Federal Government wants to come in and give the folks food stamps and welfare they will naturally take it! Why look a gift horse in the mouth? The fact of the matter is; they would survive just fine without these handouts. They are not terribly interested in fine housing and excellent roads. They have sense enough to know if they had fine roads and fancy houses it wouldn't be long until they were inundated with the so called "educated" and "socialized" phonies from up North.

Ty had been trying to hum a tune of some caliber, but rain running down the side of the mountain and across the road had created a washboard pattern in the red earth and his effort at humming became more and more like a series of hic-ups as the steel wagon wheels dropped in and out of the ruts, so eventually, he gave up and became quiet. "Okay, tell me about it" I said, finally breaking the silence. "Bout what?" He exclaimed. "Why did you stop preaching?" He turned and looked into my eyes for a long instant. "Well, Tommy, to make a long story short, I just lost the fire." He paused and I stared back at him with a questioning grimace. "But you told me you were called to preach, -that God had called you to be a preacher!" "Well, I ain't the first man that ever quit the ministry," was his instant retort. I continued to stare at him, waiting for him to continue. "I told you," he said. "I just lost the fire-I lost the faith!"

There was a long silence. I was trying to digest his explanation and at the same time perhaps find some words of encouragement, but when he mentioned faith, that tenuous concept that no man yet, in my opinion, had fully fathomed, I found myself momentarily tongue-tied. "Look," he finally began. "I was doing just fine in my ministry for a while. I was preaching nearly every Sunday at one church or another around the county. But, I was barely able to keep body and soul together from my share of the offerings and there was no prospect of ever getting the opportunity to become a full time pastor. I'm not actually that concerned about money, I don't need a lot, but I wanted something more permanent, more steady, where I could settle down in one place. You know, establish some roots. Hell, you know what I mean! I got tired of floundering around from church to church. And, I was well received everywhere I preached and folks seemed to like me. I was always invited back. But the constant study and preparation for my sermons left me feeling like I was living in a monastery. You know, I'm a young man with human appetites and I couldn't seem to reconcile that with the responsibility of preaching the Word. I became bland and then boring. I lost the enthusiasm required to be a successful preacher. That's about it. I have decided to give up the ministry temporarily. I have been doing some real soul searching lately and have generally concluded that I have a lack of self-confidence. When I start to preach I'm never quite sure my interpretation of the Bible is correct. I lack the authority of a man with credentials, you know, like a man with a college degree. I would like to have a degree from an accredited seminary. Right now I need a sign from God! I need a sign that I'm a called man of God! I guess I'm just confused. I don't know whether I'm called or not to tell you the truth. To be honest, I've been guilty of a few things pretty unbecoming of a preacher. That's why I've decided to take some time off and collect my thoughts. I'm still waiting for that sign. I believe God will let me know one way or another." He paused briefly while sucking in a long deep breath. "Hell," he blurted, "I'm just a dumb country preacher! A man needs a good education and a degree in order to be able to speak with authority on any subject!"

I allowed my memory to momentarily flick back across my own life and was inclined to agree with that statement to a certain extent. However, my question would be: to whom would that person with implied experience and knowledge be speaking? Evidently, his idea of a "country preacher" and mine was pretty far apart. A country preacher speaks to country folk about "thus sayeth the Lord!" He speaks a simple message of how incontrovertibly disobedient and imperfect man can be ultimately reconciled to the perfect God! I had witnessed firsthand what happens to a country preacher when he attempts to become too "hifalutin." He will slowly become ostracized and drummed out of his "country" church. Appalachian people are as intelligent as people anywhere. It's just that their wants and needs are simple. They will ultimately ignore rhetoric and get straight to the bottom line.

But since my return to the mountains it was becoming more and more obvious to me that drastic change was in the air. It was obvious that some of the radical changes in morals and ethics I had witnessed immediately upon arriving in the "queen city" was insidiously taking place here in the mountains as well. I had not yet figured out whether these were changes that just naturally occur over time or whether these folks were being overly influenced by re-treads like me. Many folks had gone North to work in the defense plants during the industrial boom of the forty's and fifty's but were now returning to Appalachia, and, inadvertently bringing the city customs and lax morals back with them. I did not even know how to convey my feelings to Ty on the subject of religion but pretty soon he began again.

"Did you know that the earth is at least four billion years old? Why, if you were to stop right here I could pick up a fossil anywhere along this stretch of road, like a trilobite or brachiopod that's at least a few million years old. Why, the smartest men in the world claim that we were not created. According to them we just evolved over millions of years from lower forms of life, like apes or chimpanzees!" He starred incessantly into my eyes as if he expected some shocked response to this startling revelation that he had chosen to make me privy to. But I had heard it all before during my "indoctrination" to the process of "modern education and socialization." I could identify perfectly with what Ty was feeling. I had been just like him after a couple of introductory courses in

Geology, or Biology 101. All my college professors had been sincere and sold on the legitimacy of their individual areas of expertise and during my two year stint at the University I found myself concurring with all their theories. Those guys were good. They had been brainwashed and indoctrinated as to the validity of all scientific theory. They assumed this validity simply because the word "scientific" had been applied. I have never discounted the concept of the "scientific method" but when they started to construe tenuous hypotheses to fact, I started doubting their conclusions. In the first place, the extent of the fantastic numbers they attempt to deal with is impossible for the human brain to compute. I was informed that the fossilized trilobite I was examining during my first "lab" in Geology 101 was several millions of years old and that a particular star we were discussing in astronomy 102 was seven million light years distant from the earth! When I tried to wrap my mind around these figures, my brain would freeze for a minute and then I would just throw up my hands and surrender. I didn't have to accept any of it but it was evident that if I were to pass the course I was expected to acquiesce.

It wasn't until a few years later when I began to surmise that a few of those sheltered professors needed to re-examine carbon fourteen dating and space/time warp. After some time I realized that as far as I was concerned all scientific speculation and theory on space and time was wishful thinking on the part of these guys who had been nurtured inside one of those scientifically oriented cocoons and were hoping to one day publish that earth shattering theory upon which they would be catapulted into the scientific hall of fame. It seemed impossible for these wannabe "guru's" to stop and smell the proverbial coffee and to get in touch with reality and their personal mortality. The word spirituality was not in their vocabulary for the most part, and they seemed to be intent on destroying the concept of Christianity and the importance of the holy bible to civilization. All I know is I could not even begin to fathom the existence of billions of planets, stars, suns and galaxies. Nor, did I care how old a fossilized bug was and what's more I was still waiting for someone to discover the missing link.

Ty was staring straight ahead with sort of a pouting expression on his face. I expect he was feeling exonerated for his vague implications and belief that man was not created by God but had simply evolved by chance from some slime pit during the eons past. He was wrestling hard with his faith. He wasn't sure what he believed. But if I were to ask him point blank whether he believed in the Christian doctrine of creationism or the theory of evolution I know he would choose creationism without hesitation. He would never admit his doubt. I knew that in time, if he was lucky, he would have to put his biblical knowledge and his faith to the test, and that if he survived the test, then all his doubt would be removed. I felt he was still at the point where he was experiencing "head" faith. Something has to happen in a person's life to give him "heart" faith." When this happens, doubt and disbelief in spiritual matters will leave him. I thought it best not to press the issue of Ty's decision to stop preaching, and wait for a more appropriate time to discuss it.

The stream valley began to widen some, and the forested hills on each side were becoming less steep. The scrub oak and black jack bushes which had made the near vertical hills a vertical jungle were now being choked out by white oak and walnut the size of which would have brought a smile to the face of the most particular lumberjack. We started down a long but gradual incline when Ty leaned on the brake and motioned for me to stop the team. I pulled back on the check lines and the team stopped abruptly. Ty leaned over to me and whispered, "Hand me the shotgun." I hesitated for a second and then figured what could it hurt so I retrieved the twelve gage from beneath the spring seat and handed it to him. Ty pointed toward a clump of briars and stunted elder bushes and whispered "mad dog!" I didn't have time to compute what he said. I just stood and attempted to look in the direction he was pointing. About that time he fired. The mules bolted and Ty fell across the spring seat and down into the wagon bed. I pulled back on the check lines as hard as I could and started hollering "whoa, whoa." By that time the mules were in a gallop.

I began to get control of the team after a couple hundred feet but they were still in a hard run when we reached the bottom of the incline. Water percolating across the road at the bottom of the hill had exposed the bedrock. The right front wagon wheel was badly damaged when it struck this outcropping. Ty had dropped the shotgun when the mules bolted and had leaped out of the wagon to retrieve it. When I finally got the team calmed down he was nonchalantly approaching as though nothing had happened. A few choice words of criticism passed through my mind concerning his attitude and carelessness. "Why didn't you warn me that you were going to fire that thing?" I questioned. His smile quickly turned to a frown. One of the spokes had been splintered from the wagon wheel and the vehicle was now useless. I knew I could not repair the contraption and doubted anyone within a hundred miles could.

I was becoming very agitated with Ty's disengaged attitude. He was acting like we were on one of our teenage excursions. I un-hitched the team from the wagon and Ty and I each boarded one of the animals and set out up the road toward Steve's place. I was hoping he would have a spare wheel to fit my wagon. But even if he did have one, I knew that by the time we had the thing repaired it would be too late in the day to attempt the return home.

Under ordinary circumstances I would be enjoying the ride on the sweaty smelling mule along with the rattling of the trace chains and squeaky leather harness. It propelled me back to the day when I was a kid and my granddaddy allowed me to ride the workhorse to the barn after a long hard day of plowing. As I gazed in front of me at the green valley which had opened up between the mountains, I was once again proud of my decision to leave the city and return to Appalachia. The definition of a serene and peaceful life was incorporated into this scene. The fear of losing a job, the cutthroat competition for the shiniest car, the fancier house and the best-tailored clothes, all seemed to belong to another world. It was no wonder Steve House had returned to Huntin' Shirt after a four or five year stint in Baltimore. He too must have listened to the man who said "you can only live in one house at a time, eat one meal at a time, wear one suit of clothes at a time and drive one car at a time. Everything else is vanity and a waste of effort." Ty was half singing, half humming, "When the roll is called up yonder" while gesticulating with his arms as though he were leading the church choir. "Hey," I hollered at him. You think you killed that mad-dog?" He turned and looked at me with that pouting expression of his. "Hell, I don't know! I never saw the damn thing after I shot and the wagon lurched out from under me!" "Well how do you know the dog was mad? What made you think the dog was mad?" I asked. "Well, hell, I know it was mad! I know what a mad dog looks like!"

"O.k. then, what did it look like? How could you tell it was mad?" was my retort. "It was standing on one front leg with its head sort of droopy, and it was foaming at the mouth. It looked to me like it was just ready to fall over," he explained. "What did the thing look like? Was it a big dog, a little dog, a black dog, spotted dog?" Ty studied for a long minute. "Well it was sort of a little spotted dog! No, you know it was sort of white with tan patches." He paused again. "But it was mad! I told you it was mad!" he shouted. "I told you, I know when a dog's mad and when it's not! Hell, if I hadn't killed that thing it just might be following us now!" He turned and gazed long and hard over his shoulder toward the spot where we had left the wagon.

We were on Steve's farm now. We proceeded up a short incline and that's where the valley ahead really widened. We rode past haystacks, pig stys and pieces of equipment that revealed the fact that some serious farming was taking place. A little farther on we passed a large hog-lot that held what looked like five or six huge sows and a couple of dozen piglets. Steve's house had been erected on higher ground and closer to the timberline near a grove of tall pines. The five or six room double boxed frame house of white oak was typical Appalachian; which simply means the dwelling was built for its utility rather than aesthetics. The rusty metal roof was beginning to sag a bit at the center of the crown, giving evidence of the longevity of the dwelling. A wisp of smoke was curling above the chimney which meant a fire in the cook stove and dinnertime fast approaching.

As we got closer to the fence a matronly woman with her hair done up in a bun at the nape of her neck exited the front door and proceeded to a dinner bell mounted on a frame erected over the well. She gathered her apron and wiped her hands while gazing long and hard in our direction. She was trying to discern the identity of these two untoward looking travelers aboard fully harnessed mules. After a time she collected her thoughts and began to yank the rope which swiveled the bell back and forth. The mule's ears stood erect and a cur dog lying in the shade near the front porch began a long drawn out howl as the bell tolled loudly, signaling to family members in the fields nearby to come on in for the noon meal. The lady waved a hello to us and I shouted back a salutation. She introduced herself as Mrs. House and I informed her of my intended purchases. We followed her to the house and she invited us to have a seat on the porch. We found a pair of cane bottomed rocking chairs and sat enjoying the spring breeze. Pretty soon Mrs. House returned with a bucket of fresh water. She informed us that it was not well water but fresh spring water. "The coolest and sweetest drinking water in the land," she bragged. I was thirsty and quickly helped myself. I drained a dipperful between breaths and concurred as to the quality of the water. When Ty and I had fully quenched our thirst, the lady informed us that Steve and the rest of the family were somewhere nearby clearing a new ground and would be coming in for "dinner" very soon. She excused herself and told us to "just make ourselves at home" and went inside. Pretty soon I heard the rattling of pots and pans from the kitchen. It was a pleasant sound and the smell of freshly baked cornbread wafting through the screen door was like a dose of healing medicine to me. A long time had passed since I could remember a mother in the kitchen at midday cooking and taking care of "woman" things. I smiled as I remembered how I had been affectionately ridiculed when I first arrived in Cincinnati by calling the noon meal "dinner." I had been politely informed that "dinner" was the evening meal and the noon meal was called "lunch." I think it was about that time when I started becoming aware of the idiotic movement of "political correctness" which is nothing but a psychological tool used by the rich and influential to try and separate themselves from the "common man." "Political Correctness" has not one damn thing to do with "correctness!"

Ty propped both feet upon the porch railing and leaned back with his cap down over his eyes like he was going to take a nap. I was content to sit there and admire the accomplishments Steve had forged out of what must have been at one time a veritable jungle. He had left only a few trees standing on the forty or fifty acres of rolling pasture stretching out in front of the house. The intermittent tinkle of a cowbell drifted up from among a couple dozen whiteface cattle grazing there in the knee high crimson clover. This was living! This was far removed from the effects of the industrial revolution. A secluded place nestled here in the mountains where time seemed to stand still. A place where a man could live the way man was intended to live- tilling the land and earning his bread by the sweat of his brow. Everything else, the so-called technological and economic advancements of society became moot and irrelevant.

Ty stood abruptly and brought me back to reality. He stretched and yawned and walked down the steps and around the corner of the house. I assumed he was going to find the outhouse. Pretty soon Mrs. House came out and sat in the rocker Ty had been occupying. She was a tall lean woman. She wore a gray gingham dress that came to the top of her brogan shoes. She was carrying what appeared to be a half-peck or so of apples gathered up in her apron. She sprawled heavily in the chair and nestled the apples in her lap. She drew a paring knife out of the apron pocket and began peeling one of the fist sized "Jonathans." "Whew," she blew a long breath. "Its gonna git hot agin today! Want one of these apples?" She held one of the red and yellow striped fruit up for us to view. "I generally save a few back for a few days 'till they get meller enough to eat." She turned the apple in her hand and mashed it hard with her thumb. "Yeah, this one's pretty meller. These "Jonathans" are so hard when you first pick'em that a mule can't bite into 'em." Ty held up his hands as if to catch a baseball and she tossed the apple to him. She looked inquiringly towards me and I shook my head in the negative. Ty clamped down on the big apple two or three times in quick succession while apple juice began to trickle down his chin. Mrs. House started again. "I figured I'd go ahead and use the apples up while I had a chance. I'm going to make a pie out of these. I've got about two bushel picked that I'm going to can tomorrow. They're a lot of work. They make awful good pies and they're awful good for canning too but you got to cut 'em up into pretty small sections and make sure you cut all the worms out of 'em." I looked over at Ty and he was giving what was left of his apple the once over.

It was now close to noon and I had been awake since four A.M. I was tired. But then, a three-hour ride over a gully washed road in a farm wagon seemed to be a day's work in itself. I relaxed again in the rocker and closed my eyes. A couple of June bugs and a handful of honey bees had been drawn by the nectar of apple peelings which Mrs. House was discarding in a dishpan at the side of her chair. The monotonous hum of these creatures hovering about was like a sedative and adding to the soporific feeling about to overtake me. A faint, almost undetectable aroma of freshly plowed earth was on the breeze. This smell is unmistakable. More than once during my sojourns in some Northern metropolis at about this time of the year, I had imagined myself behind a team of mules and a plow, preparing the land for spring seeding. The olfactory sense would begin to play tricks and it would seem as if I could smell that fresh turned earth as distinctly as if I had been transported back in time to that tranquil and peaceful existence on the farm.

Suddenly the sound of heavy boots on the wooden porch jolted me out of my reverie. I opened my eyes and Steve was standing in front of me. "Hey Tommy," he bellered. "Good t'see ya', welcome to my cave," he chuckled while extending a hand of greeting. After a warm handshake I introduced Ty. "He's a preacher!" I said. Steve gave Ty an inquisitive eye before he turned his attention to the water bucket. "This water fresh?" he asked his wife. "Yeh, just drawed it fresh a few minutes ago for these fellers," she replied. While Steve stood there quenching his thirst, five youngsters lined up behind him in single file awaiting their turn at the fresh water. They appeared to range in age from about sixteen to five or six. They had lined up in chronological order with the youngest directly behind Steve. There were four boys and one girl. All the boys wore bibbed overalls but the little girl had on a calico dress and apron, which was customary for girls there in the mountains. She stood out like a crown jewel in the crowd. Her head was covered in golden ringlets and her blue eyes were heart melting. The boys were all of ruddy complexion and sandy hair just like their daddy. Mrs. House excused herself and gathered up her apron full of peeled apples and went inside. Steve then came and occupied the vacant chair and the youngsters sat in a row on the edge of the porch letting their legs dangle over the side. The eldest son picked up the pan of apple peelings and scattered them about the yard. "Chickens 'l git em," he explained.

Steve House was a big man. He looked to be about six feet six and straight up and down. His overalls and brogan shoes were spotted with mud and his hands were broad and gnarled. He had one of those perpetual, abbreviated smiles, which, in my opinion is a sign of strength coupled with humbleness. The tidiness of his domain and his well-behaved brood gave witness that he was a man of principle.

While I was relating our misfortunes of the morning concerning the broken wagon wheel a little gray and brown beagle came hobbling around the corner of the house. One of its front legs was just dangling by a strip of flesh and the stub of leg swung back and forth as the dog limped along. One of the middle-sized boys ran and cuddled the animal in his lap trying to comfort it. Steve was quick to act. He seemed to bounce down the porch steps and squatted in front of the boy and dog. "Hey, one of you boy's bring the alcohol and something to wrap this little fellers leg up with. You better bring that bottle of linseed oil and some axle grease too," he shouted. One of the children brought a pan of water and sat it near the dog. Steve jerked a pocketknife from the bib pocket of his overalls and quickly severed the dangling tendon. "This dog ran in front of my mowing machine yesterday and got his leg cut off," Steve said. "It's a wonder I didn't cut all four of 'em off but I stopped just in time. Last I saw of this little feller he was high tailin' it for the woods. We looked for him but finally figured he had crawled off and died. Looks like this dog has also been shot. A lot of the hide's been burned off his back and he's full of birdshot. Good thing it was bird shot or he'd be dead for sure." I kept waiting for Ty to speak up and let them know what had happened concerning the imaginary "mad dog" in the woods but he did not respond. After considering the situation for a minute I figured it best just to let the whole thing blow over.

After Steve finished doctoring the dog we resumed our places on the porch. Steve said he had two or three broken wagon wheels in the barn and felt sure he could find enough parts to repair my wagon. Mrs. House brought a dishpan full of water and placed it on the marble washstand near the door. "All right you young'uns," she shouted. "Come on and get washed up. Dinner will be on the table in a few minutes." When the youngsters had finished washing Steve emptied the wash pan over the porch railing and filled it with fresh water for Ty and myself. Steve had been sort of scrutinizing Ty from the time I introduced him. After washing up we just sat around making small talk about the weather and farming. Suddenly, Steve turned to Ty and said; "now I remember you! Ain't you the preacher that shot that drummer up there in Harlan County?" Steve had a big smile on his face; almost laughing as he blurted those words. Ty looked surprised. He dropped his head and was evidently embarrassed. After a time he weakly responded. "Yeh, that's me!" "Man, I've been trying to place where I had seen you for an hour!" Steve said. "I attended one of your revivals at the Benham church of God! Fine meeting, big crowd, Lots of souls saved at that revival." "Well, thanks for saying that," Ty replied. "We had some fine churches up there in Harlan. There are a lot of good faithful church families in Harlan. I was proud to be a part of it." A long period of silence followed. We all kept waiting for the other one to speak. I was waiting for an explanation on Ty's part. What had happened there in that little town? Why had Ty, of all people, shot a man? I waited but he just stood there staring into space. Mrs. House finally broke the silence and called us in to dinner.

It was now two o'clock in the afternoon and far past dinnertime according to my calculations, but I surmised that the lady had gone to some extra pains being as she had unexpected guests. Extra pains or not she had proved her excellent cooking ability in my opinion. It was an exquisitely seasoned meal of comfort food; a meal of customary as well as necessary victuals required for sustenance of the human body during long days of hard work and activity, which is, after all, the hallmark of mountain life. Cornbread, soup beans, fried potatoes, fried corn and ham meat, topped off with rice pudding and warm apple pie. When everyone was seated around the huge oaken table, and the customary prattle of children had abated, Steve cleared his throat loudly sending the signal for everyone to shut up. You could hear the proverbial pin drop. "Preacher," Steve said, looking directly at Ty. "Would you do us the honor of asking the blessing?" I glanced over at Ty and noticed a crimson tinge creep over his face. "Be glad to," he whispered. He bowed his head, mumbled a few incoherent syllables and ended with a somewhat louder "amen." I was confused. He seemed embarrassed, him, -a preacher, for being called upon to invoke God on behalf of this sumptuous fare spread out before us. There seemed to be no embarrassment for anyone else, however. They began to pass the steaming bowls of country cooking around, and back and forth, while each person helped himself. When all the "pass me's" and "would you like some's" were over and all the bowls and platters were back on the table in their original spots, Steve picked up his fork and began to eat and everyone around the table followed suit. It was a happy time. There were laughs, smiles and happy remarks all around. I thought to myself, this is living. This is the way life is supposed to be. A fine healthy and happy family gathered together and enjoying God's bounty. Suddenly I thought of Maggie and the fact I was cheating myself out of these blessings and the chance of leaving a meaningful legacy.

Afterwards, we retired again to the front porch. Steve moved his chair near the edge of the plank structure and produced a twist of "King Bee" from the bib pocket of his overalls. He sliced off a generous portion of the twist and placed it in his mouth and rolled it around from one side of his jaw to the other until he evidently situated the cud into just the right spot. He re-wrapped the twist and returned it to his pocket. He put the knife blade to his mouth and you could see the shiny black licorice, which had adhered to the blade. He then meticulously licked the knife blade a few times as he savored the sweet residue of "King Bee." I was thoroughly impressed by the way this giant of a man could turn the simple task of taking a chew of tobacco into a delicious and mouthwatering ceremony. I was beginning to want a chew myself when in reality I couldn't stomach the stuff. I did the next best thing by pulling a pack of Camels out and lighting up. I wondered how I could be so relaxed with everything I had to do, but, of course, that delicious meal was the answer. I was anxious to get my wagon repaired, loaded up and headed for home. I mentioned the wheel to Steve and he assured me that he could get it repaired in short order. "Just as soon as I let that good dinner settle," he laughed, rubbing his stomach. "You got to remember," he said. "When I get those broken spokes replaced and a section of the outer ring whittled out, then, I got to fit the steel band and let the whole wheel soak in water till it swells up good and tight. That's going to take the rest of the day. In fact, we ought to let the thing soak in the creek tonight and lay it out in the sun in the morning so it will dry out real good. That way it should be as good as new." I was not at all enthused about spending the night, but again, it looked like I had no alternative.

Steve sat up straight in his rocker, puckered his lips and shot a long stream of tobacco juice over the edge of the porch and out into the yard. It looked to me like he was aiming at one of several Rhode Island Reds that were still scratching around in the previously discarded apple peelings. He wiped his mouth with the back of his hand and squirmed a little in the chair sort of like a setting hen trying to make a nest. "Hey, preacher!" he blurted as he turned and looked directly at Ty. "They didn't even indict you for shootin' that feller up there in Harlan did they? What was it, self-defense?" "Well, yeh" Ty responded. "The guy was trying to kill me! He pulled a pistol and shot at me right in front of a hundred witnesses!" "They tell me it happened inside the church house, is that right" Steve questioned. "Yeh, that's right. In fact I was in the middle of my Wednesday night sermon. I'm thankful I was the only person behind the pulpit. I was about to make the altar call when the guy stood up and shot at me. The shot busted a vase of flowers sitting on the lectern. I was startled out of my wits but I had enough sense left to hunker down. I peeped around the corner of the lectern and saw the guy standing there still holding the pistol pointed in my direction. I did the only thing I could do! I pulled my pistol and shot him right between the eyes."

There was a long pause and then, "What? You mean you were standing there preaching with a pistol in your pocket?" Steve laughed. "Yeah," Ty replied. "One member of the congregation sent me word that a guy had it in mind to kill me. You know I got scared; I started carrying my pistol everywhere I went. Fact of the matter, I slept with it under my pillow." Evidently Ty was getting a little hot under the collar. He began to raise his voice and his face was taking on that crimson tinge. "You don't expect a man to just lounge around and let some ignorant sum-- let some nit wit shoot him down do you?" He paused and drew in a deep breath evidently recognizing the level of his intensity. Steve let out a loud guffaw, leaned back and sent another stream of tobacco juice out into the yard. "Well, how come the guy wanted to kill you? Are you one of them womanizing faith healers?" he said, and let out another good-natured laugh. "No, nothin' like that," Ty responded. "Somebody told the guy I had been foolin' around with his wife!" "Well, had you?" Steve laughed. Ty frowned and resumed his somewhat sullen attitude. "Well, it wouldn't do me any good to deny it I guess.

She kept bringing me covered dishes of her favorite recipes and such things as that. Her old man was a traveling drummer. You know, he drove around the country selling notions, and elixirs, and dry goods, and stuff like that. She told me he would get drunk every time he came home and then flail the hell out of her. She always ran to the church in order to get away from him. I counseled her to leave him but she just kept going back for more. Then the rumors started that we were having these love fests. Next thing I know the guy was following me around. He was a mean sum--rascal, so I started packing my pistol. I tried to avoid him but he just kept pushing and you know the rest of the story. In that brief instant, within that split second I had committed the un-pardonable sin and I haven't set foot in a church since." He leaned forward with his head low, and sat there silently. We were all silent for a long time. "Hey Bessie, have one of them young'uns go draw us a good cold bucket of fresh water!" Steve hollered. Pretty soon one of the sandy-headed boys brought a bucket of water and sat it in our midst.

Steve put the dipper into the water and swirled it around a few times and stared into the water like he was trying to read the ripples. He finally brought the dipper full of water to his mouth and began to drink. I watched his Adam's apple as it moved slowly up and down. He was staring at Ty over the dipper. His demeanor had changed instantly from one of levity to dead seriousness. We continued the silence as each man tried to make some sense out of what we had heard. Ty had always been a bit mischievous and spontaneous and I wasn't exactly surprised by his story. After all, we were like brothers and I felt I knew his heart. But, I was hurt for him and I was concerned of the apparent affect this incident was having on him. But then, a series of my own indiscretions flashed through my mind and momentarily trivialized Ty's fall from grace. He was still a better man than me.

Steve finally spoke up. "I think you are wrong about the "un-pardonable" sin. From my understanding, the "un-pardonable sin" is pride. That is, pride so strong it can prevent a man from truly believing in God. Some folks think they are too smart to believe in anything they can't see, therefore, they go through life doubting the existence of God. To put it simply, I think, the "un-pardonable sin" is the refusal of an individual to invoke the redeeming grace of God until the day they die! When that happens there is no pardon. It's too late to ask forgiveness after you are dead! A man like that, being inherently disobedient, is condemned to eternal separation from God. I don't like to sound like a know-it-all but I too am a student of the scriptures and have tried my hand at preaching." I was aware of Steve's ministry but Ty seemed shocked. Evidently, Steve picked up on his astonishment.

Everything was quite for a minute when he started again, but this time in a lower, more deliberate tone. "I don't talk much about preaching anymore. That preaching is a hard business. It's a thankless business. I still wrestle with the idea. Most of the time I feel like I'm letting God down but I finally had to choose between feeding my family and feeding those lost souls that frequented the missions there on skid row where I practiced my ministry. When I think about it for a minute I can almost smell the gin mills, stale beer, cigar smoke and excessive makeup of the two dollar whores. Believe me; I can sympathize with you when it comes to a determined woman such as the one you were referring to. They can be mighty persuasive. There was more than one of them that tried to get me in the sack! To be honest with you, I sometimes wonder just how long I would have lasted if Bessie hadn't been right there with me. Who knows, maybe I'll take up preaching again one of these days, but right now I've got to support my family." He looked at both of us if he were expecting our approval.

Steve's two older sons were coming toward the house riding a loaded down sled filled with wagon wheels and wagon wheel parts pulled by a flop eared mule. The animal seemed to be straining severely under the load. "You boy's should have used that small sled," Steve hollered. "That sled's too heavy for one mule! Sometimes you boys act like you don't have a lick of sense!" he said to his brood. "You've got to take care of your animals, they're the only thing between us and starvation sometimes, you know!" He walked up to the mule and began to stroke its ears. "Whoa boy, whoa Jim, that's a good mule" he almost whispered. "These boys must think you're a rock." "Hey, Arron," he shouted to one of the young men. "Go get that feed bag and give this mule a little bit of that loose corn. This beast looks to me like he's starving to death."

Steve then set about repairing my busted wagon wheel. I offered to help but he said he would probably make better time if he just went ahead and did it all by himself. He said he could concentrate better that way. Ty and I sat there on the porch steps and watched. Every move Steve made was deliberate. He first layed all the parts he was going to use out on the grass and then removed the outer steel band and broken spokes from the broken wheel. He then began to cut and scrape and file and pound and glue. About an hour later the broken wheel was once again whole. "Okay boys. Take it down to the creek and roll it in. Make sure it's completely submerged. We'll lay it out in the sun tomorrow morning. It'll dry out good in a couple of hours and be as good as new." Two of the young men rolled the wheel down through the pasture toward the creek and I helped Steve pick up his tools and place them back on the sled.

We resumed our places on the porch where a fine breeze was starting to give us some relief from the humidity. Mrs. House brought another bucket of fresh cool spring water and Steve sprawled lazily in his rocker and appeared to be dozing off when little Maybelle, Steve's only daughter of about six years came skipping up the steps. Her little pink and blue dress was badly soiled and it was apparent she had been playing in the dirt. "Hey daddy, she shouted. "Look at these pretty worms I found back there under the porch!" Steve straightened a bit and opened his eyes. Suddenly he stood erect. "Good God a'mighty!" he shouted. "Throw them things down, them's baby copperheads!" He ran to her and started brushing at her arms and hands. The baby snake she had been holding was about four or five inches long and about the size of a pencil in diameter. The thing flopped to the floor and wriggled through a crack in the planks. "Good gawd, you got any more of them things honey?" Steve bellered. "Yeh, right here in my apron pocket. Ain't they purty?" She laughed. Steve ripped the apron off the child and began shaking it. Two more of the baby snakes hit the floor and they too slinked away between the cracks. "Bessie, Bessie," Steve hollered. "Get out here! This young'un has found a nest of copperheads and she's been playing with 'em."

Mrs. House instantly burst through the door and stood there askance trying to assess the situation. When it was clear that Maybelle was not concealing any more of the vipers, the parents began examining the child for any possible bites. "Oh my God!" Mrs. House cried. There's one on her arm!" "Yeah! And here's two on her little thigh" Steve announced. Ty and I were dumbfounded. We just stood there with our mouths open trying to internalize the situation. I asked about a doctor and Steve said it was no use. "It's five miles to the nearest highway across that mountain there" he pointed. "Then its three more miles to Manchester and a doctor. It would take all night to make that trip. All we can do is pray. Bessie, take her in the house, clean her up and put her to bed. I'm not sure but I've heard the baby snakes are about as poisonous as the big ones. One way or another we'll find out in a few minutes."

The parents led the child into the house and the rest of us picked a place and just sat quietly praying. Oh, our hearts were heavy and we were concerned, but the look in Mrs. House's eyes would break your heart. Somehow, I felt more sorry for the mother than I did little Maybelle. I felt that I had just witnessed the only real and true emotion in creation-a mother's love.

Time seemed to slip away and night was falling fast. Mrs. House came to the door and informed us she had set some leftovers on the table and for us to just help ourselves when we got hungry. I wasn't hungry but I figured it bad manners to ignore the hospitality. About sunset one of the children lit a few coal oil lamps and placed them on the mantle over the living room fireplace and at various other places inside the house. Ty and I agreed that it just made sense to try and eat a little something. An eerie feeling came over me when I walked inside. The lamplight cast flickering shadows all about the room and I had to wait until my eyes became accustomed to the semi-darkness before I could make my way to the kitchen. A lamp had also been placed in the center of the kitchen table and the leftovers were neatly arranged pretty much as they had been for the noon meal. We made our selections with the intentions of taking our plates back to the porch when we heard voices coming from one of the inner rooms. I walked over near the door and listened. They were praying. The door was slightly ajar and I peered in as best I could. Steve's arms were outstretched above his head. "OH God", he was saying. "Heal my baby girl if it be your almighty will!" I felt right sacrilegious and backed away. I was intruding on something far too profound for the likes of me. Nonetheless, I had to choke back a tear as I made my way to the porch.

It was a beautiful night. Not a cloud in the sky. I had completely forgotten what I had come there for. I felt like I wanted to pray but I didn't even know how to pray anymore. Ty had begun to snore. At any other time I would have been tempted to play some kind of trick on him but this was no time to play pranks. This was a serious time. There was a beautiful little girl in there at deaths door and I was totally impotent to be of any help. I finally dozed off for a while and then about two or three A.M. I woke up thirsty and went in to the kitchen for a drink of water. The door to little Maybelle's room was still ajar. I tiptoed over to the door and heard the same monotone of prayer. Curiosity overpowered me and I decided to slip inside and check on her condition. It appeared that Steve and Bessie had not moved. They were still sitting with bowed heads praying for their little girl. I inched slowly forward to where I had a good view of the sick. The lamplight added to the grotesque scene. Her face and left arm were badly swollen and had taken on a blackened hue. It was heartbreaking. If the parents detected my presence they did not let on so I retreated and went back to the porch.

The sun was just coming up when I was awakened by activity within the house. A few minutes later Steve called to me from inside. "Hey Tommy, coffee's ready if you want a cup!" Ty had slipped down in his chair and his arms and legs were twisted up like a contortionist. I gave his chair a sound kick and his reflex caused him to slide out of the chair and he hit the porch with a thud.   He rubbed his eyes and gave me a disgusting look. "Think you're funny don't you, you crazy sum-- you crazy rascal" he barked. We went inside and Bessie was standing in front of the stove stirring up a skillet of gravy while Steve was seated at the table. Mrs. House poured each of us a cup of coffee from a large galvanized coffee pot. It was boiled coffee, the kind I had grown up on, the kind that would wake you up in a heartbeat and possibly remove hair if the need be. "Well, how's little Maybelle?" I asked. Steve sort of chuckled. "Well, see for yourself. Here she comes now." Maybelle came out of her room and ran straight to her daddy and climbed upon his lap. "Mommy, I'm hungry! Can I have a biscuit with some jelly?" she called out in a plaintive tone. Steve laughed and hugged her tightly. "See there, fit as a fiddle!" I couldn't believe the change from what I had witnessed a few hours earlier. "Praise God!" Ty exclaimed, drawing the "God" out into a long "Gawwwd." "Yep, it's a miracle!" Steve bellered. We all seemed to be silently in awe of the situation as we peered questioningly into each other's eyes. "The faith of a child has always's amazed me," Steve began.

121

"It's so easy for them to believe. I told her last night God would heal her. Well, she believed and here she is."

We were loaded up and ready to head for home by noon. I didn't want to waste any more time so we declined the offer to stay for dinner, but Mrs. House insisted we take along some left over sausage and biscuits in case we got hungry later. Steve's sons had been a great help. They put the wagon back together and loaded it for me. The wagon bed was filled to the top of the sideboards with corn and above the corn they had stacked twenty bales of hay. They fashioned a rope halter for the cow and tied her to the wagon. The three-month-old calf would just naturally follow the mother. I had planned to purchase a couple of weaned pigs for slaughter the following fall but we had no way to haul them. Steve, being a practical as well as a good hearted man, said if I would agree to buy one of his big sows, he would throw in a couple of the sow's piglets for free. I quickly agreed to that deal. The sow already had a ring in her nose, which prevented her from rooting beneath the fence and running free, so we attached a small rope to the ring and tied the sow to the wagon. Steve said not to worry. The piglets might wander a bit here and there but they would, by and large, follow along obediently after their mother. It was times like these that you missed your camera. We surely must have looked like a band of wandering gypsies.

We traveled for an hour or so in silence. I think we both were trying to understand and internalize the events of the past few hours. Of course we hadn't been in bed for at least thirty-six hours and trying to sleep in a cane bottomed chair only added to our lethargy. Finally Ty spoke up. "Well, what do you think happened back there? A look of great consternation came upon his face. Then he added, "something strange for sure!" He waited for me to comment and when I only shrugged in puzzlement he began again. "You know, it must have been four or five in the morning. I woke up and when I couldn't go back to sleep, I slipped into the house and got a look at Maybelle. She was turning black and swelling up like a foundered cow." He got a deep breath and blew it out long and hard. "And then, and then, this morning it appeared that nothing at all had happened to her! She seemed fit as a fiddle. What the hell happened?" He waited for me to answer and when I shrugged again he continued. "Do you think Steve healed her?" "I don't know" I responded. "They sat there and prayed nonstop for her all night long. Miracles have been known to happen." "You didn't answer my question!" he said. "Do you think Steve healed her?" I thought the question over for a minute. "Well, in the first place, neither Steve nor anyone else can heal a person. Now they can pray, and go on, and holler and cry, but in the end, God does any healing that gets done!" "Then you don't believe in spiritual gifts, do you?" Ty questioned. "Sure, I believe in spiritual gifts. Even the most primitive cultures believe in spiritual gifts in one way or another. The American Indian described it as having the "power." According to some historians Geronimo had "the power." He would wade right into the thick of battle with soldiers firing at him from all sides. He ended up dying from a fall from his horse when he was a very old man!" "Ah, you don't know what I'm talking about" Ty responded.

The wagon held together okay and we arrived home around four in the afternoon. When we rounded the bend in the road there at the little hill just below the house I noticed a strange car parked behind my old truck. I pulled the team and wagon inside the barn and checked to be sure everything was still intact. I discovered right away that we were missing one of the piglets. Ty sensed that I was anxious to find out who the car belonged to and agreed to begin unloading the corn and hay. Since I didn't have a pen for the hogs or a pasture for the cow fenced yet I just tied them inside one of the empty stalls. I started walking toward the house when I saw the missing piglet rooting around in the ditch by the side of the road. I was relieved since I would not have to go searching for it. As I neared the house, my ex-wife Maggie walked out onto the porch. I was not altogether surprised and had been hoping for that moment for some time but the many disappointments of my past life had rendered me immune to spontaneous elation. After some serious hugs and kisses she informed me that she had sold the house and what furniture I had. She had arrived about noon and had been trying to familiarize herself with the place. I sensed her disappointment. While I busied myself with drawing a bucket of fresh water and building a fire in the cook stove she went through the house examining it room by room. I boiled a pot of coffee and after the lovemaking was over we sat there at the kitchen table asking and answering questions of one another. I tried to explain why the bed was sitting a-top lard cans and why there was no indoor plumbing, no electricity and no telephone. "It'll take some getting used to, but if you can stand it I'm sure I can," she said with a good-hearted chuckle.

That was Maggie, good hearted! She was no stranger to poverty and hard work. She had grown up in the cotton country of south Texas. Her father sharecropped a few acres of land and worked his family from daylight to dark while he lay in the shade drunk most of the day. He had started trying to pimp Maggie and her younger sister out when they matured physically and when Maggie reneged he beat her. She ran away from home and got a job in a mattress factory near a bar where I used to work. Probably, because of our rural background and southern upbringing, we became close friends and confidantes. After about a year, we made the decision to get married since we were from the old school, and agreed on the old saying that "two can live as cheaply as one." We pooled our resources and pledged our allegiance to one another but whether or not we were "in love" remains to be seen. At least we were loyal friends and watched each other's back. We both knew how important a trusty friend could be among a throng, or maybe I should say a herd of unscrupulous people.

Maggie was by and large a pretty woman. She had a beautiful set of teeth and a radiant complexion. She was about five feet six and a shade on the hefty side. I'm not sure but I imagine she would tip the scale somewhere around a hundred and forty. I was confident she would be able to endure that first year or so without any of the modern conveniences she had been accustomed to and at the moment I was hoping against hope that she would have the grit.

When I got back to the barn, Ty had everything pretty well under control. The hay was in the loft, the corn was in the crib, the cow and pig were in separate stalls and the mules had been watered and fed. Since Maggie's car was now available in case of emergency, I allowed Ty to use my truck. I asked him if Maggie's presence was going to cause him to change his mind about working for me that summer and he reassured me that when he promised something he always kept his word. He said he would be back bright and early the following morning.

The nights were still a bit cool so I stoked up a fire in the fireplace for Maggie's benefit. I could tell she was a bit perplexed about what to do for supper so I showed her how to stir up a pan of cornbread. Then I opened a can of pork and beans and fried some bacon. After supper we sat in front of the fireplace discussing the future. I was thrilled to have her there and found myself inadvertently and indirectly inquiring as to how long she intended to stay. The question was could she and would she be able to survive this primitive way of life until I could add a few modern conveniences. The only thing standing in the way was money. We had enough now from the sale of the house in Cincinnati to go ahead and modernize the place but if we did that we might run short before the first tobacco crop was sold. And even then, there might not be a tobacco crop since there are so many variables to consider in farming. I figured two years at the most until I would be able to turn the old place into a reasonable facsimile of a modern home. When I informed her of that, she seemed to accept the situation as it was. In fact, she seemed thoroughly enthused and said she would chalk it all up as a great adventure.

Although I had slept very little for the past two days I found sleep to be fleeting that night even when I was in a relatively comfortable bed and back among more familiar surroundings. I had a million things to accomplish and very little time in which to accomplish them. First of all the plowing had to be done. I would need at least four acres for the tobacco, which I realized was not a lot of plowing if you have a tractor. I would also need land cleared for a good crop of corn and hay. All in all I estimated at least twenty-five acres of clearing and plowing. Besides that I would need to find someone with tobacco plants for sale since there was no time to sow a tobacco bed and grow the plants. That chore should have been accomplished in February. On top of that, if I had to plant the tobacco by hand, that is, a plant at a time on my hands and knees, that would require several extra days. It was the same thing with the corn. If I had to plant corn with a hand held corn planter, that is, enough corn to feed my animals through the winter, I was out of luck. I wouldn't be able to accomplish all that until the middle of July, which would be too late for the crops to mature. Even with Ty's help I would not get finished in time. I had to find someone with a tractor, a dozer, and the necessary attachments to get what was looking more and more all the time like an impossible task accomplished.

I had finally tossed and turned enough so I built a fire and boiled a pot of coffee. After a couple of cups of that thick concoction and a half pack of camels, I decided to go on down to the barn and feed the animals. About halfway down the driveway I suddenly remembered ol' rattler so I returned to the smokehouse where I had been keeping him. I didn't want Maggie to accidently discover him. It would scare her to death, so I carried him down to the barn and turned him loose in the corncrib. This would solve the problem of my having to remember to feed him since there were plentiful rats and mice around the barn.

When Ty showed up I informed him of my plans to hire most of the clearing and plowing done providing I could find someone close with the necessary equipment. He agreed this might be the only feasible route to take if we were going to get the planting done on time. He told me of an out of work strip miner he knew who lived only a few miles away. This man owned a small bulldozer and would be tickled to death to get the work. When I asked his name I discovered him to be the same fellow who had done the original job clearing around my house and barn. When we found the guy he agreed to do all the clearing and the heavy plowing.

From that time forward everything started to materialize the way I had planned. By the last week in May all the clearing and plowing had been accomplished thanks to the assistance of the guy with the dozer and tractor. Ty and I sowed about twenty-five acres of timothy and crimson clover by hand. During the first week of June, four acres of tobacco plants were in the ground and we had planted ten acres of field corn. Maggie had pretty well taken over the vegetable gardening and all the root vegetables had been planted along with the sweet corn. We had been working long hard hours and by this time we figured we could slow down just a bit. Maggie was doing swell. She was adjusting fabulously to a way of life that most people today would describe as primitive and demeaning. Reading by a coal oil lamp, bathing in a wash tub, doing laundry on a washboard and being deprived of the luxury of going to the refrigerator for a cold drink or a plate of leftovers would have been more than most modern housewives could endure.

But Maggie actually seemed to be enjoying the challenge. At one point she made the comment that the whole life change was like a healing tonic to her. Ty, on the other hand, seemed to become more despondent and withdrawn as each day ended. I'm not implying that he was not a good worker, he was. He attacked every project with the enthusiasm of a man killing snakes. He was as concerned as I was about turning that little patch of forsaken earth into a successful and viable farm. His only motive as far as I could tell was his promise and his friendship for me. He was a true friend and I worried that he was losing all enthusiasm for life. Many times after a hard day's work he would have his supper with me and Maggie and then go down and sleep in the barn rather than drive home. More than once, when I had occasion to go back to the barn after nightfall, I found him there reading the Bible by lamplight.

On one occasion after I completed whatever I had come there to do and started to leave he called me back. "Hey, have you heard anything from Steve lately concerning little Maybelle and how she's getting along after that snake bite?" "No, haven't heard a word" I responded. I walked back to where he was and sat down beside him on a bale of hay. I sensed maybe he was finally coming out of his shell a little since he wanted to have a conversation. "Do you believe what happened was actually a miracle or do you believe maybe her immune system was just in excellent condition and she healed herself?" he asked. "Well, to be honest, I doubt you could prove anything one way or another. The way I understand those things is that only people who are filled with, or are led by the spirit of God are able to bring about physical healing. I don't doubt such things but to tell you the truth I don't have enough sense to figure it out." We sat silent for a minute and then in an agonizing voice he said "Aw-w. Gaw-wd! I wish now I would have just let that guy up there in Harlan kill me. All I ever wanted to do was become a good preacher. I don't know why but that's all I ever wanted to do! But now it'll never happen. Like a damn fool I had to go ahead and kill that man. Me, like Steve said, carrying a damn gun on me right there in the pulpit. What was I thinking?" We were silent for another minute and then, I don't know why, but I blurted out what is probably the most stupid remark I will ever make. "Well, I've always heard that a stiff pecker has no conscience!" I was sorry for it the moment I said it. He turned his head away from me and I sensed how terribly hurt he was. I figured I would find him gone the next morning but he was still there.

It was now mid-July and our crops were thriving beautifully. Of course everything had been planted in relatively new ground and we had not spared the fertilizer and nitrogen. It had been an extra-long workday for us but we were now finished with most all the cultivating for the summer. I was trying to get the milking finished before dark and Ty was tending to the mules. When he opened the door to the corncrib, ol' rattler nailed him on the arm just above the wrist. I dropped the milk bucket when I heard Ty squall. "God-damn, I'm snake-bit," he hollered. I ran to him and by that time he had pulled the viper out of the corncrib and was stomping on him with both feet like an Indian doing a war dance. "That sum-bitch bit me! You hear me? That sum-bitch bit me," he rasped, while still dancing on the snake. Finally ol' rattler stopped wriggling and lay there at our feet, limp, and lifeless. I looked at the wound on Ty's wrist and sure enough there were two pucture marks left by snake fangs. Blood was oozing from each hole.

I had never mentioned my initial encounter with ol' rattler to anyone. I guess I figured the whole episode would sound preposterous so I had just kept it to myself. I knew that if in fact it was ol' rattler, and I was sure it was, that Ty was in no danger and there was nothing to worry about. In fact, I stifled a laugh but acted genuinely concerned. Ty finally stopped dancing and stood staring down at the corpse. "Good God! He's a big sum-bitch ain't he? Probably had a quart of venom in him! Matter of fact, I think I can feel it going up my arm already! What do you think I ought to do now?" "Well, big as that snake is, the poison will act awfully fast" I said. "We'll never make it to town in time, and even if we could, we probably wouldn't be able to find the doctor." "Well, do you want to try and open the wound and suck the venom out?" he asked. I thought for a minute on how to get out of that one. "Hell, I'd be afraid to do that! I got a hollow tooth. That would be likely to kill me too!" "Well, hell, do something! I'd help you wouldn't I? Tell you what, you slice open the wound and I'll suck the poison out myself." I jerked my knife out and got a firm grip on his wrist and just in the nick of time he said, "Wait a minute! I've got a hollow tooth too! Aw hell, now what are we going to do?" There was only one thing left to do, I thought.

I led him out onto the driveway and found a place for him to sit and then I brought a bottle of horse linament and prepared to apply the stringent concoction to the bite, but then I stopped. "Ty, I said, you're my buddy. I'd do about anything for you and I think you know that. But, I've been thinking. Maybe this is all God's will. Now let me ask you a question. Why do you think that snake was in that corncrib?" Ty shrugged his shoulders as if to say he had no idea. "Well, I continued, rattle snakes don't normally hang around barns and places where there's other animals and people. They like the mountains and rocky places; places where they can roam free and un-impeded; a place where they can crawl out onto a warm rock and sun themselves. Ain't that right?" He shook his head in the affirmative and mumbled, "I guess so." "Ok", I went on, "now you are a man called by God almighty to preach the gospel. I've heard you say so more times than I can count. But lately, you have been doubting whether you were actually called or not. I can tell! You are not the same old Ty I used to know! Now listen to me. Let's not do anything to alter this situation. Let's not try to doctor it or anything because I believe that snake was put there for a reason." I waited for a minute to let what I had said sink in. "You know, this could be your "road to Damascus." This could be your own epiphany!" He continued squeezing his wrist near the bite and gazed up into the sky. After a minute or so he began to quote a scripture: "Saint Mark, chapter sixteen, verses seventeen and eighteen-'And these signs shall follow them; in my name shall they cast out devils; they shall speak with new tongues; they shall take up serpents; and if they drink any deadly thing it shall not hurt them; they shall lay hands on the sick and they shall recover'." He waited for a second and added: "Praise God forever and ever, amen." We sat there in solitude for a while.

Night was falling fast. The swamp frogs near the creek behind the barn had begun their nightly chorus. The moon was full and the myriad of stars appeared brighter than usual. I left Ty there alone, just him and his God. He was bowed foreward with his head in his hands, softly praying. I made my way slowly up the driveway towards the house. The dead silence was broken only by the mournful baying of a coonhound, which had evidently treed in some distant hollow. And, in spite of all my shortcomings and hypocrisy, I felt at peace with the world.

Ty was banging on my door the next morning at daybreak. He thrust his arm up to my face and said, "See there, not a sign of a bite." "Well, miracles will never cease I suppose," I said, acting thoroughly surprised. His attitude completely changed after that. He talked incessantly of God's grace and infinite power. If he wasn't talking he was singing a hymn. Along about the middle of July Maggie told me she was pregnant. That made me happy. We were a happy trio, going about life with a new outlook on the future. The concept of faith, that elusive idea which I had been wrestling with all my life was beginning to make just a little sense. I looked it up in the Bible and the best definition I could find was in the book of Hebrews, chapter one, verse one: "Now faith is the substance of things hoped for, the evidence of things not seen." I had hoped for Ty's enlightenment, and Maggie's pregnancy was evidence of things not seen. I realize that's a lame analogy but its best I can do.

Ty kept his word and helped me through that first difficult season. I did not make any money but by and large I broke even and that's another miracle. The tobacco matured a little early and we got it cut, housed, cured, stripped and to the market in Richmond by the first of December. I didn't see much of Ty after that. In fact, when winter really set in, I only got out of the house to feed the livestock, do the milking and chop stove wood. It was a terrible winter with six and eight-foot snow drifts. Maggie and I spent most of the time in front of the fireplace trying to keep warm. They voted Ty in as pastor at New Bethel, which I surmised was the height of his ambition. I only got the chance to hear him preach there one time due to the inclement weather. By springtime he was gone. He left New Bethel and became an evangelist. Now and then they would run an occasional piece about him in the weekly paper concerning his huge success on the road and the large crowds he was drawing.

Our new daughter was almost a year old when Ty's daddy, Frank, brought me the news. Ty was dead. They had found him in an Indianapolis hotel room, shot in the head. Those are the only details I ever received concerning his death. They were shipping him back for burial there at the local graveyard behind the post office. Frank wanted me to help dig his grave. It had always been customary in that part of the country for friends and family to help in digging the grave of the deceased.

His body arrived late that afternoon and they held an all-night quake for him there at his parent's house. Maggie and I attended along with several neighbors. It was a sad time with lots of crying and hugging. There seemed to be a mysterious aura surrounding that all-night vigil. I still have not been able to completely understand that ordeal. I was probably the closest person to the front door and about midnight I happened to detect a faint knocking. I opened the door to a lady dressed completely in black mourning clothes. Actually I was a bit astonished. She appeared a specter standing there in the dim light. As far as I know, she didn't speak a word to anyone the entire time she was there. She made her way to the casket where she viewed the body for quite a spell. Afterwards, she sat alone in the back of the room until about daybreak and then she was gone. After she left, I enquired of some of the other mourners as to whom she was but no one seemed to know her. The only telling thing about her was a gold wedding band on her ring finger. It was just a curiosity. I know Ty wasn't married.

It seems there are always little incidents happening in life that just become more and more perplexing the longer you think about them. But to tell the truth, Ty Hardy was a perplexing man. I knew Ty had killed a man in self-defense. But, I also wondered to what extent a man is supposed to carry the commandment of "turn the other cheek." I couldn't help but wonder whether or not Ty really did have his epiphany. If not, could it have been because of my little indiscretion of being less than honest with him about "ol rattler." I honestly thought that incident, along with little May belle's apparent miracle, had helped to restore Ty's faith in himself and God. There is still no doubt in my mind that a man who has fallen from Grace can also be redeemed. But then I couldn't help but wonder if that old twelfth century tentmaker, Omar Khayyam, had been right when he concluded in one of his famous quatrains: "The Flower That Once Has Blown Forever Dies."

THE END

I sent my Soul through the Invisible,
Some letter of that After-life to spell:
And by and by my Soul return'd to me,
And answer'd: 'I Myself am Heav'n and Hell

"The old tentmaker"
Omar Khayyam circa 1120

"I SENT MY SOUL INTO THE INVISIBLE
SOME LETTER OF THE AFTERLIFE TO SPELL"

"Hope springs eternal in the human breast. Man never _is_ but always _to_ be blessed." These debatable words of wisdom had been rattling around in my brain for many days. I have no idea why they popped back up just at the moment I awoke that morning. Perhaps it was due to my discomfort with that sliver of sunlight streaming across my face through the slit in the window curtain. Or maybe it was because I had been searching for a sliver of hope, something substantial, something true and dependable during that period when my whole world and the world in general had gone to hell.

I tried to swallow. It was difficult. My throat was dry as ashes from remnants of the cheap wine and cigarettes of last night's debauchery. I automatically reached toward the night stand in hopes of finding something wet to help soothe that parched sensation. The empty wine bottle tumbled to the floor and I sat up on the side of the bed. I wobbled over to the antiquated sink in the corner of the room and drenched my head in cold water. "My God" I thought. "What am I becoming?" A quick glance in the dirty mirror revealed a wrinkled face that looked like forty miles of bad road and a set of cadaverous eye-sockets. As this pallid image stared back at me I pictured myself in a coffin and was not shocked. "I don't care," I whispered. "The sooner the better."

My wife and five year old son, the only people I had ever really cared about were dead. It happened three years back during the "great pandemic" as most people refer to that catastrophic event. Every family was affected. Millions of Americans died. It was more like a continent consuming conflagration. It was suddenly upon us. It was as if a single wave of diseased air had swept across the land from coast to coast decimating half the population in the span of a week. Then, just as suddenly as it had appeared it was just as suddenly gone. I later heard only scraps of news concerning that grotesque malady. Some say it had continued on to Europe and Asia, but I sort of lost track. The news media was out of sponsors, and transmission had all but ceased except for those sensational tidbits slanted to favor the current political party in power.

Anyway, those of us who had been spared the physical effects of the bug were kept busy reporting the dead, burying the dead or cleaning up after the dead. We were a population of simulated zombies. There for a while we were all expecting our imminent demise. But days, then weeks, months and years went by while most of us who had been left alive felt we too would have been better off if we had just passed on into oblivion. There had been no effective preventive measures against the scourge. There were no vaccines or oral remedies. The pharmaceutical companies had stopped producing; they had been taxed and regulated out of business. Seventy five percent of the countries hospitals were little more than empty shells and seventy five percent of the doctors were deceased or had just stopped practicing.

"Yes, the sooner the better, I whispered again. But then, in a little while, as usual, that old God instilled desire to live came back. I knew that somehow, someway, I had to get it together. I hadn't been to the newspaper in over a month. I had made weekly visits for the past year or so always hoping for some news about going back to work. However, it appeared the presses had stopped for good. I decided then to go on down, clean my desk out and maybe head on back to the mountains where I had been born and raised. I retrieved my pistol from under the mattress. I didn't particularly like the thing, but I would not have set foot outside without it in this day and time. A state of anarchy was upon the land.

I pulled the chair away from where I had wedged it under the doorknob and stepped out into the rancid smelling hallway. I started down the stairs and saw a couple of homosexual winos cuddled up on the second floor landing below me. I knew they were queer since they seemed to be slobbering in one another's mouth. I thought of how this minority of misfits had insidiously continued to push their abhorrent lifestyle upon the general public over the years until normal folks had begun to more or less accept their nasty acts and abnormal way of life. Regular folks were just too worn out from trying to keep their families fed, and the wolf away from the door, to pay much attention. I was hoping I could pass them without incident, but before I had taken three steps one of the men jerked the others trousers down and mounted him. He made several quick thrusts and then uncoupled. A long slider of feces came slinking down the man's thigh, and my stomach churned. I hadn't eaten for some time, and there was nothing in me to throw up, but I heaved and gagged until cold droplets of sweat formed on my forehead. I finally pulled myself together and passed the two sicko's. A few more steps and I was out on the street. "Jesus!" I muttered. "What in the hell has happened to the human race."

It was mid-July and I hadn't gone ten steps before my cleanest dirty shirt seemed to be welded to my back by the rivulets of sweat trickling down between my shoulder blades. Rotting garbage was piled waist high all along in the gutters. I kicked a dead rat out of my way. The city, like most of the inhabitants was broke so I assumed the sanitary workers hadn't been paid either. I had a long walk ahead of me. I was pretty lucky to still own a car, but I had to leave it in the garage there at the newspaper if I wanted to keep it in one piece. Most of the misfits popped their heads out of their rat-holes only after the sun goes down and would then descend upon a vehicle and strip it clean in a matter of seconds. Anyway, it didn't matter much whether I had a vehicle or not; who could afford twelve dollars a gallon for gas? The streets were near destitute of people except for an occasional vagabond slinking from one empty storefront to another attempting to spot out something that might be worth stealing, or if there was someone around drunk or invalid enough for him to rob. I began trying to think of something pleasant, you know, practice some of the tips I had heard on the power of positive thinking or some such bullshit you hear from all the wanna be guru's in the self-help media. But being the proverbial glutton for punishment that I am, my mind began to drift, and before long I was back into that mental syndrome of trying to make some sense out of this thing we call "life."

I'm just a guy who has been going about the country side for twenty years digging up and resurrecting any old story that may be of interest to the reading public. Oh, I've got problems, and I've had my troubles, but I actually can't fault anyone for those misfortunes. I just happened to arrive in this world one September day. I had no choice in the matter. The die was cast, and it "is" what it "is." As Job said "Man that is born of woman is of few days and full of trouble."

Well, you know, we are pushed and grunted out upon this globe a bloody and greasy mess, weaned off the teat, jerked out of bed every morning before daybreak; await the school bus for thirty minutes before dawn; travel for an hour to a public school where we are detained for five hours in the name of public education by glorified baby sitters. During this "school day" we are indoctrinated with a thousand "thou shall" and "thou shall not" instructions in the hope of molding us into malleable and compliant "citizens." Then we travel for another hour on the bus back to our homes, eat a supper of cheeseburgers and French fries prepared by the local "greasy vest" restaurant; watch three or four hours of television, and then are shuffled off to bed so our parents can sit and commiserate with one another about how they failed to receive the coveted promotion, and how they were mistreated at work that day.

We finally finish school; are emancipated from parental custody, and, if we are lucky, find some way to make a living. Then we spend the next forty or fifty years chasing the Yankee dollar. The irony of it all is that the majority of us end up broke and in debt anyway; Doctors, lawyers, hospitals or the government get our money. We find that no-one is really there for us when we are down and out, and all our so called friends are just acquaintances who really wouldn't piss in our ass if our guts were on fire. Finally, we get too old to work so we rattle around with our aches and pains for a few years and then we die. Or, we may be among those unfortunates who linger far past their time and are shipped off to a county nursing home to be harassed by some lard ass, sadistic, sex deprived aide and then we die! Two or three weeks later we will be all but forgotten except for an occasional "oh yes, I remember him! - He was a good old boy!"

But, what do I know? Like I said, I'm not an expert at anything. I realize I'm a cynic, a skeptic and lack the ability to trust. I imagine if I were to be analyzed by a competent shrink, I would be labeled and pigeon holed as an out and out misanthrope. I've even prayed a lot concerning my eccentricities and short comings, but it seems there's no way to change what I am. I have long since concluded this inescapable personality is to account for my inferiority complex, my addictive idiosyncrasies and my lack of sympathy and charity toward humankind. I, like most members of twenty first century society, have wasted a lot of time searching for someone to hang a reason for my failures on. I've heard it from too many people. You know, like "we were too poor to afford nice school clothes, or my daddy was a drunk and my mother never told me she loved me", and all that kind of bullshit. Well I know what they mean, but I certainly can't commiserate with them. When I get alone with my thoughts, especially when I lie down to sleep at night and the past begins to flood my mind, I finally have to get honest and admit the fact that no one is to blame for my failures except myself. I was too hard headed to take advice, so everything I learned was by trial and error. I got a lot of knots on my head with that attitude, but at the same time I got a priceless education from that proverbial school of hard knocks.

Of course, on the other hand, when I get real serious and take an objective look at the whole picture, there's no doubt about it; I'm a lucky man. But, I've made my own luck. I grew up in a small college town in Southeastern Kentucky. My father was a college professor of chemistry and we lived the average middle-class life until I was about ten. He was also a womanizer and a rake, according to my mother. He loved his pretty young women and sold our house and left town with one of them in a shiny black Cadillac one summer. We never saw or heard from him again. Homeless and almost destitute, a widower with a good sized farm offered to give us board and lodging in return for our labors. Thus began my eight years of tilling the soil and "earning my bread by the sweat of my brow." During the growing seasons I was out in the field behind a plow looking the mule in the ass that was pulling the plow until I was eighteen years old. But, I count those eighteen years a blessing. I know what it is to be poor and how it feels to be hungry. I also know the world would be a better place if every man alive were forced to experience at least a short season of such destitution.

That's exactly what I wanted for my old man. I wanted him to have to stand behind that plow smelling mule farts day after day; cultivating just enough food to keep body and soul together until he worked himself to death. I knew that would never happen so I finally just vowed to hunt the son of a bitch down and kill him for what he had done to my mother. The day I graduated from High School I kissed my mama goodbye and caught the first Greyhound bus headed north. I learned fast that a country bumpkin is like a sitting duck in the city, so I carried what little money I could come by in my shoe and tried to keep a low profile for the first five years. I washed a lot of dishes, carried a lot of bricks and mixed a lot of cement while going to school at night. Ten years later the hard work paid off, and I graduated from college with a degree in Journalism.

The paragon of the cocky optimist, I carried my credentials here to the Nation's Capital and proceeded to commence living the so called "American dream". I was hired by the leading newspaper, got married, and became the father of a handsome son and proud owner of the quintessential stucco cottage with the proverbial white picket fence. My reputation as a "go get 'em" reporter grew, and I was able to write a very impressive resume.

I was still in college when the world started turning to shit. Our soldiers ran Saddam Hussein and his henchmen out of Kuwait. Most of us had assumed our problems with the Arabs were over after our success in "Desert Storm" but were we ever wrong. These Muslim fundamentalists hated America for invading their part of the world, and to be honest, I couldn't blame them. America had been sticking her nose into the business of other countries since the Korean conflict of the nineteen fifties. I'm not making light of the world trade center catastrophe. The senseless murder of three thousand innocent Americans was a tragedy to say the least, but I believe the incident could have been resolved without getting thousands more of our young men and women killed, devastating two sovereign countries, and killing and maiming thousands more innocent people at a cost of billions of American tax payer dollars.

Oh, it was a horrific act, killing three thousand people, but the president made too much of a handful of thugs trying to make a statement. At the time, those nineteen "terrorists" and their cohorts were no more of a continuing threat to America's freedom than the common thugs walking the streets of every U.S. City. Those nuts could be rounded up and put out of commission at any time. But, the president wanted an excuse to prove he was a fearless leader, so he inadvertently escalated the whole incident way out of proportion. A little of the right kind of diplomacy and the ensuing fifteen years of war could have been avoided. Those Muslim fundamentalists just don't like us invading their countries and attempting to impose our decadent and immoral ways of life upon them. They didn't like our whores and whore-mongers, our free love, our seemingly general acceptance of homosexuals, the murder of late term fetuses, and our women leaving the home to work while their children were left to roam the streets and fend for themselves.

The Muslim radicals were evidently persuaded that all Americans were like the Hollywood misfits glamorized by television, movies, and magazines. The money grubbing publicity agents had turned many a wonderful and talented actor and singer into literal perverts in the eye of the general public. However, most of that Hollywood set has no talent to begin with. They can't act, dance, sing or play a musical instrument so they paint themselves up, let their tits and ass hang out, dance and prance around to some ungodly drum beat and ear splitting guitar sound and call it music. Then, if that isn't enough they trot out the professional athletes who in the main have no brains, just brawn. Some old timer hit the nail on the head when he said "to be merely an athlete is to be nearly a savage." Of course if they get enough publicity the young folks will begin to idolize these knuckle dragging Neanderthals and begin to emulate them as well.

Those Muslim fundamentalists had made a loud and unforgettable statement when they destroyed the twin towers: "keep it over there, don't bring your greed, lust, avarice and immorality over here!" they seemed to say. Hasty decisions for retaliation were subsequently made by America's incompetent elected leaders who hurled the United States into a long and ridiculous war. Immorality, dishonesty greed and the goal of the bleeding heart leftists in America to proselytize the rest of the world and tell them how they were going to live had finally tipped the scale. The National economy began to collapse and in an effort to bolster the system congress and a green and progressive president enacted spending bills which quickly bankrupted the nation.

I, as most able bodied Americans, continued to spend the great majority of my day trying to make a living. But it all happened so fast, things had bottomed out before we knew what was happening. Wall Street failed due to greed and avarice; large and small businesses failed due to tight money; the pensioners, old folks and disabled failed because the checks stopped coming in, and the

United States Government failed because it had printed worthless money and borrowed and inflated the American dollar out of existence.

But this was only a symptom of what was yet to come. "Climate Change" was becoming more and more apparent. Like most, I had shrugged it off. But the day of reckoning finally arrived. Whether or not it was due to man's negligence or some natural change is immaterial; it happened. Glaciers melted and sea levels rose wiping out much of the most expensive and beautiful property in the nation. Devastating straight line winds and hurricanes occurred with far greater frequency. Subterranean earthquakes toppled many of the deep water oil rigs. The broken and abandoned wells perpetually regurgitated the slimy and toxic black ooze upon the pristine beaches and wetland waterways. The oil companies finally went broke and out of business trying to clean up the mess and plug the wells. All efforts seemed futile; the oil kept spewing while turning the shorelines into virtual tar pits and slime bogs. It's only a matter of time until many major cities along the coasts will turn into virtual swamps.

The sun was out full force now. Man it was hot. I unbuttoned my shirt to the waste and wished for a little breeze. Suddenly a tall, thin, grimy appearing man stepped from a doorway and pulled a knife on me. I was ready. The instant I saw him I wanted to kill him. I jerked my revolver, cocked it and thrust it to within an inch of his nose. His eyes grew as large as silver dollars, and he quickly turned and ran on down the street. This wasn't the first time such an incident had happened, and I was tired of such bull-shit. I knew if I hung around that neighborhood very much longer I would end up killing one of those bastards, and I would be penitentiary bound.

My office building was now in view, and a few minutes later I was what sounded like "stomping" my way up the iron stairs to my vacant office. The building was empty of people, and in the old days you couldn't hear your footsteps or anything else for that matter over the deafening roar of the presses. The room was almost dark except for a faint light that came through the dirty windows. Most everything had been carried off except the heavy desks. "The end of an era", I muttered; "The printed news industry has gone with the wind." I had to chuckle at that analogy. I tried to wipe the caked dust from my old desk with my handkerchief, but my efforts were futile. There was not even a pencil left in the drawers. I did find a picture of my wife and son and an envelope with just my name on it. I shoved these articles into my pocket and hurried back out into the sunlight. I slipped the picture into my wallet and then quickly tore open the envelope. A single page read as follows: "Dear Mr. ....you come highly recommended to us from an anonymous source. We understand from your reputation as a very competent investigative reporter that you are the "go to" man when it comes to finding a missing person. We are in the position to offer you a very substantial remuneration for your efforts in such a matter. If interested, please contact Mr. James Dever at the law offices of Mason and Dever, Esq., 536 Poplar St, at your convenience." I welcomed any opportunity to earn a little money so I figured I would see what Mr. Mason and Dever had in mind.

No guard or watchman was present anywhere around the old building; not a soul in sight. I had to break the lock on the parking lot gate to retrieve my old ford. Poplar Street was three miles South and I made it there in about twenty minutes without incident. Five-thirty-six Poplar was an ominous looking place to say the least; dirty two story brick; nasty windows and a rusty drain pipe hanging from the front eave. A rusting wrought iron fence surrounded the building. There was a cast iron plaque implanted in the front yard which read "Mason & Dever Attorneys at law." This sign would have been attractive at a much earlier date, but the black letters on the white background were almost illegible due to the chipped paint. A cobblestone walk led up to the concrete encased portico. Huge fluted pillars on each side of the entrance made me feel for an instant I was about to enter the Parthenon.

I rapped on the great oaken door several times, but no sound came from inside. Finally I tried the doorknob. The door was open. I stepped inside to a musty smelling hallway that only a hundred and fifty year old brick building with little maintenance can have. Immediately to my right was Devers' office. I entered to find a man in his seventies all decked out in a striped suit, white shirt, necktie and all. It just seemed odd to me. Why would he be so formally dressed when evidently not another soul was within a mile of the place? But then I surmised that some old farts just automatically dress that way every day out of habit. If they tried to dress casually they would just look like any other old geezer waiting on the grim reaper. He was holding a cigarette filter between his teeth, but the cigarette was missing. No wonder, I thought, cigarettes were near fifty dollars a pack! I introduced myself as he leaned back in his chair and gave me the once over. "We were expecting you two weeks ago" he quipped, in a high pitched effeminate tone. "I only got your message a little while ago. What's the deal?" I said.

"Let me get right to the point!" he sang. "Dr. Samuel Thompson, a man of renown, and chairman in the department of chemistry at a well-known Ivy League college, left on sabbatical more than a year ago, and is now way overdue. He has been nominated, and favored to win, a prestigious award for his research on Carl Jung's theory of a collective unconscious in man. We are pretty sure he is alive and well, as he was spotted right here in this city not more than a month ago by an impeccable witness. The people who want him found must remain anonymous, but are willing to pay you ten thousand dollars when you locate him. You must personally bring me proof of his whereabouts. You will be paid five thousand when you sign this contract and the other five when you return with the information. Mind you, this must remain entirely between you and me. I am also providing you with what current information we have on the man." He handed me a small manila envelope along with a legal looking contract which read almost exactly as he had just stated. I intuitively smelled a rat. There was something he wasn't telling me, but the five thousand cash I could not afford to turn down; especially since I was busted. I signed the contract, and he handed me fifty one hundred dollar bills. Not another word was spoken; not even a "good day." I expect we both thought it wise. I left the place elated but also with a gnawing sensation that something was amiss.

Naturally, the first chore facing me in my quest for locating this illustrious person was to collect the names and addresses of those who had last clapped eyes on him. Mr. Dever had provided me with access to his personnel file, his office at the university and what turned out to be his very palatial appearing home just a few blocks off campus. I quickly surmised him to be no pauper by any estimate. The home was immaculate; a little dusty and stuffy since it had not been lived in for a couple of years, but by and large, immaculate. Dr. Thompson had been a widower for five years before his disappearance, and a man living alone would not have been that meticulous in housekeeping. Actually, the discovery of his whereabouts after that deduction was rather simple. A Ms. Eve Gordon had been his housekeeper for the past fifteen years as I found various items of correspondence addressed to her spread about the residence. I had only to inquire of the Bureau of Motor Vehicles and a local credit reporting organization in securing her current address.

She was presently residing in a small village not a thirty minute drive from the University. I phoned the lady and she graciously made an appointment for us to meet. She was a fine specimen of a middle aged woman, and you could tell at a glance she was smart and had taken good care of herself from a physical standpoint, but her apparent nervousness made me a bit uncomfortable. She fidgeted about and could not sit still the whole time I talked with her. When I mentioned Dr. Thompson she became despondent almost to the point of tears. She began to ask questions as to his health and sanity. When I assured her that I had not seen the Doctor but was searching for him, she demanded to know why. When I apprised her of the news concerning his nomination she immediately became more conciliatory and quickly wrote out the address and directions to where she thought I might find him.

She asked me if my intentions were to get some help for him, and when I informed her that I did not know of his need for help she reluctantly began to convey details of her extensive relationship with the Thompson family. She had been employed by the Thompson's as housekeeper and general caregiver for Mrs. Thompson. She had nursed the old lady through ten years of pain and torment from what turned out to be an incurable cancer. After the lady died she agreed to stay on with the Doctor in the same capacity. She spoke highly of him and said he had for the most part been a kind and gentle man and a good employer up until the time he began contemplating retirement. He became very private and withdrawn at about that time. He rarely came out of his room except to attend his scheduled lectures at the college. She said he read incessantly day and night from the stacks of antiquated and dog-eared books strewn about his library.

For a few months, while taking a short leave of absence from the university, he kept very late hours and often came home in the wee hours of the morning in a state of apparent inebriation. The

Thompson's had owned a retreat in the Pocono Mountains of Pennsylvania for the entire time Ms. Gordon had known them, and one day he informed her of his plans to go on sabbatical there. He asked her if she would be willing to go along and continue to keep house for him. She agreed to the change hoping he would come out of his shell and return to a more normal way of life. This did not happen. He became even more reclusive and belligerent.

Six months before my meeting with Mrs. Gordon, Dr. Thompson had fired her. He had become impossible to please and ranted and raved at her every time they came into contact. He ate and bathed very little, and she was becoming concerned with his physical as well as his mental health. I reassured the woman that if and when I found the man I would try to help him if he would allow me to do so. "There is one more detail that I must make you aware of," she said as I opened the door to leave. She walked towards me slowly, almost sheepishly with her head bowed as if she were embarrassed. "You must promise that you will not repeat a word of what I'm about to say to you." I was really curious now so I agreed to the promise. She put her head close to my ear and whispered "he eats raw meat." Startled, I asked her to clarify the statement and give me an example. "He eats raw steak and raw chicken livers! That's another reason he resented me so. When I told him he could get salmonella, or worse, from eating uncooked meat, he became furious and ran me out of the house with his walking cudgel. He also had other choice names for me like bitch and queer. His final words to me are still ringing in my ears: "the cave man ate raw meat did him not, you stupid bitch." I tried to conceal my astonishment, and told her it was probably just some fetish he had acquired. I bid her good day with the assurance I would keep her informed of any ensuing developments. Upon leaving Ms. Gordon's apartment I once again got that uneasy feeling. She was not being totally honest with me. Her demeanor, coupled with her body language told me she was not the woman she outwardly portrayed.

I arrived at a small town in eastern Pennsylvania late in the afternoon and checked into a motel. From my calculations I was not more than a couple of dozen miles from the Thompson retreat. After finding my supper at a small diner in the little town, I sat on the motel balcony and enjoyed the stillness and the fresh mountain air. I could understand why a person wanting to get away from the hustle and bustle of the city would choose a location of that sort to do so. Compared to Washington D.C. it was a virtual paradise of silence and serenity.

It became obvious the following morning that Ms. Gordon's directions were far removed from being precise. I must have driven back and forth over at least twenty different country roads before I discovered the Thompson retreat. The mailbox with the address was partly concealed by a roadside bush and I had driven past the rusty thing several times. I made the turnoff from the county road onto a partly graveled driveway. After a couple of hundred feet, the lane became so boulder strewn I thought it best to park my sedan and walk. I was beginning to think I had made the wrong turn off when suddenly I emerged out upon a grassy clearing. The house was situated at the far end of the clearing at the bottom of a cliff which over-towered the building. In a place so secluded you would have expected to hear a barking dog or at least some sign of people, but there was only dead silence. The house looked to be constructed of dark stained clapboard with a long porch running the entire length of the building along the front. The windows seemed to emit a brownish hue with lighter vertical streaks where rivulets of moisture had trickled part of the way down the panes. I don't know why, but I felt a nervous trepidation as I attempted to sort of ease up the six or eight wooden steps leading to the porch. The boards squeaked with each step and due to the relative silence of the area those squeaks seemed louder than they normally would have. I tapped lightly on the rusty screen door several times and waited. There was no answer; no sound from within. I was dreadfully hot and by that time sweating profusely.

The air seemed stagnant and the temperature must have been ninety five. I paced slowly from one end of the porch to the other and attempted to peer through the grimy windows but could detect no living thing or sound from inside. I figured by that time the place was destitute of life and was about to leave when I decided to give it one more try. I opened the screen door and rapped loudly on the glass. I heard a faint noise from inside and waited. That ominous feeling was still with me. What was I doing in this Godforsaken place? My trepidation continued and only escalated when the door was flung open, and I was confronted with a replica of Lazarus fresh from the tomb. An old man dressed only in a soiled set of

147

boxer shorts stood before me. He was at least six feet tall and all but skin and bones. Shoulder length hair and a scraggly iron gray beard partially concealed his agitated scowl of contempt for this obnoxious intruder. I had evidently awakened a modern day Robinson Crusoe from a sound sleep.

"What the hell are you selling?" was his gruff greeting. I swallowed hard and responded in a subdued tone "I'm in search of a doctor Samuel Thompson." "And what the hell do you want with him?" he blurted. Embarrassed by my cracking voice I informed him in as few words as possible as to who had hired me and then added something to the affect that I was only a simple investigative reporter. "Investigative reporter 'eh" he scowled while his steel gray eyes bored a hole in me. "Well, come on in if you can get in," he added. I wriggled through the partially opened door and waited for his next response. The place was a mess. There were books and stacks of papers piled all about. He pointed to a table and a couple of chairs at the far end of the room and I immediately took a seat. "Investigative reporter 'eh? Tell me what it is you investigate!" "Just anything of public interest! I write it up and try to sell it to newspapers or magazines willing to print it or report it to the general public," I replied. "Ever investigated and reported on anything worthwhile?" he smirked. "Well, as a matter of fact, yes!" I stammered. "I helped in the investigation and conviction of those five guys responsible for the toxic waste dumping from the tannery near the Tennessee boarder." I waited briefly for some response, and when he only grunted I added; "That outfit was poisoning the drinking water of the entire community." I gulped a few times and waited again for him to say something. Nothing! I thought hard for something more impressive to add. "I actually helped to secure a multi-million dollar settlement for those residents," I quickly added. "Oh yeah, two years or so past, wasn't it?" he questioned. I nodded in the affirmative. "How much did you make off the deal?" he quipped. "Well, I only did the reporting and a lot of footwork. The lawyers made the money. However, I earned the reputation for being a crack-shot reporter!" I waited for his response, and when he was silent I softly added "Well, looks good on a resume I suppose."

He started to speak, but then hurried into the bathroom and slammed the door. There was no mistaking that sound of heaving and retching. He was sick and the reason was obvious. There were whiskey bottles and dozens of medicine bottles sitting on the utensil island in the middle of the room. White powder dust and mixing bowls with the little pill crushers were everywhere. I wanted to get up and inspect all this pharmaceutical paraphernalia but I thought it best to wait.

Pretty soon he returned wiping his face with a soiled towel. A small and fantastic looking dog staggered along at his heels. The animal had the appearance of a Dachshund when viewed from one perspective but a Poodle when viewed from another, and yet had the head of a rabbit in profile. The dog's fur was curly and fluffy with large black spots on a white background. An amazing looking creature, I surmised. The dog did not walk in a straight line as a dog would normally, but sort of staggered haphazardly along as if half conscious. They make a good pair, I thought to myself! I was totally startled when the mutt sprang unexpectedly into my lap. The thing turned completely around a couple of times like he was getting ready to lie down and fall asleep but thankfully Dr. Thompson intervened.

"Come on Adam," the doctor was almost whispering. He picked the animal up and placed it in the chair which he himself had previously occupied. He then procured a bowl from a pile of dirty dishes near the sink and filled it with a milky like substance from what appeared to be a milk bottle. "You do know that milk alone will cause worms in a dog don't you?" I sporadically interjected. "Yes, I do know that, my friend, but this is not exactly milk. It's more like a vitamin. I'm preparing Adam here for a long journey he and I are going to take pretty soon now." He pulled another chair up alongside Adam's and flopped heavily into it. He began to stroke the dog's head and murmur soothing words of comfort to the animal. Adam quickly lapped up the contents of the bowl and then leaped to the floor where he curled up behind Dr. Thompson's chair and seemed to immediately fall asleep. Dr. Thompson poured himself half a water-glass of whiskey from the bottle of "Old Crow" which had been sitting near the edge of the table. He downed the whole thing in one gulp. "Hair of the dog you know" he sputtered. "Want one?" he offered. I shook my head in the negative and he poured himself another.

I was astounded at his attitude. Here was a man about to be awarded an international prize for some discovery, some innovation which he had pioneered for the benefit of mankind, acting like a skid row alcoholic getting his morning fix. He was as far removed from the stereotypical college professor who had spent his entire life in the academics as you could imagine. The question foremost in my mind was what could have happened in this paragon of virtues life to turn him completely about as had apparently taken place. "I suppose I should apologize for this rat trap", he laughed. "Thing of it is, I've about stopped paying attention to manners and protocol. I've come to the conclusion that most of what I've believed in or given credence to over the years has been nothing more than out and out lies or half-truths." The half pint or so of whiskey he had consumed was now beginning to take effect. He had not attempted to get dressed. I was actually embarrassed. His soiled shorts would often come agape at the crotch revealing his pubic hair and I would have to look away. The man had no shame and certainly no respect for me. I thought once I would just get up and leave and forget the whole thing, but the thought of another five thousand dollars blew that idea all to hell. I had come this far so I figured I would stay and tough it out.

Pretty soon he stood to his feet and wobbled over to the stove. He cracked a couple of eggs into a blackened skillet. As the eggs began to sizzle he asked me if I would like some breakfast, and I declined. He brought the plate of "sunny side up" eggs back to the table and flopped down into the chair. I thought for a second the eggs were going to slide off onto the floor, but he leveled the plate just in time. He wiggled around in the chair sort of like a chicken making its nest. When he was comfortable he hiked one leg and let a tremendous fart. "Better out than in" he laughed. I was growing very agitated. This disrespectful son of a bitch was beginning to really piss me off. When the eggs had cooled sufficiently he held the plate in his left hand and began to stir the eggs with the index and middle finger of his right. He picked up a portion of the greasy concoction and crammed the dripping glob into his mouth. I couldn't believe it, but I didn't say anything. "Guess you think I'm nuts eh? Well fingers were invented before forks I've always heard." He laughed again. I'm not sure whether he was laughing at his statement or at the look on my face. "You think I'm nuts, don't you?" he blubbered again, as a drizzle of egg yolk oozed off his chin. "Well, I'll tell you something my young investigative reporter friend. I don't give a damn if the whole rotten world thinks I'm nuts. I'm through putting on airs for any son of a bitch. This modern society can have their rules and etiquette, their special eating utensils for each course and their finger bowls and napkins. I'm through trying to impress anyone!"

He paused and caught a long breath. "Look-- say, what's your name anyway?" "My name is John, that's good enough for now", was my contempt laden answer. "Well John, you seem like a nice enough kid! I know you are reasonably intelligent since you have already made a complete mental inventory of the contents of this room. I've noticed you're eye-balling of my medicine vials and mixing bowls. You need to know, there is a reason for all of this, and I would like nothing better than to explain to you what has been going on with me and the reasons I have been AWOL from the university. But, before I divulge anything further, I would need a commitment from you. In fact, since you are a genuine bona fide "investigative reporter," I would like to hire you myself!" There was a long pause as he licked the remaining egg yolk off the plate. "Well, what do you say my young friend?" "First of all, you don't have to belittle my profession," I began. "I know a reporter is many levels below that of PHD in chemistry, but still, it's an honorable way to make a living." "I did not mean any disrespect", he said. "Matter of fact, I'd trade places with you any day." "But I can't imagine why you would want to employ me. Don't forget, others have already hired me and are paying me pretty well just to locate you."

He thought for a minute and then responded. "Well John, I have no problem with your reporting my whereabouts and collecting your fee but only when and if I give you the okay. But, at the same time, I'll pay you handsomely to assist me for a few days in my own enterprise." I thought it over for a few minutes and then asked how it was I would possibly be able to assist a man of his stature. "After all" I said, "You are a man of letters with a PHD in chemical engineering." "You too?" he vigorously responded. "What makes you think I'm any different from most other men of average intelligence? That mind-set which has been peddled for centuries by some of our "influential" citizens is one of the reasons I have decided to just drop out of this so called "society." Hell, anyone with a brain can accomplish what I've accomplished. What? Do you think all PHD'S are genius? You probably think all physicians and surgeons are genius! Oh, I'll admit there are a few specially gifted folks in the field of medicine and the academics who are brilliant-but damn few! There's thousands of us PHD'S but basically we are just average people like you who have persevered and studied our asses off trying to digest and internalize what others have published. Don't sell yourself short my friend, and above all, don't put any man on a pedestal!"

I must have appeared a bit dismayed at his self-degradation and no doubt he could see that look of consternation in my demeanor. "Tell you what" he began. "Let me pour us a drink and if you have a little time I will fill you in on what I'm about. Afterwards, you can decide whether or not you want to become my assistant." He drained the remaining inch or so of whiskey from the bottle into his glass. "Well, how 'bout that! A spider! That one's free and on the house" he giggled. He walked briskly to the kitchen counter and brought back another bottle of the "Old Crow" and another glass. He poured himself a tall drink and was about to pour me one when I held up my hand and said "no thanks- none for me." I really wanted the stuff, but I was not about to let him in on any of my shortcomings. "But I am willing to listen to your proposal," I added. "O.K., I'll try to give you a rundown on what I've been doing for the past year or so and where I am now." He squirmed a bit in his chair trying to get comfortable and began.

"Competition within the halls of the so called "Ivy League" can throttle the college professor. Success depends upon research, writing, and publication of articles and books. Hell, if you're not published, you can forget it! There is little time to cultivate or pursue one's personal hobbies or interests. I was always afraid of failure and refused to let my guard down. I suppose I enjoyed a reasonable amount of success during those years. But then, a peculiar uneasiness concerning this success began to haunt me. I had never taken the time to analyze that minor annoyance until I started to consider retirement. I asked myself what would be my personal legacy to academia; what had I brought to the table? I suddenly realized I had simply been mimicking or parroting all those teachers and "professors" who had preceded me, and quoting from textbooks and research papers they had written. I suddenly realized that nothing "totally" new or original had ever fallen from my lips. I realized just how impotent I had been. Of course, this feeling of inferiority may not have been justified since few, if any of us, have ever attained to "a-priori" cognition. It has been said that "original" thoughts are only realized by modern man while dreaming or demented--if at all, and that the prophet or genius is a brother to the mad man." He had suddenly assumed a relaxed demeanor and was speaking more slowly and succinctly. I thought it strange since the amount of whiskey he had consumed would have rendered me incoherent.

He sucked in a long draw off a cigarette and began again while allowing the smoke to slowly escape his lips. "My parents were strict taskmasters, and I was constantly pushed in the direction they wanted me to go. My personal interests were never considered. And, being a conscientious person, I never got a chance to slow down after having "arrived" in my career. I'm a tenured professor of chemistry, but my real interest is in genetics, and I naturally take a certain amount of pride in my spurious accomplishments. But towards the end of my career and my impending retirement, I began to wonder just what it was that I "professed." All along there had been something nipping at my conscience concerning my abilities. I started to feel empty and began to suspect that I was a phony." He bowed his head and got silent for a minute as if in deep thought. I sort of felt sorry and a bit embarrassed for him.

"Hell, don't feel like the lone ranger", I spoke up. "I haven't gone nearly as far nor been nearly as successful as you, and I always feel like a phony! I'm like a scavenger making a living off of the other person's misfortunes. There's almost always a victim in my stories. I rarely ever report on anything good. Hell, people don't want to hear about goodness! They won't read my articles unless it has to do with some blood and guts crap." He gave me that "I know" look while nodding his head in the affirmative.

The old man was beginning to get fidgety again. His hands were starting to shake, and he was often squirming in his chair. Small beads of sweat began to form on his brow and under his eyes. "Guess I'd better put me on a pair of pants" he said. He walked unsteadily into what apparently was a bedroom and pretty soon came back dressed in a pair of wrinkled jeans and a pair of open toed flip-fops. He re-assumed his chair at the table and poured himself a half glass of the "Old Crow." He licked his lips a couple of times before starting to guzzle the stuff. I watched his Adam's apple as it floated up and down like a yo-yo. He coughed asthmatically a couple of times and placed the glass back on the table. "Damn!" he exclaimed. "I'd like to find something a bit more compatible with my stomach than this stuff, but so far it's the only thing I have found that will calm my nerves after a night of those fitful dreams. Seems I have to have a pretty good buzz on, or I go all to pieces. He found the nasty towel and wiped his face before beginning again.

"Anyway, after such bouts of negativity there was little left to excite my fancy. I felt as impotent as a castrated man caught up in a sex orgy. I became less energetic, and a state of lethargy set in upon me. I thought long and hard about what I actually knew and whether or not it really mattered. I often sat for days with my mind constantly whirring like a computer running an endless loop of binary tape. I was helpless to shut it off. Even my sleep was a re-run of that wretched whirring.

I was in desperate need of a new challenge to restore my enthusiasm for life. But then, during one of those sleepless nights, I happened across a theory set forth by the renowned psychologist Dr. Carl Jung. The theory was that concept having to do with the "collective unconscious." This idea is only mentioned briefly in a few of Jung's writings since it's highly controversial and would be very difficult to prove. Nevertheless, I continued to dwell on the idea for some time. I surmised, in a nutshell, that if the theory had any truth to it, knowledge and experience could be transmitted genetically; that I knew at least in part some of those secrets that had gone to the grave with my ancestors. An interesting idea you must admit." He paused briefly and sort of squinted at me as if he expected some comment. "I had always heard that a man uses only ten percent of his brain and I'm sure we have all wondered what the other ninety percent was there for. I felt sure that if any such phenomena as a collective unconscious did exist it would be found in this dormant gray matter. All that remained for me to do was to find a way to tap into it--to unlock it." He paused and squinted intently at me again as if expecting some comment. "By this time, since you have a bright and deductive mind, you may be making some connection between my words and the whiskey and barbiturates you have been eyeballing." "No, but you are beginning to interest me" I said.

He had another drink and continued. "One of the more common phenomena that may give this idea of a "Collective Unconscious" a bit of credence is that feeling of déjá vu most of us have experienced at one time or another. It's common to think we recognize a familiar face in a complete stranger or a familiar house on a familiar street in a city which we are presently visiting only for the first time. But my most memorable of such incident's occurred when I was in some natural and unaltered habitat. For instance, one of the times I went hunting as a youngster. I had just fashioned my first bow and arrows. As I chased along after a rabbit I had wounded and was getting close to the kill--somehow I knew I had been in that exact location and participating in that exact activity sometime in the past. The trail, the rabbit tracks in the snow, the peculiar shaped boulders that I had to dodge and the terrain in general was totally familiar to me. But that was my first rabbit hunt, and I had never been in that area in my life. The place was a hundred miles from my home. That experience was so surreal and so vivid, I thought about the incident off and on for a few years. Then at the age of about twenty, my parents and I journeyed to a farm in Tennessee for my grandfather's funeral. One afternoon I was out for a casual walk and came upon what it seemed was the exact spot of my deja' vu experience as a boy. Come to find out that was the family farm where many of my ancestors had lived for a couple centuries.

That incident came back to me in a profound way when I first read about Jung's theory. I meditated for hours, sometimes days, on this theory of the collective unconscious. I developed a compulsion to explore the idea to its limit. I even had the audacity to consider the great leap possible in human development by the unlocking of such a phenomenon. The individual who found that key would be revered for all time. But then, as it is with most tenuous ideas, my enthusiasm would wane and in many respects the whole thing seemed to be preposterous. I deduced that if the thing had any semblance of truth to it at all, a new born babe would spring forth from the womb with a brain full of data and images which would be, and evidently must be, subsequently crowded out by new and more vivid experiences. Perhaps crowded out would not be the better way to describe the process. Perhaps the data is simply stored in that dormant part of the brain. You know, much like the recycle bin on your personal computer!" he paused with a low chuckle.

"I could remember more than once looking into the eyes of an infant and wondering whether or not there was more than just that blank stare behind those wide and seemingly knowing orbs. Of course this concept would nullify the age old notion of the Tabula Rasa, or an infant's blank mind as described by the famous philosopher. But was there original ideas behind those babies' eyes? According to a few psychologists, the prophet and genius on occasion, and always the madman, think in a-priori thoughts, or thoughts that have never before been congealed in the human mind or within the ether of space and time. The only exception, according to a few of our leading theologians, would be that you attribute the origin of these thoughts to God. Although, if you prefer, to some omniscient and omnipotent spirit.

Now the idea of the latter held a great deal of significance for me. You see, in spite of my scientific background, I am a Creationist. I believe that the concepts of God, time, and human events can be explained with a very simple analogy. You see, God can be explained as a being impervious to time who wrote a great Novel. God isn't involved with "time!" Man invented the concept of "time." You see, within a "time" of six days, God created everything contained within that Novel. The six days are inserted only for man's understanding. All the heavenly spheres, all the plants and animals, and all the events which would happen to his creation from beginning to end are incidents contained within the plot of that Novel. That includes the events taking place here in this room right at this minute. He completed it all, and simplified it for man in a short span of time called "six days," "And It Was Good" according to His Word. Everything that has happened or is going to happen is contained within this Novel which I alluded to and has already happened in the mind of God, the Novelist."

"Most of us would like to believe that we are far removed in every respect from the stereotypical "cave man" or "wild man." But are we really different or do we differ only in appearance? It doesn't require an extraordinary imagination to stroll down a crowded street and see a walking composite of *Neanderthal* or *Cro*

Magnon but for his attire, and as far as his intelligence is concerned, a few modern folk would need to take a "course" in order to be able to live the life of a cave man where the only requirement for existence would be to stay warm and dry and forage for food. Just consider some of the older men of our society today with the grizzled beards and the oily iron gray hair hanging over their shirt collars; their fat stomachs distended like a pregnant elephant and the young men having to walk along with their legs spread apart in order to keep their trousers from falling completely off. The women can't wait until warm weather to strip off nearly naked and reveal as much of their flesh to any onlooker as the law will allow."

"Actually, these anomalies should not shock us since the cave man still abides in us and among us. We are his kin, and his blood still courses through our veins. Supposedly, "modern" man has been civilized and socialized and I suppose I must agree with this if only to avoid extensive deliberation on these very tenuous and fuzzy concepts. But I would speedily concur with the idea that man has simply been indoctrinated. It all begins the moment we pop from the womb. To the extent this process of indoctrination is internalized within the individual controls the extent to which he can live peaceably among other men. Man has learned by way of this process to keep his wild side suppressed, but with some of us it seems the process is incomplete.

We have all read accounts of sexual perverts who cannibalized the genitalia of their victims or the senseless bludgeoning and dismemberment of children by sane adults in a fit of rage. It is during these intense episodes of mental agitation when the wild man rears his ugly head and finds the surface. Just steal a man's money or try and take a woman's' child away from her if you want proof. And by all accounts from experts, we are "civilized" even though we continue to kill one another whether by outright cold blooded murder or murder by the state in the form of capital punishment."

"While I considered the ninety percent of the untapped brain in conjunction with the possibility of the phantasmagoric theory of the collective unconscious having some degree of truth, I again began to reflect upon my personal learning. When I considered the source of the information I had gleaned over the years from a thousand or more textbooks, graduate theses and research articles,

I started doubting the validity of my knowledge. These authors were all well- known, respected and influential scholars. But, when I asked myself if they had all actually performed the research and conducted the experiments and analysis contained in all those volumes I had spent a lifetime internalizing, I had my doubts. I believed many of these text book authors to be no different than I was. As I mentioned before, my work was not original. All my teaching had involved paraphrasing from these volumes of lore that had been written and published by influential scholars. I started to wonder who it was that influenced the influential.

Here I was, about to retire and walk away from my profession without leaving anything to posterity that was entirely my own. I could not accept the idea. I couldn't help but wonder if some of the ideas I had been teaching all those years were nothing but a hoax. Consider this possibility: A renowned scholar of the past decades had discovered in his waning years on the job that he was as impotent as I suspect I am. He happens upon a theory with possibilities. He throws out some feelers and gets feedback from all his colleagues. They tell him he may be on to something. But then, a little further along in his research he discovers a flaw in his theory. It's a very minute flaw, but nevertheless, this very small flaw, however undetectable by even the most learned of his colleagues would render his theory invalid. This being his last shot at fame; he publishes the falsehood and goes down in history, at least during his lifetime, as a man of great renown and genius.

It only required the hoax of "Piltdown man" to convince me I was on to something. Bones had been planted by aspirant archeologists /geologist's in the county of Sussex, England. The bones were then excavated in nineteen eleven and claimed to be a newly discovered species of prehistoric man. The whole thing was not proved to be a hoax until nineteen hundred and fifty three. The perpetrators of this falsehood had a lifetime to bask in the lie. The possibility of such an act occurring with greater frequency caused me great consternation. I became a skeptic and doubtful of the printed word. I started to religiously read the major newspapers and tune in to the world news on a regular basis and discovered something almost diabolical going on within the political arena and the world of academia. I realized that the largest changes taking place in the world had come about due to theories and presumptions and not fact. Here is just one example."

"In case you haven't noticed, the United States of America is about to be hijacked by a group of hedonists, wanna be do gooder's, crooked politicians, homosexuals, reverse racists and irreverent fools in general." I think my mouth must have dropped open and my eyes bulged at that tirade. Dr. Thompson's reddened eyes were boring a hole in me as he waited for a response of some kind. "Look, I said, I don't want to comment on my opinion of the state of the nation. I simply came here to let you know people are concerned about you and would like for you to contact them at your earliest convenience." He seemed to regain his composure before continuing on. "Hell, don't you think I know those nit-wits have been looking for me? Why do you think I've been hiding?" Man he was agitated and worked up. He paused only briefly and then began his tirade again. "There is a great debate concerning the theory of evolution going on in the world. I had never considered the theory to be debatable. As I said before, I didn't question what the influential touted as fact. I just passed the information on to my students. But, I found to my dismay that the theory of evolution of species was being trumpeted throughout the world as the fact of evolution; including the evolution of Homo sapiens. The idea of man evolving from a lower form of life such as the Chimpanzee is highly debatable and not a fact! There would have to exist that proverbial "missing link" which we have all contemplated if that were the case. After considerable research on the subject I concluded that man has not basically changed since he first came into existence. No doubt we are healthier and live a bit longer due to the inventions of soap, antibiotics, and a more nutritious diet. But you and everyone else knows that most of the important discoveries of the nineteenth and twentieth centuries were accidentally discovered through trial and error.

It was not Charles Darwin who perpetrated this farce. It was the hedonists of the world who were driven by some malicious demon to destroy the concept of a first cause; in other words, God! Or, if you will, that omnipotent and omniscient spirit which of necessity must, and does, pervade the eternities. Evolution had to be accepted as fact by all if these fools were to be successful in brainwashing the general population. The idea of evolution leaves

God, and the concept of God as being creator of all, completely out of the equation. Oh, I know, there are a few scientists and church leaders who tell the tale that they have in some vague way "reconciled" evolution and creationism but in fact, they are simply liars. These two extremes can never be "reconciled." All the old standards of truth from the Bible to the United States Constitution and the Declaration of Independence are being disputed under the guise of "progressivism." Adherents to Biblical truths and constitutional government are being marginalized by a handful of "leftists" who have learned that under ordinary circumstances the "squeaking wheel gets the grease." So these loud mouthed few, continue to squeak the loudest and overwhelm and fatigue the majority of the people to the point where the people just throw up their hands in surrender since the average man is too busy trying to make a living and provide for his family to take the time to challenge these extremist "liberals." There is always a bunch of bleeding hearts who are largely overcome with guilt due to their own greed, lust, pride and crookedness and deceitfulness in general, that they search for some cause or other, like helping the poor, hugging a tree, or serving the sick, in order to assuage their own sinfulness and shortcomings.

They will jump on any bandwagon in order to get a little attention. They beat the drums and fly the flags of the bleeding heart humanitarians, when their real motive, a motive often hidden even to themselves, is to rub a little balm on their own conscience and try to pass themselves off as charitable people, when in fact, if the truth be known, they themselves are the rotten apples in the barrel. But then, the thing that really ticks me off is when some of these bleeding hearts die, the media will piss and moan and cry for a solid week and eulogize that individual. They will place his body in repose at some well-known shrine and make a big to-do about him. Then because of all the publicity, not necessarily because of grief or respect, thousands of people will show up, file past the coffin, cry piss and moan again even though they had never before given that individual a second thought. Ninety nine percent of those who show up are there simply out of curiosity. But, these "dumb driven cattle" will hang around and march behind his coffin to the graveyard never stopping to think that he was just a man pretty much like themselves, who too had to put his pants on one leg at a time."

"But getting back to the theory of evolution, since there was little serious debate, and the average man had little access to the press or media, the perpetrators of the farce assumed they had been successful in getting away with the scheme and began to publish the idea in all the newspapers, magazines and textbooks. Ignorant and lazy teachers and those who thought themselves too smart to believe in a creator picked it up and we see where it is today. The point being, we cannot accept theory as fact just because it is easy to believe and easier to teach. Since man is by nature greedy, lustful, prideful, inquisitive, jealous, combative and erotic, this nature must be controlled in some way. Laws must be instituted to protect ourselves from ourselves, not from "others" since we are the "others." No-one wants anarchy and the law of "might makes right" to prevail. Nor do we want to live in a society where the only way to keep the peace is by the swinging of the policeman's club. True peace and harmony within a society must be attained and maintained in a more subtle way if it is to last. It should be common knowledge that 'a person changed against his will is of the same opinion still'. If a person is going to change, the change must come from within himself and of himself. This quasi ideal society can only be realized through supernatural authority. In other words, religion must be allowed and promoted by the authorities. A nation cannot be strong unless it believes in God. Wise leaders have allowed the concept of God, and the worship of God to flourish all down through the ages, and in no wise has anyone been successful in its total denigration or subjugation. It's been said that if God did not exist, man would need to invent one. The laughable idea that man just evolved from a one celled organism congealed in a slime pit must be addressed by sane people and once and for all proved false. Incidentally, I hope to be able to shed considerable light on this subject and that is one of the reasons I hope to employ you."

I was about to ask him to elaborate on the subject of my employment but before I could advance the question he began again. "Let me ask you something, do you believe in God?" "Sure, what the hell do you think; that I'm a damned atheist or something?" The question just ticked me off that much more. I was growing wearier of this windbag and his arrogance by the minute and more tired of his philosophy. Although, after I had a minute to internalize the question, I realized I wasn't bothered by the question but rather by my instant response. I was brought up in a Christian home and had generally tried to maintain a positive attitude on anything concerning God and the Christian doctrine. But secretly, I had a few doubts concerning Christ and some of the Christian doctrine in general. Ordinarily, when these doubts would creep into my mind I normally forced myself to change the subject. I had never admitted those doubts to anyone and I certainly was not about to start with this babbling rejection from Bedlam. "So, you probably don't believe in the theory of man evolving from some lower primate, do you?" he began again. I was already planning to cut out before long so I figured I'd just let him ramble.

"How about Metempsychosis? Have you ever given any credence to that concept?" I studied for a minute or two on that question before responding. "I'm sorry, but I don't know what you are talking about." Dr. Thompson chuckled and said "I like to refer to the idea with that word. It's a quick way to get attention on the subject. Metempsychosis is a more or less archaic term for reincarnation or transmigration of the soul." "Well, I follow you now. What about it?" I said. "Well if you believe in God you certainly believe in His perfection, and a perfect creator doesn't have to engage in a "do-over" so to speak. The Bible states that God "created," Not that He was "creating" or is continuing to create. "Creation" is finished, and as the Bible says, "It was good" and "He was pleased." He had created all seeds and formed man from the dust of the ground. Man grows from a seed. But without God's breath of life man would be like a tree. But God breathed his breath into man and man became a living "soul." The body of man and the soul of man are different entities-hence the concept of Des carte's theory of "Dualism". The soul of man is essentially the breath of God. The soul of man is eternal. The soul of man will never die. You can't see the soul of man. You can't taste touch or smell it but it exists."

I could stand no more of his fucking diatribe. "Look man," I said. "You are beginning to really creep me out. What's this all got to do with anything anyway? You talked about me doing some work for you so let's get to the bottom line! I'm getting tired and hungry!" Mr. Thompson stood up and stretched and yawned. Then he began to march around the table. I kept a close watch on him. This son-of-a bitch was likely to lay my head open with something. I was beginning to feel more uneasy all the time. After a couple of rounds he stopped and faced the bottle of "Old Crow." He squinted at the bottle as if hesitant to reach for it but then poured himself a tall drink and downed it. I was thoroughly pissed and now I started to yell. "Maybe if you'd stop hitting that bottle you could get to the point. I demand to know for what purpose you want to hire me and how much you are willing to pay!"

Apparently he had not detected my aggravation. After coughing and hacking for a while due to the effects of the drink he looked at me and held up ten fingers. I tried to assimilate his meaning from the gesture and then said "what does that mean? Ten dollars, a thousand dollars, or what?" "How about ten thousand" he said. I'll give you ten thousand dollars for assisting me a bit and then reporting the events which will be taking place here within the next several days." I thought about it for a while. Ten thousand for hanging around and writing up the events of the next few days was beginning to sound like an offer I could not refuse. But, I was naturally suspicious. I was the only soul around except for this nut. What if something happened to implicate me in some sort of a crime or nefarious event and no-one other than myself as witness? If I was going to spend any more time in that Godforsaken place I certainly did not want to be alone there with Thompson. I suddenly hit upon an idea.

"Sir!," I began, I do not wish to be disrespectful and attempt to dictate to anyone as to how they should live, but do you not think this residence could use some tidying up?" "You are right kid!" was his thoughtful response. "I've always been very particular about my living conditions, personal grooming and hygiene. We generally kept a housekeeper but she retired and I was never good at woman's work." Seizing the opening I had been waiting for I quipped "Oh, you mean Ms. Gordon." "You know Ms. Gordon?" he blurted. He had not been expecting that. "Yes, we've met. She said that you two had some sort of falling out and that you finally drove her away." "That poor mixed up soul" he said. "She's lesbian, you know!" I had to laugh. "She didn't look like a lesbian to me" was my quick retort while simultaneously realizing I would not be able to determine a lesbian if confronted with one. He shot me an amused smirk. "Yes, she and my wife carried on some sort of diabolical affair. I always thought the whole thing to be shameful and an abomination but as far as I can determine that was my wife's only fault. So, I thought it best to overlook the whole thing. They were so discreet that no-one but myself ever suspected anything so atrocious was going on. Actually, it never bothered me. I couldn't believe they were lovers. I could never determine in my mind how two women could copulate, so I guess I was never convinced. Aside from being barren, my wife was the paragon of wives. My wife looked after me in every respect and I felt sure our sex lives were satisfactory. Of course after my discovery of the lesbian thing I often wondered if our relationship was all it could be.

Anyway, I was very busy with my work and by and large just tried not to concern myself with the whole affair. But then, I had never been with another woman and actually had no way to compare. And, my wife was very sick for many years and one could not expect normal sexual relations under those conditions. Then, after my wife died and I had the opportunity to sow a few wild oats so to speak, I discovered what I had been missing all those years and consequently developed quite a dislike or rather a contempt for Eve Gordon. I think the straw that broke the proverbial camel's back was the time shortly after my wife died and I found Eve sitting on my wife's bed crying into a pair of my wife's panties. I could stand the site of the bitch no longer and fired her and drove her out of the house on the spot."

I was pretty amazed at all this information but none of it had altered my own fix. I could not spend any more time with that man in that place. "She was a good housekeeper was she not?" I said. "Yes, excellent" he replied. "Well, if I could persuade her to return and resume her duties and get this place cleaned up a bit would you agree to such an arrangement?" I paused and then added "at least during the time required for you and me to complete the task at hand." After a few minutes of deliberation he acquiesced to the idea. "Well, I suppose I will be able to tolerate the bitch for a few days. That is, if you can convince her to return."

If I was going to collect my finder's fee I would need some proof of my having found Dr. Thompson. When I explained this fact to him he immediately, and without hesitation, penned an affidavit as to his whereabouts along with his present address. He added a postscript promising to personally appear at Devers office in ten days. When I descried my objection that such a document was without legal status he explained that Ms. Gordon was a Notary public and could legitimize the affidavit with the customary Notary stamp. It all seemed so simple but I still held some tenuous reservations. After all, what concerned me most was receiving my finder's fee in hand. Whether such a document would be sufficient to satisfy Dever was doubtful and I was suspicious that anything less than habeas corpus would be evidence enough to convince him to release the rest of my money. Then I remembered Dever stipulating to simply bring proof of Thompson's whereabouts.

It was around five pm. when I left the Thompson retreat. I refused, over Thompson's insistence, to spend the night there. My nerves were frayed enough. I made it back to the motel of the night before; had a light dinner and was in bed shortly after sunset. The drive back to the city was pleasant enough-beautiful weather. Ms. Wilson seemed in good spirits, and was elated when I relayed the news of Dr. Thompson's good health. I presented the affidavit to her which she read, signed, and stamped with the notary seal. I witnessed it and at the same time questioned its legality but thought to myself "what the hell. It won't matter anyway." She seemed pleased that Thompson wanted her back but was also reluctant. She made it clear that she could not tolerate another one of his fits. I reassured her that I would be there the whole time and she would be absolutely safe, and, if she wanted to leave when I did she would be welcome.

I found Dever as I had left him: sitting alone in the antiquated office behind the great oaken desk. He was still dressed to the hilt with the cigarette filter clinched between his teeth. After the normal salutations I presented him with the affidavit. He appeared to examine it carefully, then pulled out fifty one hundred dollar bills and handed them to me without a word. I was amazed! It was just too easy! Now, I definitely smelled a rat. I was sort of pissed so I figured I'd do a little fishing. "Alright fucker, what's this all about?" I shouted. "Sorry John!" he exclaimed in a rather effeminate voice "I have done my job, good day!" The son of a bitch looked and sounded queer and I couldn't abide a queer so I left without another word. I really didn't care what was going on now. I had ten thousand bucks in my pocket and on my way to another ten thousand. I was just hoping the next ten would come as easy as this one.

Ms. Wilson wasn't even packed when I arrived back at her place. It would be really late when we got to Thompson's so I suggested we spend the night there at her apartment; that I was not about to drive those country roads after dark and then walk across that literal jungle the last quarter mile to Thompson's retreat. I remarked that I could sleep on the couch or just anywhere. She graciously agreed to that arrangement. It was past my time for a drink and when I asked if she had any liquor in the house she seemed quite pleased to finally have someone to drink with. She mixed a pitcher of martinis and we relaxed in the living room just talking about the weather, politics, and the state of the nation. She insisted I see the rest of the place and the room I was to sleep in. Her immaculate abode was nothing out of the ordinary; just the normal two bedroom apartment with ample space for one person. My room was sparsely furnished with a bed, dresser and a chair. There was also an electric fireplace with a mantle. A ten by twelve picture centered on the mantle immediately caught my eye. I don't know why, it just did; perhaps because of its size. The man and woman in the picture were both standing with one leg propped up on the front bumper of a black Cadillac. The woman appeared to be a very young Ms. Wilson. The man, I assumed, to be her husband or maybe an old beau. When I asked if he was her husband she quickly retorted "oh no, I've never been married!" and immediately changed the subject.

We sat in two matching overstuffed chairs in the living room with the pitcher of martinis on a small table between us. After a couple of minutes she got up and switched on the lights in the decorative fireplace. "There, that's better" she remarked. She was right. The artificial fire gave the room some welcoming atmosphere. Obviously she knew how to decorate. There were prints and copies of a few masterpieces attached to the walls it seemed, in exactly the optimum places for the relaxed observer to admire.

After a couple of very dry martinis we both became more relaxed and our conversation naturally drifted towards the professor since he was the central subject of our coming together. "How long have you been acquainted with Dr. Thompson?" I asked.

"Oh, we met when I was about twenty" she quipped. "I was one of his students!" "Oh shoot, I forgot the olives" she added and quickly excused herself and went into the kitchen. The lady's got a lot of class, I thought. Her pronunciation and enunciation was flawless-the way she carried herself was light and graceful. I guessed her to be in her mid-fifties, but devoid of close scrutiny she could easily pass for forty. I could not think of sufficient words to describe her except she appeared immaculate in every way. Her speech, the mellow voice, not too slow, not too fast and very succinct. The way she carried herself-like a debutante; with a slim, well-proportioned figure. When she returned with the olives it was plain the drinks were loosening her up. She seemed out of character and heavily plopped back into her chair.

"Did you graduate from college?" I asked, just trying to make conversation. "No, unfortunately I didn't. I, like most young women with overzealous hormones fell in love-or at least I thought I did. The man of my affection was twenty years my senior. He was a brilliant man but sad and in a rut when I met him. He was shackled to an instructor's position at a small college in the South. I was a sociology major and had transferred there just for one summer hoping to get a better perspective on Appalachian living; you know, the coal mining region, life there, the company store, the alleged poverty and life in general within that backwoods region. I was born and raised here in D.C. And since my father worked at the Pentagon and was in the upper echelons of government I guess we were quite wealthy and I was quite privileged. Daddy was unhappy with my choice of men but in the end he capitulated and pulled a few strings and secured my man a research position here at George Washington. I never went back to school after that." She suddenly looked directly into my eyes with a long hard stare as if trying to read my mind-then rolling her eyes she turned the stare back to the direction of the fireplace. "She thinks she's talking too much" I mused to myself "or she said something she shouldn't have".

It was obvious from her conversation that Dr. Thompson had been the lover. I filled our martini glasses again and began to munch on an olive. The gin was beginning to give me that "I don't give a damn attitude." Then, without thinking, I asked: "well why didn't you marry the good doctor?" She sat as if in a trance for a couple of minutes. She then downed the martini I had just poured and slammed the glass onto the table. I looked to be sure she hadn't broken it. Then she directed her gaze into my eyes and slurring her words just a bit said "because the rotten bastard married my mother!" I was naturally shocked and could only exclaim "well I be damned!" The gin had not only loosened her tongue but her brain as well I surmised. Some things were now beginning to jell in my own mind. I couldn't exactly put it all together yet but it was happening and I was getting more curious by the minute. I had to ask "well, why did that happen? Why did he marry your mother?" After a couple more minutes she blurted it all out.

"Well my folks were very rich and the professor and I had not been here in the capital more than a couple of months when my father suddenly died of a heart attack. He had made mother his sole heir with a small exception." She poured herself another martini. "He left me a few stocks and bonds and a few inexpensive odds and ends just so I couldn't contest anything. My mother liked the professor right from the start and was actually only four or five years older than him. By that time the professor was only interested in money-money to supplement his research grants. So, we schemed the whole thing up. I would pretend to hate him, leave town, and he would be free to marry mother. Oh, he's a silver tongued bastard. It was no time until he had mother eating out of his hand. She obeyed him like a three year old. If he said piss she would ask how much and how far!" She caught her breath and giggled that quaint laugh of hers. "Anyway, not long after they were married I returned hoping that he and I would take up where we had left off but it never happened. He treated me like a chamber maid and mother even worse. He used us both for sex and that was it. If we complained or did not do exactly as he dictated he would literally beat us. He tried not to injure us in places where it was visible. At least that's what he aimed to do but one of us seemed to always carry a fat lip or black eye as he often misjudged his punches. They had been married about a year when mother became bedfast with one of those slow growing cancers."

"She lingered for ten years in that condition. The professor was becoming more and more successful with his research and new discoveries. He was widely published and received millions in contributions and grants. He finally stopped the beatings as well as the sex. I rarely laid eyes on him as he became more prominent.

After mother died he began to call me a queer but that was only an excuse to drive me away. You know, I think he had actually conditioned himself to forget exactly who I was. After all, I had been the catalyst to his success! And, although he would never admit it, I was his stepdaughter. I finally had no alternative; I had to leave. My father had left some stocks and bonds in a lock box for me from when I was three years old. There was no way the professor could touch that money. I feel sure there is enough to sustain me until I die if I'm careful! Well there you have it my young friend." She giggled some more and waved her empty glass in front of my face. "There, I've spilled my guts now." Laughing a bit louder now she said "hell though, that's what I usually do when I'm half drunk!" I hadn't put it all together yet but it was coming along. It was sort of like a jigsaw puzzle. It seemed I had put a lot of it together but there were still a few pieces left to find.

We retired to our respective bedrooms shortly after Ms. Gordon had "spilled her guts"-her words, not mine. I think I must have fallen asleep before my head hit the proverbial pillow. The gin had done its job! I awakened to the unmistakable smell of bacon frying and coffee boiling. I went into the kitchen and found Ms. Gordon flitting around like a twenty year old making breakfast. She was humming some catchy tune and upon seeing me, pointed to the coffee pot. "I think I'll get a shower first if you don't mind" I said. She handed me a clean towel and a wash cloth and pointed the way to the shower. She didn't seem to be a bit hung over and I surmised that she must be a regular drinker. Then I thought she might be happy that she was going back to the professor with the possibility of getting long dicked again. I stifled a laugh all the way to the shower with that thought in mind.

We had a pleasant enough drive back to the professors' retreat and arrived in midafternoon. He was already well into the tank and had evidently just downed a glass of whiskey as his breath near anesthetized us when he opened the door to let us in. His only welcome was an unconcerned grunt. Ms. Gordon set in right away attempting to tidy up which by any imagination would be an overwhelming task. The minute I sat down old Noah, as usual, leaped unexpectedly into my lap. Thompson resumed what he had evidently been doing before our arrival. He was crushing pills and mixing elixirs. He was totally disheveled. His gray hair and beard were frizzed up like he had just touched the poles of powerful magneto. This crushing and mixing continued for at least another thirty minutes without anyone saying a word.

Thompson finally ceased what I laughingly considered the mad scientist routine and after downing another stiff drink, plopped his nasty looking ass down in the chair opposite me. He sucked in a deep breath and exhaled long and hard in my direction. His pungent whiskey saturated breath was nauseating. "Well, I'm done" he exclaimed with his usual nicotine rasp. "Tonight's the night! I'm going all out this time!" "Tonight's the night for what?" I had to ask. "I'm going to delve deeper into the human psyche than any one has ever dared to go before." He paused while he lit a cigarette. The thing literally crackled as he pulled in a long drag and exhaled again in my direction. The motherfucker has no decency I thought as I tried to wave the cloud of smoke from my nostrils.

"Okay, care to elaborate a bit?" I asked. He thought for a moment, and then slowly, almost methodically and in a near whisper responded. "To put it simply" he said "I'm going to turn off my everyday brain and turn on my dormant brain. You know, that ninety percent of our brain anatomists and psychologists say we never use-the gray matter." I didn't need to deduce anything from these words. He was going to render himself comatose! Simple as that! Ms. Gordon had entered the room and was gathering up some of the dirty dishes which he had left about. She was going about this very quietly trying not to upset the professor. Suddenly he yelled "come here and sit down, Eve!" Ms. Gordon placed a couple of the dishes in the sink and wiping her hands on her apron came and sat near the man. She clasped her hands in her lap and stared at them not saying a word. "You are still that beat down little bitch you always were. Aren't you Eve?" he said, in a callous and scorn laden tone. She quickly glanced at him and then lowered her head once more. "Eve knows of my experiments don't you honey?" He queried her in a low, almost tantalizing whisper. She more or less only scowled at him this time. Recognizing her disdain he said "Pity you didn't bring one of your partners so you and she could slip off somewhere and make out!" Ms. Gordon quickly rose and stood stiffly in front of the man. "I knew I shouldn't have come you miserable old bastard! You'll never change! Would to God I had left you in that miserable hick town! You would still be a half assed instructor there at Unity College! I rue the day I ever laid eyes on you!" They continued to babble back and forth but I was no longer listening.

That foreboding and ominous gut feeling upon seeing the picture of the man and woman and the black Cadillac on Ms. Gordon's mantle came suddenly to fruition. "This old son of a bitch is my daddy just as sure as hell" I thought. I had been looking directly at the professor and when Ms. Gordon mentioned Unity College he turned instantly and glanced at me. I had caught the significance but did not at all let on. She was the bitch that had destroyed my family and he was the son of a bitch I had wanted to kill for so long because of what he had done to our family. It had all clicked and come together in my mind instantly. "So you have finally found the right combination of chemicals to produce such an effect?" I asked. I noticed my voice crack as I spoke but I tightly clasped my hands together to conceal my nervousness and keep my composure. "Oh, I've had the right combination for some time! It's the exact amount of each chemical to add to the concoction that had me stumped. To be honest it's a wonder I haven't already killed myself with all the experimentation. Hell, I've injected myself at least a hundred times and each time I got closer to unlocking the door to the past. Just imagine the benefit to humankind. Old crimes could be solved; great ideas that have gone to the grave with ordinary men could be revived and resurrected. The benefits to society are countless." He was staring intently at me as he spoke-waiting for my response. I was thinking again that he was nuts. Just a frigging crackpot! This bastard might just kill himself for sure this time I was thinking-what about my fucking money?

"You see" he began again. "Only the most profound events that occurred during a man's life can be passed on, and I believe are passed on to his offspring genetically. In fact such knowledge could be dominant in the brain of a six month old infant human. But then, as these infants are insidiously indoctrinated to ways the parents and siblings wish them to respond. Most of the inherited knowledge is pushed deep within the psyche and only bits and pieces of it ever reach the surface again. These ghosts affect the individual's behavior throughout his whole life. The real and practical evidence of this is best understood by the old de ja vous experience." He stopped, lit another cigarette, had another four fingers of liquor and left me to ponder what he had said. To me it was all gibberish. I hadn't been trying to follow his reasoning. All I knew was that I was sitting in the presence of a diabolical witch and the man from whose loins I had sprung; the man who had at one time been a brilliant scientist but was now as mad as the proverbial hatter. "Okay doc." I blurted, "What about the rest of my money?" He slowly walked into the bedroom, came back in a few minutes and handed me fifty one hundred dollar bills. That's all I was waiting for. I wanted to just simply bolt! Just get the hell out of there but I managed to calm myself within a minute or two. I was still nervous but still curious. I figured I would hang around awhile and see what was going to happen next.

No one spoke for a few minutes. It was so quite we could hear old Noah snore. Finally Thompson went to the kitchen counter and brought back two different colored syringes. One was filled with a clear substance and the other with a milky white concoction. "Okay, now here's where it gets dead serious. You must, and I repeat must follow my instructions verbatim, understand? It's very simple. I will lie there on the cot and inject myself with the contents of this syringe." He held the syringe in front of my face. "I will fall asleep almost immediately. If I do not awaken within twenty four hours you must, and I repeat must, inject me with the full contents of this syringe. It is totally imperative you do that. Otherwise I could slip into a coma or even death within a very short time. Have you ever used one of these things?" He held the syringe up for me to plainly see. I nodded slowly several times in the affirmative. "Okay, that's all there is to it. Within twenty four hours I should have tapped deeply into that gray matter of the brains of my parents and then, who knows, perhaps even generations beyond that." He paused and lit another cigarette. "That is really the great unknown variable I'm dealing with. If I am not rendered conscious within twenty four hours I could recede back in time to the beginning of my very essence, and then inevitable death, since there would then be no more subject matter for the brain to think on and the brain must think in order to "be!" Okay, so let's do it!"

While he was reclining and making himself comfortable on the cot I thought about letting him know I was wise to the whole scheme. Old lawyer Dever was just a front to lure me into finding my father. The professor had no doubt been keeping up with my career and whereabouts for who knew how long. My stories and even my picture had been published in the paper numerous times but why had he wanted me to be present and witness perhaps his last rodeo? It was, at that moment, mind boggling. I figured there was no point in starting what could end up being a serious altercation at that point, so I kept my mouth shut. Hell, it would all work itself out one way or another! When Thompson pulled the blanket back on the cot I saw four leather shackles attached to the cots frame: one at each corner. "Now don't be alarmed" he said. "These are only for precaution. It's possible I could try to get up and if so, could injure myself. Now right after I inject myself I want you to strap me down and lock the shackles. The key is there on the counter." I nodded in the affirmative.

He then injected himself with the milky concoction in his lower abdomen and drifted off immediately. I did as he said and strapped him down by all fours. Ms. Gordon must have noticed the stillness and came in. She stood staring down at him. "He's doing it again huh?" she muttered. "Did you know I was his son?" I inquired. "Not exactly" she said. "But I was beginning to suspect it very strongly." "Do you even know what pain and suffering you caused my mother you fucking bitch?" I yelled. She stood face to face with me. She wasn't in the least intimidated. "I never knew your mother and yes I do regret any pain and suffering I may have caused. I too have paid for it and lived with the pain all these years. But you can't just turn love off like you can a light switch. I was truly in love with him at first and would have done anything for him but eventually the love turned to hate." She looked down at the man again. "I hope the son of a bitch never wakes up!" she said through clinched teeth. She was right and I knew it. Actually I felt a bit sorry for her at that moment. I too had experienced spurned love and realized love is not something you can't turn off at will. Thompson was resting peacefully; not even snoring. It was six PM. And I knew I had to be awake and alert at six a.m. in order to fulfill my end of the bargain. I set the Big Ben alarm clock and placed it on the end table beside my chair.

Funny thing, it was at times like this when I was relaxed and drowsy my mind would begin to reflect on what it all meant: life, reality, love, beauty! I had read a lot of the old philosophers: Plato, Aristotle, Augustine, Bacon, Des Carte and even some of the more modern sages like Kierkegaard and Sartre and Heidegger, the so called Existentialists. I was never really able to fully comprehend their elusive thought. All of those readings would, here and there, spark moments of deep feelings and profound wonderment. But, the next day when I was once again faced with the reality of life, such philosophy did not apply. I stared at my father lying there. What the hell is the meaning of anything, I thought. He is a brilliant man, a knowledgeable man, an educated man. But in the end just another man with a fucked up mind-a waste! There was only one short way to describe him in my opinion: The son of a bitch was crazy!

The hours wore on and I dozed off. Pretty soon the Big Ben rattled me out of some half ass dream. Thirty minutes to "D" day old man, I thought. Ms. Gordon had heard it too and got busy with the coffee pot. A little later on she brought me a cup of the soupy black liquid and we sat waiting for six A.M. We both silently prayed for his awakening but he snored on. At six o'clock on the nose I went to the counter and brought back the syringe with what I thought of as the antidote. As soon as I sat down by the old man's side, Noah leaped into my lap and knocked the syringe out of my hand; shattering it to pieces. The liquid leaked out and formed a puddle on the floor. "Dammit," I shouted as I stood gazing into what could very easily be the old man's life draining away. I panicked for a second but then went back to the counter in hopes of finding a second syringe filled with the essential liquid. But, as I suspected, the search was futile. Bewildered, I sat at the old man's bedside and prayed for him to wake up. His respiration and heartbeat was strong and steady and his color was still good. Two hours passed and he snoozed on. I realized finally that I had no alternative. I must summon professional help.

Ms. Gordon and I waited for five days at the hospital anticipating either the professors' demise or recovery; neither happened. We finally went our separate ways with a promise from the attending physicians to let us know of any change in the professor's condition. Sixty days passed and I received a registered letter from lawyer Dever requesting my appearance at his office concerning matters pertaining to the professor's last will and testament. I had been named heir to any and all of the professor's estate contingent upon his death or total impairment.

So I'm going to cut this short! It seems the professor had been rendered and adjudicated totally impaired. The last time I saw him he was squatting in the corner of a padded cell and evidently awaiting his feeding time of bits of raw meat. He could not speak. The only sounds he made were continual grunts. He seemed quite paranoid and fearful; burrowing his head in his folded arms and grunting frantically when anyone approached his cell.

Even though the world was falling apart and no-one seemed to give a damn I managed to live in luxury for several years. There were still a few places left where a rich man could appease his nihilistic urges and appetites. But this carefree self-indulgence soon began to wane and I once again found myself asking the age old question of "is this all there is?" I suppose the sage who said "the fruit never falls far from the tree" was right. After I had tired of watching "people," the scum and scourge of the earth, in their daily debaucheries and Godless ways of living, I journeyed once again to the professor's old retreat. I was, upon my first arriving there, determined to live out the rest of my days as a recluse. This worked out great for a year or so. I had my little garden and a few things to tinker with but eventually boredom got the best of me and I kept wondering what the professor would be able to tell me if I had been successful in administering the antidote which may have prevented his mind from being locked up somewhere in the past. I found a few of his notes on combinations of chemicals for unlocking the collective unconscious. I decided I wasn't too enthralled with life anymore so I did a little experimenting. The chemicals I ingested had little or no affect. But then, by accident, I discovered whiskey to be a catalyst to the desired effects of these chemicals. No wonder my old man was also a boozer! After a few experiments and self-injections I realized he had really been onto something.

It's been two years now and I'm getting closer and closer to that final dose. Up until now the past traumatic incidents experienced by my ancestors have only come to me by bits and pieces. But I feel sure I have concocted the right combination of chemicals to make these incidents come together and make sense. I often think to myself what a breakthrough for humanity! But then during my more lucid moments, I know, just like my father must have known that my efforts are all ego and vanity driven. Fuck humanity! I'll be famous! The fucking world will be at my feet. After all, its fame and fortune we seek whether we admit it or not!

I have engaged an ex-nurse to assist me much like I had assisted the professor. I discovered her on one of my very infrequent visits to the city. She was sitting passed out on a barstool with her head drooped over into a half filled bowl of soup. She, like most people, had been cast out upon the street with no job and no future. She was just an old trollop now; a streetwalker. The only thing she lacked was the proverbial shopping cart but I imagine all the shopping carts in the world had been taken. I was sure she would do exactly as I instructed for the ten thousand dollars I had promised her. After all, her job would be so easy: just administer the antidote at exactly the right time.

Well, all is prepared. The gurney with the shackles is waiting! But my hands are shaking so I doubt I can hold the syringe. I best have another glass of liquor! I hope my trusty assistant will be faithful and bring me out of the coma if anything goes awry. Ah, that word "hope" again. Hope is to man as rain is to grass or gasoline to an automobile. Hope is man's fuel. Without hope man would stall, wither, and die! And then, if what he had hoped for in this life did not materialize, he could always <u>hope</u> for a better life to come!

THE END

ABOUT THE AUTHOR

John Fee Gibson was born and raised in the Appalachian foothills of Southeastern Kentucky. He moved to Ohio as a young man where he graduated from The Ohio State University. He was employed in the metals removal industry for several years as a tool and die maker, designer, and computer aided drafting and machining engineer. He received his teaching credentials later in life and held teaching positions with the Southern Ohio College, the Community College System of Kentucky, and the Public Schools of Ohio.

Mr. Gibson presently resides in Fairfield, Ohio and is retired.

www.ingramcontent.com/pod-product-compliance
Lightning Source LLC
Chambersburg PA
CBHW031454260626
47154CB00017B/2733